I0588877

The Route from San Francisco to Finland

That's what the red line below indicates. From Finland, we hopped to the Åland Islands, which you can see in the inset box to the right. Don't forget, we went to Paris, too–briefly. And then it was back to San Francisco and up to the Napa Valley, which you can see details of in the box below.

Napa Valley

You can see Rutherford, where Grandpa Nick and I both live, just about in the middle of the above map. Mt. St. Helena is just above Calistoga, towards the top left.

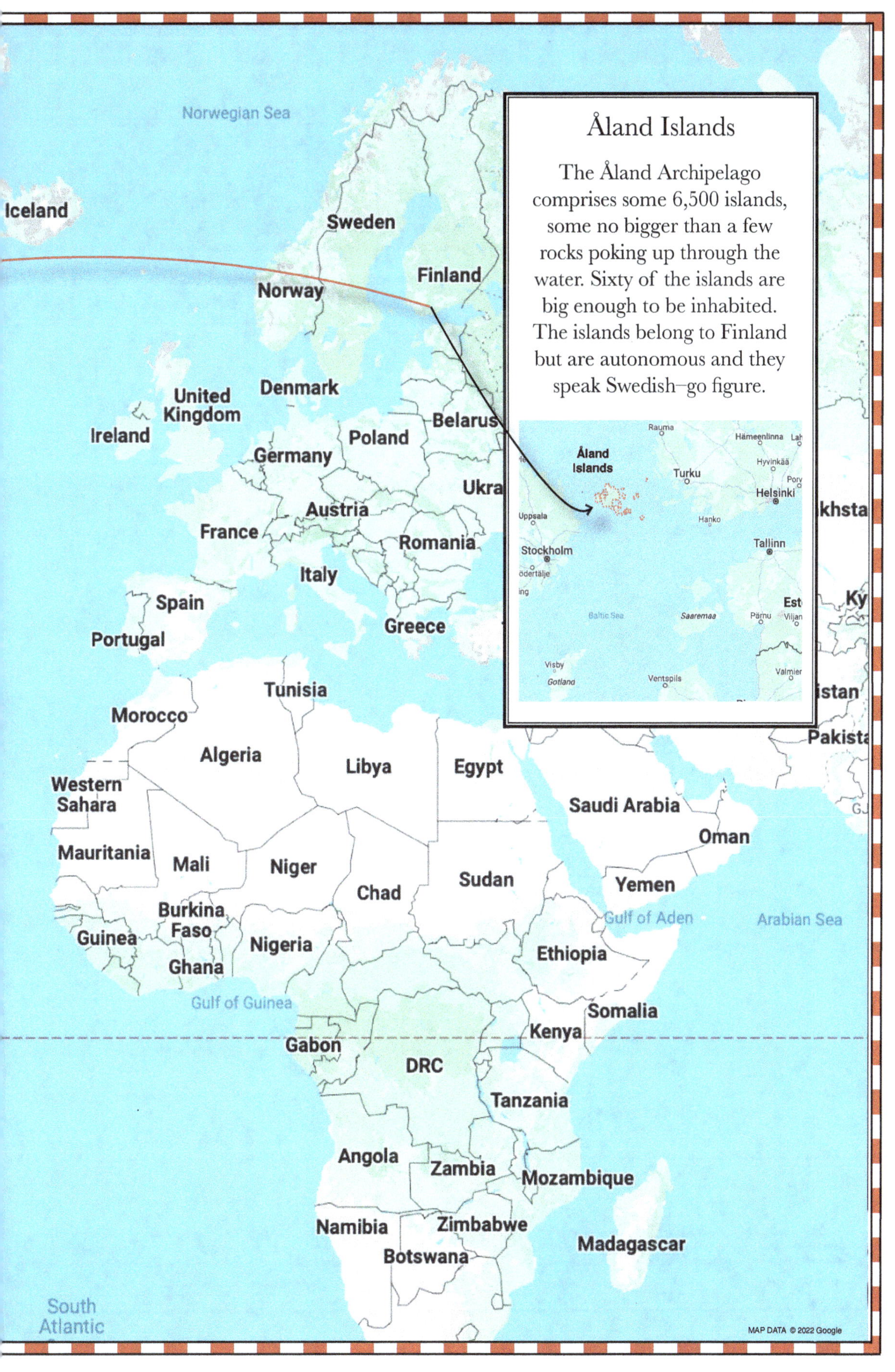
Norwegian Sea
Iceland
Sweden
Finland
Norway
Denmark
United Kingdom
Ireland
Belarus
Poland
Germany
Ukra
Austria
France
Romania
Italy
Spain
Greece
Portugal
Tunisia
Morocco
Algeria
Libya
Egypt
Western Sahara
Saudi Arabia
Oman
Mauritania
Mali
Niger
Chad
Sudan
Yemen
Burkina Faso
Nigeria
Gulf of Aden
Arabian Sea
Guinea
Ghana
Ethiopia
Gulf of Guinea
Somalia
Kenya
Gabon
DRC
Tanzania
Angola
Zambia
Mozambique
Namibia
Zimbabwe
Madagascar
Botswana
South Atlantic
khsta
Ky
istan
Pakista
G.
Åland Islands

The Åland Archipelago comprises some 6,500 islands, some no bigger than a few rocks poking up through the water. Sixty of the islands are big enough to be inhabited. The islands belong to Finland but are autonomous and they speak Swedish–go figure.

Rauma
Hämeenlinna
Lah
Åland Islands
Turku
Hyvinkää
Pory
Helsinki
Uppsala
Hanko
Stockholm
Tallinn
ödertälje
ing
Est
Ky
Baltic Sea
Saaremaa
Pärnu
Viljan
Visby
Gotland
Ventspils
Valmier
MAP DATA © 2022 Google

Escape to Silverado

Also by A. Cort Sinnes

The Silverado Trail

The Voyage of the Silverado

Escape to Silverado

Written and Illustrated by

A. Cort Sinnes

Printed in the United States of America

Alfred Cort Sinnes
P. O. Box 571
Napa, California 94558

This book was designed and produced by Hearth & Garden Productions

A. Cort Sinnes, Text, Design and Illustrations

Library of Congress Cataloging-in-Publication Data

Sinnes, A. Cort *Escape to Silverado*,
written by A. Cort Sinnes
All artwork by the author unless otherwise indicated

ISBN 978-0-578-98345-5

Front cover illustration: *Lars to the Rescue*, by A. Cort Sinnes

For my grandparents,
Nels and Lempi,
with fond memories and
renewed appreciation of our
1970 trip to Finland

Preface

Many of the most unlikely people and events in this book are, in fact, real. In 1880, the great Scottish writer Robert Louis Stevenson, spent his honeymoon on Mount St. Helena, in an abandoned mining camp named Silverado, from which this book takes its name. And Gustave Niebaum, a Finnish sea captain did, indeed, found a famous winery in the heart of the Napa Valley in 1879. Not only that, but an aristocratic family in Europe really did provide the British government with an enormous amount of gold to assist the Duke of Wellington in defeating Napoleon at the Battle of Waterloo in 1815, thereby ending the Napoleonic Wars. The ancient non-bank banking system known as *hawala* remains very real to this day and, yes, crows do speak to one other in surprisingly sophisticated ways and, of course, there are humans who can talk back to them. No fooling. As to the diminutive folk at the center of this story, as Joaquin says at the end of this book, "stay tuned." Things could get interesting.

A.C.S.
Napa 2021

Table of Contents

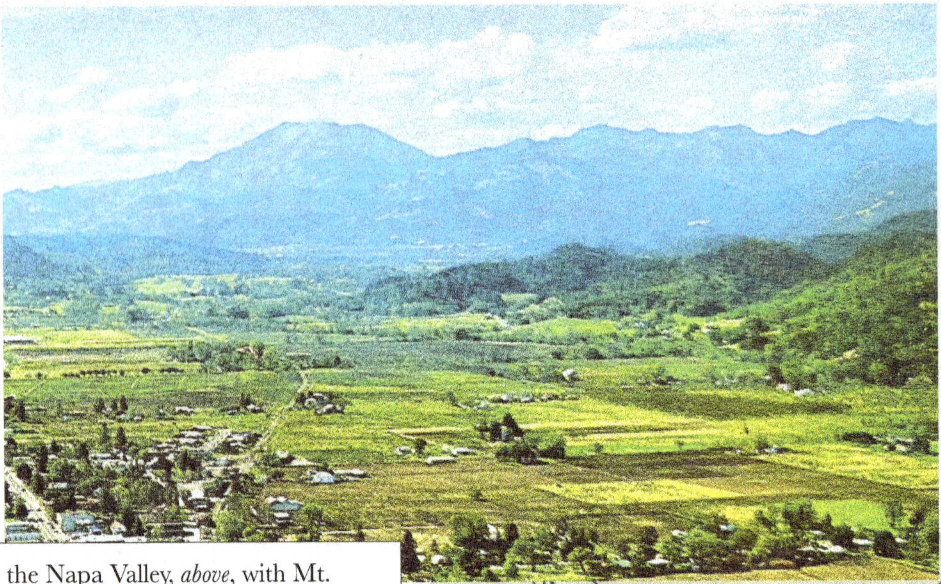

VINTAGE POSTCARD – COLLECTION OF THE AUTHOR

That's the Napa Valley, *above*, with Mt. St. Helena looking particularly majestic, reigning over the valley at its northern end, above the town of Calistoga.

Right: On the way home from Finland after an intense seven days. I asked Grandpa to do a quick sketch of the inside of the plane, just so we'd have something to remember it by.

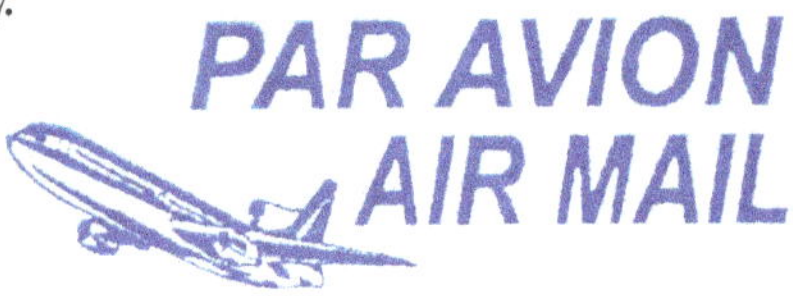
PAR AVION
AIR MAIL

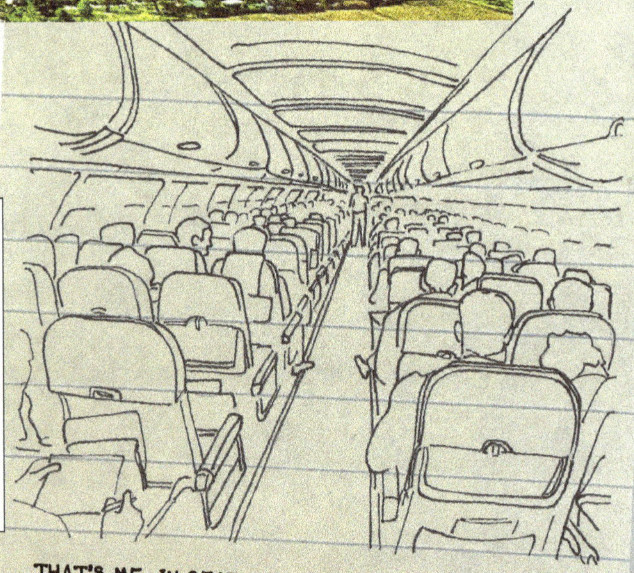

THAT'S ME, IN SEAT 19-F, NEXT TO THE WINDOW.

Below: Postcard showing a few of the more than 6,500 islands and islets in the Åland archipelago–some of which are barely big enough to stand on.

CURIOSO – SHUTTERSTOCK.COM

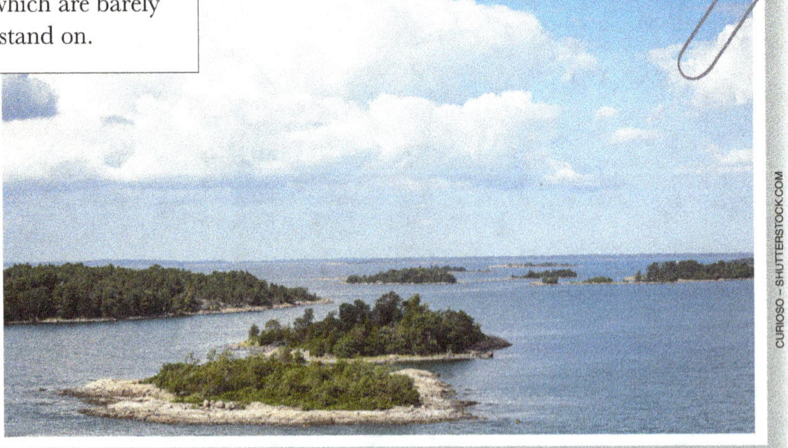

Prologue

June 27, 2013

En route, return flight from Helsinki to San Francisco
Finnair flight 1337

Day Seven of our week-long trip to Finland

Joaquin writing:

I'm sitting in Seat 19-F, next to the window, on Finnair flight 1337, returning home to San Francisco from Helsinki, writing in what was, just a week ago, a brand-new journal. Now it's almost full. My grandfather and I spent the last seven days on the Åland Islands and in Helsinki, Finland. Don't worry if you've never heard of the Åland Islands; they're way small and not on most people's radar. There's a map that shows where they are (between Sweden and Finland in the Gulf of Bothnia) inside the front and back covers of this book. We also went to Paris, but I don't know if it counts because we were only there for dinner and we came right back afterwards. No kidding.

It's a good thing I took some pictures because I think I'm going to need them to convince you that some of the things that happened really happened. But first, let me explain a few things up front. This whole megillah started about a year ago when I told my grandfather about what happened at my best friend, Darren's, family's winery. A barrel of wine got stolen and someone left a leather pouch filled with gold nuggets where the barrel had been, like it was payment for the wine or something. Anyway, when I told Grandpa, it got him going, all the way to the attic, where he fished out a journal he'd written over 40 years ago, when he was like 14, and he handed it to me and said "read it."

Are you sitting down? This is wild.

First off, my name is Joaquin, I'm 15 years old and live in the Napa Valley. It's in northern California, about sixty miles north of San Francisco and as beautiful as everyone says it is. If you haven't read the first two books in the The Silverado Journals, *The Silverado Trail* and *The Voyage of the Silverado*, I'll give you the headlines. My grandfather lives in an old Victorian house, surrounded by big old oak trees and vineyards. My mom, dad, and I live down the lane from Grandpa. It's all part of the same property that includes the winery, Eagle's Nook, which my grandpa Nick inherited from his grandmother. My grandfather is an artist and writer. He's got a cool studio and workshop in a barn next to his house. I like to hang out there and work on stuff at his workbench.

I already mentioned that last year when I told him about the stolen wine and the pouch of gold at Darren's folks's place, he gave me one of his old journals to read. The story he'd written was pretty good, but it was out there–like *way* out there. I tried, but I couldn't get him to tell me if it was true or not. Not that I would have believed him if he said it *was* true, because one of the things he says all the time is "never let the truth get in the way of a good story." See what I mean?

The story in the journal takes place in 1967 when my grandfather was 14 years old and just home from boarding school for the summer. He lived with his so-called aunt and uncle, on their pony farm in St. Helena. His mom, dad, and brother were killed in a car accident when he was little. Even though his Grandma Hattie was his guardian, she thought he'd be happier living with Walter and Ma-D, the owners of the Twin Oaks Pony Farm. Although there's no way to prove it one way or the other, she was probably right: the farm *was* a cool place to grow up. My grandfather lived there with Walter and Ma-D and the miniature ponies until he went off to boarding school. On the first night my grandfather arrived at the farm in 1967, Walter's prized Shetland pony disappeared. Or more to the point, was stolen.

Let me back up and explain something important. The real beginning of this story happened in 1879 when Captain Gustave Niebaum, my great-great-great grandfather discovered stowaways aboard his ship. Any stowaway is a problem, but these stowaways happened to be gnomes, one of whom was the gnome king, King Gob. I know it's a stretch, but that's what Captain Niebaum wrote in his ship's log 134 years ago. Unfortunately, when Niebaum's ship made a stop in Kauai, five of the gnomes (tired of the long voyage and even more tired of being seasick) jumped ship and disappeared. My third-great grandfather and the gnome King made a deal: if the remaining gnomes would dig the caves for his new winery, Eagle's Nook, in the Napa Valley, he would grant them their freedom. Which is how they wound up living on (or more accurately, *in*) Mt. St. Helena. Wild, huh?

The first journal describes how my grandfather eventually got his Uncle Walter's pony back. This was interesting because, it was those gnomes who stole the horse. When a seafaring relative you've never met writes about discovering a band of gnomes aboard his ship in 1879, that's one thing. But when it's your grandfather who's telling you the story, standing right in front of you, that's where it starts to get weird, at least for me. I mean, when was the last time you saw a gnome?

By the end of the first story, my grandfather's Grandma Hattie and the king of the gnomes, King Gob, got all buddy-buddy. And the gnome king's son, Prince G, my grandfather and my grandfather's best friend, Chuy, who were all about the same age, became friends, too.

In the last chapter, King Gob and Grandma Hattie agreed to have my grandfather, along with Chuy and Prince G, go to Kauai the following summer to bring Dagywn, the gnome wizard, back from wherever he was hiding on Kauai. Are you following all this? Dagywn was one of the five gnomes who jumped ship back in 1879 and the one King Gob wanted back the most.

Did I tell you the gnomes live like practically forever? Or that my grandfather, Chuy, and Prince G sailed to Kauai on Grandma Hattie's 78-foot sailboat? That's what grandpa wrote about in the second journal, *The Voyage of the Silverado*. After I'd read the first journal, Grandpa Nick asked me if I wanted to read the second one and I said "sure." If I'm being honest, part of me really wanted the story to be real and to see what happened next. The stories were cool enough, but they wouldn't have meant that much if it hadn't been for that stolen barrel of wine and the pouch of gold nuggets at my friend Darren's place. The logical me figured there was a practical explanation for why these very similar pouches of gold were showing up so many years apart. As it turns out, the explanations are getting less and less "practical" every day.

Once they got to Kauai in 1968, my grandfather, Chuy, and Prince G teamed up with Mad, a 16-year-old girl (her real name was Madison) who lived on the island. She knew everything about the island and then some. After a lot of looking, they finally found Dagywn the wizard and brought him back to King Gob on Mt. St. Helena. In that second journal, my grandfather mentions that he and Prince G used homing pigeons to communicate with each other. Basically it was the only way they *could* communicate, considering gnomes don't use electricity or any other modern devices. I accidentally discovered that not only was the dovecote (the place where the pigeons live) kind of hidden in Grandpa's garden, there were pigeons living in it. They must have been descendants of the ones Grandpa and Prince G used, back in the day. I didn't tell Grandpa I was going to re-activate the "pigeon post" (which is what he and G called their message system) to try to communicate with Prince G because I was sure he'd say it would never work. I counted on Doyle, who lives with us, to help me attach the messages to the pigeons, which is kind of tricky. And then one day, lo and behold, one of the pigeons came back carrying a message attached to its leg. The message was from Prince G.

That changed everything.

First, it meant that the whole frigging story was true. This took a while for me to process. Two, the message from Prince G asked if I'd meet him on Mt. St. Helena and to bring Grandpa. Prince G wrote "there's a plan afoot."

After he read it, Grandpa said to no one in particular, "It's a little late. Like some 40-odd years late."

That said, this book is about how that plan became real. And then some.

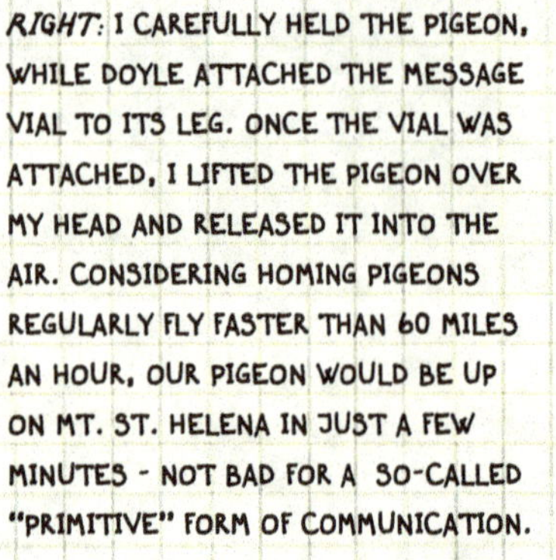

Left: The paper people use to roll their own cigarettes makes perfect, lightweight paper to write messages on and is the right size for putting in the small metal vials.

Above: You need a good, sharp pencil or pen wth a very fine point (one with a 0.3 point works) to write the message on the rolling paper—but be careful: the paper is very thin and tears easily.

Above: It looks big, but a message vial is small and light enough to be attached to the pigeon's leg without weighing it down. The grooved cap on the top of the vial twists off, allowing the message to be inserted into the vial. *Right:* It's fun to watch the pigeons dip and dive as they race off to their destination.

Chapter I

Fill in the Blanks

June 27, 2013

En route, return flight from Helsinki to San Francisco
Finnair flight 1337

Day Seven of our week-long trip to Finland, *continued*

Joaquin writing:
Let me give you a couple more headlines so the story Grandpa and I are about to tell will make a little more sense. I'm turning the Way Back Machine to last year when "things" started coming together:

August 14, 2012
Grandpa Nick's house
Rutherford, California

Once that pigeon came back to Grandpa's with the note from G attached to his leg, G finally became real to me and I looked at what happened in Grandpa's two journals in a whole new light. If G was real, I guessed the rest of the stuff was real, too. Which I admit freaked me out–especially when I thought about Madam Pele, who figured large (*really* large) in Grandpa's second journal. I decided to think more about that later. Right at the moment, I wanted to write G back, post haste (as they used to say) to set up a meeting. I ran into the house to tell Doyle what had happened–that our effort had succeeded. He was really surprised. As surprised as I was.

All three of us—Grandpa, Doyle, and I—sat down at the kitchen table. I had already sharpened a pencil to an extra fine point, and had one of those small sheets of that super thin Zig-Zag rolling paper ready to go.

"What should I say?"

"What do you want to say?" Doyle asked.

"It's not so much what I want to say, it's what I want to do… to go up there on Mt. St. Helena and meet those guys, like right now."

"Well, that's not going to happen, so…" Grandpa said.

"So I need to set up a meeting."

"Right. And don't forget they reverse night and day, so you need to suggest a nighttime meeting."

"Is that all right?"

"I don't know. Is it all right with you?"

"Sure. I'll meet 'em any time."

"Okay" Grandpa said, "so start by suggesting a time. I always found before midnight was good—they have their big meal of the day at midnight and a nap afterwards, so it's either before midnight or well after, which gets late for us night-sleepers."

"What about 10 o'clock?"

"When?" Grandpa asked.

"Tomorrow?"

"No time like the present, eh?"

"Sure, why not?"

"I think the day after tomorrow would be better. Those guys aren't exactly known as speedy decision-makers."

I didn't want to wait that long to meet G, but after reading Grandpa's journals, I knew what he said was true, so I wrote a message suggesting we meet on Friday night at 10 o'clock. I carefully rolled the paper tight and eased it into the vial. All three of us went out to the dovecote. I caught one of the pigeons and held it gently while Doyle attached the vial to its leg. I couldn't tell if it was the same one who brought the message. I guess that didn't matter. After Doyle attached the vial, I lifted the pigeon over my head and released him into the air. Just like before, he performed a couple of big loops and then headed north to Mt. St. Helena.

"Now what?" I asked Grandpa and Doyle.

"Aside from waiting?"

"Yeah, well, I'm not a very good waiter."

"Come on inside. I've got something you should see.

We all traipsed back to the kitchen. Grandpa pulled the locker we had taken from the attic a few days ago off the shelf next to the kitchen table. He opened it and took out what looked like another of his journals.

"Here," Grandpa said, pushing it across the table in my direction.

"Really?"

"Why not?" Grandpa asked.

"I don't know. I'm just getting caught up with things."

"You mean you don't feel ready for another adventure?"

"Something like that."

"Well, take a look at it anyway."

It felt a little strange, like he was forcing it on me.

"Well I'm not going to sit here and read the whole thing right now."

"You might."

With that, I flipped through it. There wasn't a darn thing in the journal.

"What's this?" I asked, confused.

"The third journal," Grandpa said.

"Yeah, but blank? What's the deal?"

"Basically, there was no deal. Nothing happened. I'm guessing the gnomes couldn't make up their minds how to proceed. Don't forget, their sense of time isn't like ours. It may be normal to them, but compared to the way we Uplanders do things, I'd definitely say they play a long game."

"So you didn't go to the Åland Islands?"

"Nope. I didn't go anywhere. Except back to school and my normal life. My normal Uplander life."

"That's weird."

"Yeah," Grandpa said, "I'll be the first to admit that even back then, I wasn't so sure about going off on another venture for Gob. But I'd be lying if I said it wasn't a letdown not to hear anything. Of course it could have just been their sense of time. But it still seemed strange that the whole thing just… I don't know… evaporated. It still feels that way. That message you just received is the first time I've heard from G, or any of the others, in more than 40 years."

"That's crazy."

"It *is*. What would really be crazy is if they finally decided they wanted me to go to the Åland Islands. G said in his note that there was a plan afoot. I had reservations back then. But I have completely different ones now. I'm too old for this stuff."

"That's why you have me," I said, not knowing even remotely what I was talking about or what plan was afoot. Or just how quickly one's whole world can change. And it did. But if I told you everything that happened over the next few days, this story would be way too long. So, to keep things moving along, I'm going to stick to just the headlines.

It was only a few hours before we got word back via the pigeon post Friday night at 10 p.m. was fine. Time went very slow for the next day and a half and Friday night dinner was the longest one in history. But finally 9:30 arrived and Grandpa and I drove almost to the summit of Mt. St. Helena. We parked in a turn-out in the road where we had agreed to meet G. Sure enough, he came walking down the mountain path, carrying a small lantern, lit by a candle. I tried to play it cool–like meeting a gnome was something I did everyday–but for the first few minutes I think I kind of lost it. Then I realized he was basically like anybody else, only a lot shorter, and I was chill. Although I think I probably stared at his clothes longer than was polite, but for such a small guy, he had *a lot* of clothes on–layer on layer, each a different pattern and color. It was quite the look. We followed him along the narrow trail that snaked around the side of the mountain until we came to a dark opening in the rocks. It looked like the entrance to a cave, which is exactly what it was.

If I hadn't read Grandpa's journals, I'm sure I would have been even more knocked out by being inside the gnome's cave. We had our meeting with King Gob in the incredible gold room with the black obsidian floor. It was just how Grandpa had described it in his first journal, way back when. I looked down at my dark reflection in the glasslike floor. It made me feel like I was standing on an upside-down version of myself, just as it did for Grandpa all those years ago. It made me feel a little lightheaded.

Gob and G treated Grandpa like they'd seen him last week, as if there was nothing strange about a lapse in communication for more than 40 years, picking up where they'd left off in 1968. Because I'd read Grandpa's journals, I felt familiar with King Gob and G, and they certainly treated me like we were friends. And I've got to be honest: Like I said, it took me about three minutes to get used to these guys being really short.

After a few minutes of mostly talking over each other–and Gob constantly trying to serve everyone more wine–Aalto, the wizardess, joined us. We all sat at one end of the long dining table. Aalto was very composed and focused, more or less the exact opposite of Gob. She essentially ran the meeting, with Gob occasionally making vaguely affirmative guttural noises in between swigs of wine. G didn't say much but I could tell he wasn't missing a thing.

Aalto laid it out. And although admittedly strange, the job they wanted us to do was straightforward enough: Travel from San Francisco to the Åland Islands, pick up 43 men, women, and children and reunite them here, on Mt. St. Helena, with their husbands, fathers, and sons. The job got a little more complicated knowing the 43 men, women, and children were, of course, gnomes. And, oh yeah… their store of gold–141,904 pounds of it at last count–that also needed to be transported from the Åland Islands to the Napa Valley. Like I said, straightforward enough, but all of a sudden, way complicated. And that's what this story is about…

• • •

Just so you know, Grandpa and I are going to tag-team telling this story. Considering I just ran out of space in my journal and we're going to be landing in San Francisco in a few, it's probably a good time to turn it over to Grandpa. I'll be back.

Above: Signe was a no-show at the Church of St. Lawrence at Eckerö. She chose the location because there were plenty of gravestones on the church grounds, just the right size for her to hide behind. *Right:* Those are the Åland Islands outlined in red, between Finland and Sweden in the Gulf of Bothnia. Eckerö is on the western edge of Åland, closest to Sweden.

Chapter II

No Show

June 27, 2013

En route, return flight from Helsinki to San Francisco
Finnair flight 1337

Day Seven of our week-long trip to Finland, *continued*

Grandpa Nick writing:

Joaquin and I lucked out and scored an empty seat between us. I let him have the window seat because I'm a nice guy. We both have our headphones on; I don't know what he's listening to; I'm listening to Mozart's *Divertimento in D.* He just leaned over and asked me to do a quick sketch of the inside of the plane and then mouthed the words that it was the "last page" of the moleskin journal I bought him a few weeks ago before we left on this trip.

Since he's almost out of space and we've got a little time before landing, I'll bring you up to date. I know Joaquin has written about rediscovering the homing pigeons last year and reestablishing contact with G which, I've got to tell you, kind of blew my mind. I mean, 40-plus years is a long time between conversations. At any rate, after considerable discussion, we came up with a definition of the job they wanted us to do. We also decided that instead of rushing into it, we'd wait until the following June to put the plan into action, which brings us to now.

I'm old enough to know when anyone says something is straightforward, there's a good chance it's anything but and, of course, that's how G described what he wanted us to do. G explained to me that Signe (who was nominally King Gob's wife and G's mother–but more on that later), was the very competent head of the remaining gnome clan in Åland and had planned their exodus from the island for many years. He also assured me she had a well-thought-out scheme for moving their considerable horde of gold. All Joaquin and I would have to do was to oversee the plans Signe already had in place and be on hand if anything should go wrong. And what could go wrong, right? Unfortunately, it started going wrong on the day we arrived and didn't let up for the seven days we were there. Now that we're on our way home, I'm hoping things will settle down and go according to what remains of the plan but, truthfully, I have my doubts.

I started my journal the first day we arrived. We landed in Helsinki after a 14-hour flight from SFO and then a less-than-an-hour hop to Åland in a small prop plane. Once in Åland, it was a short cab ride to Eckerö, where we were supposed to meet Signe. Both Joaquin and I were a little worse for wear, but nothing that a good nap wouldn't fix. Unfortunately for me, a nap wasn't in the cards. Here's how things started out—or didn't, as the case may be.

June 21, 2013
The Church of St. Lawrence at Eckerö
Eckerö, Åland Islands

Day One of our week-long trip

It had taken considerable effort to set up a meeting with Signe, so having some random Finnish guy approach me in the church graveyard, at the exact time (4 o'clock) and spot where Signe and I had agreed to meet, and having him tell me Signe wasn't going to make the meeting, was definitely not a good start to this "project." I explained to him that I'd just traveled more than 5000 miles for the express purpose of getting to this specific spot, at this specific time. *What the… ?* I wondered out loud, exasperated.

"Signe said to stay put and she'd get in touch with you."

"Stay put?!" I said, louder and more angrily than I intended. "For how long?"

The young man, whose name was Lars, said he had no idea, "I believe you have a saying in your country—something about not shooting the messenger?"

He was right. It wasn't his fault. In an attempt to apologize, I invited him for a beer at our hotel, which wasn't that far away. Lars followed me there in his car and went to the bar. I went to our room and left a note for Joaquin (who was taking a major nap) letting him know where I was. Walking from our room to the hotel bar, I wondered why in the world I'd said yes to this venture. Even if everything went off without a hitch, the whole situation was going to be difficult and weird enough. And for Signe not to show up for our initial meeting was simply not a good omen for the future. I'm not a quitter, but I couldn't help thinking that it might be best to just cut and run before things went, as the English say, completely pear-shaped.

I put that thought on hold as I sat down next to Lars in the pleasantly dark bar and ordered a beer. There was no one else besides the two of us sitting at the actual bar and only a few patrons sitting at small round tables in the spare, Scandinavian Modern room, one side of which was a floor-to-ceiling wall of glass, framing a view of sparkling water flashing through remarkably uniform spruce trees, everything very green and blue.

As out-of-sorts as I was, I couldn't help asking how Lars and Signe had met? I didn't think the social lives of a college-aged kid and an ancient gnome overlapped that much. I couldn't have guessed his answer in a million years.

Above: The "Land of the Midnight Sun," where sometime around 11 p.m. in mid-June, the sun barely dips below the horizon for just a few hours before it starts to rise again around 3 a.m. As a result, it may be night, but it never gets dark, just this strange, in-between twilight time, not quite dark and not quite light. *Right:* Lars's first architectural commission—his great aunt's new outhouse, built in preparation for her sister's upcoming visit from America. No one could have foreseen the consequences of such a seemingly humble undertaking.

THE NEW OUTHOUSE WAS BUILT CLOSE TO LARS'S GREAT-AUNT'S HOUSE, BUT SURROUNDED BY A FOREST OF BIRCH TREES, TYPICAL OF THE ÅLAND ISLANDS.

Chapter III

Nose-to-Nose in the New Outhouse

June 21, 2013

The hotel in Eckerö

Day One of our week-long trip, *continued*

Grandpa Nick writing:
"A new outhouse?"

Like I said, never in a million years.

"I'm afraid so," Lars said, before taking a long gulp of his beer. "I'm rather proud of it. It turned out nice, actually."

"I'm sure it did, but you're going to have to explain it to me. I don't mean to be rude, but who uses outhouses any more—let alone builds a new one?"

"Well, my great-aunt, for one. There's a certain part of the population—mostly older—no offense," Lars said, looking at me sideways.

"No offense taken," I said, self-consciously.

"Yeah, there are still those who think that, you know, an outhouse is a smelly thing and no one in their right mind would want that smelly thing inside their house."

"I get the logic. But don't they realize that modern plumbing has all but done away with the smell?"

"What can I say?" Lars said, raising his shoulders. "Old habits die hard. And my great-aunt's uppity older sister from America was coming for a visit, so she wanted to make sure she had a fresh outhouse for her."

"You live with your great-aunt?"

"For now. I just graduated from architecture school and I'm having trouble finding a job. My great-aunt, Hilma, lives by herself on the family farm. I needed a place to stay and she's got plenty of room. So when she asked me to build the new outhouse, I figured it was the least I could do, considering the circumstances. My first architectural commission. You could say I started at the bottom. At least that's what my friends said," he said, raising his beer in my direction with a wry smile.

"So what does building the outhouse have to do with Signe?"

"Everything," Lars said. "Long story short, the hole I was digging for the outhouse overlapped with her underground home. We basically came nose-to-nose one morning when I dug through the wall of her bedroom and woke her up. It didn't take long to become friends with her. She's quite the character. I don't know if I was predisposed to believe in gnomes, but for whatever reason, I wasn't resistant to the idea. I don't know what it says about me, but it just wasn't a problem. Plus, it didn't take very long for a *real* problem to develop."

"What happened?" I asked, my curiosity piqued.

"My great-aunt's sister is not a nice person. She's a busybody. She pokes her nose anywhere and everywhere. Don't ask me how, but in a matter of days after I met Signe, Grete—that's my great-aunt's sister—found out about Signe and the rest of the gnomes who lived, as she said, on my great-aunt's property 'rent-free'. Within a week, Grete hatched a plan to turn the gnomes' underground home into a tourist attraction, with tunnels and windows dug into the hillside so you could see what the 'wee folk' were doing. If you can believe it, Grete told my great aunt that she 'owned the gnomes' and they were hers to do with as she pleased. Grete went so far as to get the town's mayor to buy into the idea. *Great for business! Everyone's going to get rich!* Even my great-aunt thought it was a good idea. It was unbelievable how fast the whole thing got out of control."

"What did you do?"

"Signe was the one who did everything. I just followed orders."

"What did *she* do?"

"Came up with the idea to 'self-kidnap' the tribe."

"What does that mean?"

"There was no way on earth that the gnomes were going to let themselves get made into some kind of a, a, how do you say...*freak show*. Signe knew she had to get everyone and everything out of their underground home in a hurry. And she knew that she had to float a story out there to explain their disappearance in a way that would keep anyone from continuing to look for them.”

“Why would anyone even miss them if they just disappeared? They’ve been practically invisible for the last few hundred years, haven’t they?”

“Not exactly. You know about their gold, right?”

“Of course.”

“Well, gnome or not, you simply can’t own that much gold and not have certain other people aware of it. Even before the idea of being made into a tourist attraction came up, Signe was worried about how to move their gold without attracting attention.”

“Makes sense. What did she do?”

“I’m not sure. Signe plays her cards close to her chest. One day she just didn’t show up.”

“What do you mean?”

“We’d taken to meeting every morning at six at the graveyard. A week ago she didn’t show up. And hasn’t shown up since. The last time I saw her she said, more to herself than to me, was ‘we’ll kidnap ourselves and steal our own gold.’ Before she ran off, she said she’d let me know where the tribe was once they had settled. She also told me about your meeting today and said I had to be at the graveyard to meet you and explain what happened. At least as much as I know.”

I was quiet for a minute, trying to process what Lars had just told me. Was the smart thing to simply bail before it got any more screwed up? “Sorry Lars, for being so upset earlier. This whole thing has taken a lot of time and effort. And in less than a day, it’s morphed into a situation I’m not sure I can handle.”

“But you have a long history with the gnomes, don’t you?”

“Yeah. Several generations worth. All the way back to the late 1800s and the Original Finn, as I call him, Captain Gustav Niebaum. King Gob and his band of explorers were stowaways on his ship. In exchange for Niebaum not throwing them overboard, the gnomes agreed to dig the caves he needed for aging wines at his new winery in the Napa Valley.”

Lars put his hand to his mouth to stifle a laugh.

“Did I say something funny?” I said.

“Not intentionally. It’s just that in Finn, napa means ‘bellybutton.’ Captain Niebaum’s winery is in ‘Bellybutton Valley,’ Lars said, laughing out loud now.

I couldn’t help but laugh, too. “I forgot. My grandmother, Hattie, told me that years ago. Something tells me I won’t forget again.”

"Don't worry about it. If that's the worst thing that happens today, you'll be in good shape."

An awkward translation wouldn't be the worst thing that happened that day. Not by a mile. Once we both stopped laughing, I said, "Where were we?"

"You were telling me about your long history with the gnomes."

"Right. And the fact we're here means the story continues. As you know, my grandson is here with me. He re-established contact with the gnomes last summer, in California. After more than 40 years of no communication."

"How'd he do that?"

"With some homing pigeons with good memories. But that's another story. Speak of the devil, here he is now."

Joaquin appeared in the bar, hair every which way, blinking to get used to the relative dark.

"Joaquin, this is Lars. A friend of Signe. She sent him to let us know she couldn't make our meeting because she and the tribe had self-kidnapped themselves."

"Whoa. TMI. I just woke up. I'm not even sure where I am exactly." Joaquin pulled up a barstool next to me and ran a hand through his hair.

"Even people who know where they are aren't sure where they are when it's the Åland Islands," Lars said, chuckling.

"If you mean we're a long way from nowhere, I get that." Turning to me he asked, "Is 'self-kidnapping' what it sounds like?"

"I guess so. What do I know? Without Signe, I'm kind of at a loss here."

"How long were you planning to stay?" Lars asked.

"Not long. I figured we'd be done with our business in a week, but I'm beginning to think that's not happening."

"If you don't mind my saying, that doesn't sound like much time to me," Lars said, draining the last of his beer. "Granted, Signe acted quickly with the whole 'self-kidnapping' caper, but from what I've read, the gnomes aren't exactly known for their speedy decision-making."

"No, you're right. But I was given the impression this relocation venture was settled business and we'd do it by the numbers. I admit I was thinking more like an Uplander than a gnome. Gnome time is definitely slow time."

"Uplander?" Lars asked.

"That's what they call us tall folk."

"Will you excuse me for a minute?" he said.

"Certainly," I turned to Joaquin as Lars walked off. "How are you feeling?"

"Like I could fall asleep again sitting here."

"I hear you. I think I had an adrenalin rush when I thought I was going to meet Signe. *That* has definitely worn off. We're a couple of live wires, aren't we?"

"Good thing the hotel room has black-out curtains." Joaquin said. "It never gets completely dark this time of year, does it?"

"Nope. The sun barely dips below the horizon at Midsummer."

"That's so weird. What's winter like? Dark all the time?"

"Yep," I said.

"Man, that must be depressing."

"Yeah. That's why they go all kinds of crazy during summer."

Just then Lars came back and sat down. He didn't say anything, but his face was absolutely stricken.

Something was very wrong.

THE CHURCH OF ST. LAWRENCE AT ECKERÖ DATES BACK TO THE 13th CENTURY, AND PROBABLY THE LAST PLACE YOU'D EXPECT TO SEE A VOSLAKIAN GROUNDSKEEPER, WHICH IS WHY HE CAUGHT LARS'S ATTENTION.

Chapter IV

Voslakian Terror

June 21, 2013

The hotel in Eckerö

Day One of our week-long trip, *continued*

Grandpa Nick writing:

"What's up Lars? It looks like you've seen a ghost," I said.

He kind of shook himself and, looking at us both, said, "Do you know anything about Voslakia?"

I looked at Joaquin who raised his shoulders and shook his head. I turned back to Lars. "I guess not. Why?"

"The last thing Signe said before she disappeared was to be on the lookout for any Voslakians. They're bad news. Really bad news."

"What's the story?" I asked.

"Voslakia is one of the smallest countries that used to be part of the Russian Federation. They've always been a breed apart. A bunch of bad asses known for their crazy tempers. I don't know why, but it comes naturally to them. They'd just as soon do bodily harm as talk to you."

"What do they have to do with Signe?"

"At the top of their hate list are the gnomes. It's been that way for generations. The gnomes get blamed for anything that goes wrong in Voslakia. Whether it's a house fire, a drought, or an earthquake, it's the gnomes' fault. In the old days, the Voslakians would use any disaster as an excuse to terrorize the gnomes and steal as much of their gold as they could get their hands on. There haven't been any gnomes in Voslakia for two hundred years or so. But if you can believe it, the Vo-slakians still blame the gnomes for stuff that goes wrong."

"Why did Signe tell you to be on the lookout for them?" Joaquin asked.

"She said if anyone was going to get wind of the gnomes moving and tak-ing their gold with them, it would be the Voslakians. A international criminal en-terprise is what they've evolved into ever since they declared their independence. They're very connected. Signe said if there was a Voslakian around, there would be trouble. That simple. Getting the rumor out there that they'd been kidnapped was more or less specifically aimed at the Voslakians. Obviously it didn't work."

"So how can you tell if someone is Voslakian?" I asked.

"It's not a hundred percent. Usually they have big heads, especially the men. I know that sounds strange, but I'm not kidding. And they look kind of Neanderthal, with that raised ridge across their foreheads, above their eyebrows."

"Really?"

"Look, I'm telling the truth. I almost ran into one just now. I was pulling the bathroom door open from the inside and he was pushing it to get in. We practically ran into each other. What's really bothering me is that I'm almost certain I saw the same guy when we were at the churchyard. He was pushing a wheelbarrow around, pretending to be a groundskeeper. He had a straw hat on, so I didn't register him as a Voslakian, but now that I've seen him up close, I'm sure it's the same guy. This is not good, you guys."

"What should we do?" I asked.

"Get out of here right now. This Voslakian obviously knows you and Joaquin are staying here. He's just waiting for an opportunity to… I don't even want to think about it. Come on. Let's get your stuff. I've got a place where you can stay. As long as we're not followed, you'll be okay. At least long enough for us to figure out a plan."

The photograph along the top of the page shows a view of the sea with a small forested island with granite rocks.

Above: The island (the one in front) Lars took us to belonged to his great aunt. It was very small and essentially composed of just two things: granite boulders and stunted pine trees, surrounded, of course, by water. The cabin was on the other side of the island, so you can't see it. Every direction you looked, there were more islands of every size (most of them even smaller than the one we were on) and they all looked more or less the same. It would be very easy to get lost in this archipelago and, by the same token, hard to find–which was somewhat comforting considering who was trying to find us.

THE FISHERMAN'S COTTAGE WAS ABOUT AS RUSTIC AS THEY COME, BUT NOT WITHOUT ITS APPEAL - ESPECIALLY IN THE SITUATION WE WERE IN. "ANY PORT IN A STORM," AS THE OLD SAILORS WOULD SAY.

Chapter V

Island Hideaway

June 21, 2013

A very small, unnamed islet in the Gulf of Bothnia, part of the Åland archipelago

Day One of our week-long trip, *continued*

Grandpa Nick writing:

Considering we hadn't unpacked, it didn't take long for Joaquin and I to get our stuff and throw it in the rental car. I didn't even bother checking out. I'd figure that out later. We followed Lars on a series of narrow, curving roads through forests of spruce and birch trees, interspersed with green, gently-rolling open meadows. Pale granite boulders, large and small, dotted the forests and meadows. In different circumstances I would have stopped the car and taken pictures. It was that beautiful. But not today. Looking frequently in the rear-view mirror, I could see that we weren't being followed; I'd seen only two cars after we left the hotel, both going in the opposite direction. On an island, all roads eventually lead to the water. And sure enough, after about 15 minutes, we parked on a flat, gravel-covered clearing right next to the water. A primitive wooden dock jutted out from the parking area. Lars told us to get our luggage while he took a canvas cover off a small wooden dinghy tied to the end of the dock. He sat in the stern and we handed him our bags and got in. Joaquin sat in the bow, with me in the middle. After he fiddled with the small outboard engine, it sputtered to life, and we took off across the steely gray water. None of us said much, but there was no mistaking the sense of urgency that silently passed between us.

Once we got into open water, Joaquin yelled, "Where are we going?"

I shrugged and looked questioningly at Lars. He pointed to the horizon and said loudly, "it's not far." As tense as our situation was, as I looked around, the overall impression was one of softness. A thin, high overcast sky softened the light, extracting the bright colors and hard edges, leaving an almost monochromatic scene of faded pastels. The temperature was surprisingly mild and there was next to no wind. A number of gulls raced right above us, as if they wanted something. I caught Lars's eye and pointed at the birds.

"When my uncle used to pull up his fishing nets, he'd throw the smallest fish up in the air and the gulls would catch them. Now every time they see the boat go out, they think they're going to get fed."

As we entered an area with a lot of exposed rocks, Lars cut the engine to about half-speed. The further we went, the rocks became small islands, maybe a quarter acre or less. Some of the islets were more or less flat, others were mounded in the middle. But none rose more than ten feet out of the water. On all the islands there were spruce trees. How they grew in what looked like solid rock, I had no idea. No wonder they weren't very big.

Lars approached one of the small islands and cut the engine, expertly guiding the boat alongside a large rock. He told me to jump out and look for metal cleats that had been secured to the rock. I found them and tied the dinghy to the cleats while Lars grabbed our bags. Without hesitation, Joaquin took off like a goat, hopping from one boulder to another. From a distance, we could see him pointing at something and yelling through cupped hands, but neither of us could make out what he was saying. With the dinghy secure, we headed off in Joaquin's direction, bags in hand, zig-zagging our way across the rocks. Along the way, he explained in addition to owning a dairy farm, his great-aunt owned this island. Apparently it wasn't unusual for the locals to supplement their income by fishing, at least during the summer months. The routine was to take the dinghy out into the ocean after dinner and set nets in strategic spots, motor to the *kalastajatorppa*, or fisherman's cottage, sleep for a few hours and then pull the nets up the following morning and return to the dairy farm in time to milk the cows. The catch was either sold or used by the family. Lars explained that he had been close to his late, great-uncle and frequently accompanied him on these fishing expeditions.

"You and Joaquin will be safe here," Lars said. "There's no way anyone can sneak up without you knowing it."

"If you say so." I was not entirely convinced that someone couldn't arrive unnoticed the way we had a few minutes earlier, but I decided not to bring it up. We made our way to a small, weathered wood cabin, maybe 12 by 15 feet. The door was open and Joaquin already inside.

"It's like a kid's clubhouse," he said, looking around the rustic, single room.

"It's just meant to be somewhere you can catch a little sleep and make some coffee in the morning," Lars said, pointing to a small woodstove. Other than that, the only furniture was a small wooden table and two chairs.

"Where are the beds?" Joaquin asked.

"In the wall," Lars pointed to two narrow bunks built into the wall, one on top of the other.

"Cool," Joaquin said, "I get dibs on the top one."

"Fine by me."

"Listen," Lars said, "I'm going to go back to my great-aunt's and get some food and coffee for tomorrow. I'll be back in a couple of hours. There's a kerosene lamp over there, a shortwave radio, firewood on the side of the cabin, and an outhouse out back. Everything you need. Oh, and a deck of cards," he said, pointing to a pack on a small shelf under a clouded window. "It's not much, but at least you'll be safe while we figure out what's next."

"No dominoes?" Joaquin asked.

"Nope. Sorry."

"And Neanderthal man isn't going to find us out here?" Joaquin asked.

"No, we gave him the slip–for now. Okay, I'm going. The sooner I go, the sooner I'll be back and we can figure out a plan. I'll see you later," Lars said, waving at the door.

Joaquin and I stood in the middle of the small room and looked at each other. Were we thinking the same thing? What in the world had we gotten ourselves into?

Above right: Lars built a proper bonfire on the beach to serve as a beacon for Remi to be able to find us. *Right:* Remi said he kept his boat at Grisslehamn Harbor in Sweden. I looked it up on my phone. It was only about 50 miles from where we were on the western side of the Åland archipelago (the black dotted line on the map at right). Even so, he'd have to travel mighty fast to make his way to us in less than a couple of hours. I wondered what kind of boat he had. Once I found out, it all became very clear.

Chapter VI

Remi to the Rescue

June 21, 2013

A small, unnamed islet in the Gulf of Bothnia, part of the Åland archipelago

Day One of our week-long trip, *continued*

Grandpa Nick writing:

I sat at the table and messed around with the shortwave radio. Through the small window, I could see Joaquin sitting on a large, flat granite rock, fixated on his phone. *Good thing I brought along a solar-powered charger*, although I wondered how well it would work with the overcast sky.

After about an hour, I went outside and got Joaquin to walk with me around the island, first in one direction and then the opposite. There's nothing like being stranded on an island the size of an average suburban lot to sharpen your focus and try to answer basic questions like, how exactly did I get here? As beautiful as it was, there wasn't much else to keep me from thinking about the predicament we were in. And the more I thought about it, the more I realized there wasn't a thing I, personally, could do to improve the situation. In his own way, I think Joaquin felt a similar frustration. After a couple of hours of pretty much aimless exploring, it would be an understatement to say we were pleased to hear the sound of Lars's outboard motor. Once he was next to the docking rock, we tied up the boat and grabbed the net bags filled with groceries.

Inside the hut, Lars didn't waste any time making a fire in the wood stove, placing a small pot of water on top.

"You'll have to excuse me, but I've got to cook some potatoes—now. I haven't had any since yesterday and I'm feeling faint."

"Well, by all means, go ahead," I said.

"Are you and Joaquin hungry?" Lars asked.

"I am. How 'bout you, Joaquin?"

"Starved."

"Every man for himself," Lars said, unwrapping several packages wrapped in waxed paper. "There's bread, cheese, sausage. And I picked a few tomatoes and cucumbers from my aunt's garden, along with the potatoes," he said, holding up a pink new potato the size of a golf ball.

While the potatoes boiled, I sliced the tomatoes and cucumbers and put them with the cheeses and sausage on a plate in the middle of the table. Lars found some jazz music on the radio from Estonia, of all places, and Joaquin lit the old-fashioned oil lamp he'd found on a shelf. It's surprising how quickly a place can take on a welcoming atmosphere with only the basic comforts.

There were only two chairs, but Lars went outside and brought back an un-split round of firewood and sat on it like a stool. Once we had filled our stomachs, Lars began to ask questions.

"Do you have any way to get in touch with Signe?" he asked.

"Yes, but it's not exactly direct."

"What do you mean?"

"I can't actually talk to her in person, but I can get a message to her and she can get one back to me. It involves me calling the last remaining pay phone in Calistoga. That's the town closest to where the gnomes live on Mt. St. Helena. To avoid being seen, Prince G goes to the phone booth at 4 o'clock every morning, carrying a wooden stepstool so he can reach the phone. Frankly, the whole thing is ridiculous. He refuses to use a cell phone because he says the GPS tracking software puts them all at risk. I suppose he's right, but it also makes communicating very difficult. So, if I need to get a message to Signe, I have to call Prince G at our pre-arranged time, then he has to communicate the message to the crows and they deliver it to Signe, wherever she is."

"How long does it take?"

"Surprisingly not that long. Even halfway around the world, the crows can deliver a message in less than 48 hours."

"Signe gave me a number in Sweden," Lars said. "She said it belonged to Remi Wingrove, someone she trusted. She said to call him if there was an emergency and he'd get in touch with her. Sounds like it's a lot faster than communicating by crow.

Ever heard of this Remi guy?"

"No."

"Well, this seems like an emergency to me. What do you say?"

Joaquin and I looked at each other and nodded in the affirmative without even thinking.

"Okay," Lars said. "I'll call him. We can't hide out on this island forever."

"No disagreement on that," Joaquin piped in.

Lars looked at his watch. "It's only 8 o'clock," he said, pressing the numbers. Once he'd heard the number ringing, he placed the phone on the table and pushed the speaker button. It rang a few more times before a male voice answered.

"Mr. Wingrove?"

"Speaking."

"This is Lars Larson. I'm calling from Åland. I believe we have a friend in common. Signe?"

"Oh yes, Mr. Larson. Signe said you might call." The man had an unidentifiable accent, or more accurately, a combination of accents. Whatever his origins, his voice was measured and reassuring.

"Please call me Lars. Are you free to talk?"

"Yes, of course."

Lars proceeded to explain, about meeting me and Joaquin, and the sighting of a Voslakian, whom he suspected had been following us earlier in the day.

"Hmmm. Where are you now? Is it safe?"

"We're at my great-aunt's *kalastajatorppa*, on a small island off of Eckerö. The Voslakian didn't follow us, so we're safe. But it's not the most practical place to stay for very long."

"No, of course not. But this is going to take a little doing," Remi said. "May I call you back within the hour?"

"Yes, of course," Lars said. "We're not going anywhere," he said chuckling lightly.

Lars ended the call and looked up saying "Who wants to play gin?"

"Why not?" I said. "But there are three of us."

"No problem." Lars grabbed the deck of cards. "We can play Jailhouse Gin. Any number can play."

"It's a good game. Joaquin, are you in?"

"Sure."

Lars explained the rules and he was right. It *was* a good game. While we were playing, he explained that his great-uncle, Voitto, had taught him the game, one he'd learned in jail.

"If you don't mind me asking, what was he doing in jail,?"

"Uncle Voitto liked his schnapps and he was pulled over for driving under the influence, which is a big no-no in Finland. Part of the punishment was to lose his driver's license for a year. He managed okay until one Sunday afternoon he started on the tipple and decided to mow his lawn. He had a fancy riding mower and, after he had mowed the lawn, he got it into his head that he wanted to go to his favorite bar and see his friends. So he drove on the city streets on his lawnmower. He didn't get far before he was picked up. This time he spent two weeks in jail. He said it wasn't so bad. The food was lousy, but he did learn this great card game. Uncle Voitto always looked on the bright side of things. Unfortunately, my great-aunt didn't share his 'bright side' approach."

"Imagine that," I said.

Joaquin won the first game and I won the second. We were just starting our third game when Lars's phone rang.

"Hold on, Remi," Lars said, "I'm going to put you on speaker so Nick and Joaquin can hear you, too. They just arrived from California this morning. I'm afraid things haven't gone as planned."

"It's better not to have a Voslakian in any plan. Sorry your trip has gotten off to a difficult beginning. I'm Remi Wingrove, Nick. Nice to meet you, even if it is by phone. And you, too, Joaquin."

"Back at 'ya," Joaquin said.

"I spoke with Signe," Remi said. "We're in agreement that you need to meet as soon as possible. And we need to keep you and your grandson as far away from the Voslakians as possible. Truly reprehensible. The lot of them. Particularly horrible to gnomes. But right now we need to get you off that so-called island–no offense, Lars–and take you to Signe. Lars, can you send me your coordinates?"

"You mean my latitude and longitude?"

"Yes."

"Sure thing," Lars said.

"I've got a boat in Grisslehamn Harbor, directly east from your general vicinity. It's not that far. I'm guessing I'll be there in an hour-and-a-half or so. I've got the midnight sun to rely on, but just to make sure we find each other, why don't you build a bonfire on the beach? That way I'll have something to look for. One small island among 6,700 other small islands can start to look the same in the gloaming."

"Will do, Remi. Are you sure you're okay with this?" I asked, wondering what kind of person used a word like "gloaming."

"Any friend of Signe's is a friend of mine," Remi said.

"Well, you know what they say about 'a friend in need,' don't you?" I asked.

"No."

"It's a variation on an old saying: I say 'a friend in need is a pain in the ass.'"

Lars laughed; Joaquin looked at me like I had passed gas. Remi chuckled and told me not to worry about it, adding he'd been called on to do much worse. That may have been true, but it seemed like a big ask to me, especially from someone he didn't know from a can of paint. I wondered what kind of relationship Signe and Remi had that made such a request okay? Another mystery, at least for now.

Joaquin and I grabbed as much firewood as we could carry from the tidy stack next to the hut. We took it down to the narrow strip of rocky beach on the west side of the island. Lars used his pocket knife to whittle some thin strips of wood that were easy to light. He gradually added larger and larger pieces of wood and in about a half hour he had a proper bonfire going.

"Why don't you guys get your stuff and bring it down here? I'll keep the fire going," Lars said.

"How are we going to do this?" I asked. Was Lars going to come with us and, if he did, would he leave his boat there on the island?

"I'm not sure. Let's wait until Remi gets here and see what he thinks."

Joaquin and I went back to the hut and got our bags. I glanced at the bunks built into the wall. As small and primitive as they were, they were definitely calling my name. Extreme tiredness was setting in. I wondered when I was ever going to get some sleep again. I glanced at my watch. It was 10 o'clock local time and, of course, as far north as we were, it was still plenty light. As it turned out, we still had many miles (and hours) to go before there'd be a chance to sleep.

Left: Remi's incredible speedboat, a 1931 Gar Wood Baby Gar, out-fitted with a new 650 horsepower Rolls Royce engine. Do I need to say more? *Below:* South Harbor in Helsinki, where we docked the Baby Gar, turning more than a few heads. The big granite steps, which frame the harbor on three sides, rise out of the ocean, widening out to a large plaza, where there's a busy farmer's market. It's like the city just rose out of the water, fully formed. Fishermen and farmers alike pull their boats up to the steps and sell their wares right from the bows. Very cool.

SOUTH HARBOR, WHERE THE CITY OF HELSINKI, FINLAND STEPS DOWN INTO THE WATERS OF THE GULF OF FINLAND.

Chapter VII

Pounding Towards Helsinki

June 22, 2013

En route from the islet to Helsinki via Remi's speedboat

Day Two of our week-long trip, *continued*

Grandpa Nick writing:

Joaquin and I got back to the bonfire with our bags and even though it wasn't particularly cold, the warmth felt good. The sun had dipped just below the horizon creating an odd atmosphere the likes of which I'd never experienced before–like a barely perceptible fog, every microscopic droplet reflecting and refracting light. The effect was extraordinary. I found myself moving my hands through the air to see if I could feel it–move it, swirl it–but no, it was there in effect only. I wondered if Joaquin noticed how strange it was. Lars was sitting on a boulder looking away from us to the illuminated horizon. Very low, at first, almost humming, he started gently singing in Finn, something I would later learn is almost a national trait–spontaneous singing. The sheer magic of it–the liquid, diffuse light, the shimmering orange stripe along the horizon, the ocean lapping timelessly against granite rocks, shades of gray comingling, the snapping fire sending golden sparks and trails of blue smoke curling heavenward, all bound together by the lilting thread of a human voice. I didn't understand the words and yet, in a way, I did. It was unmistakably a love song, bearing witness to the beauty of the moment. Everything about the scene was totally enchanting. And then from out of nowhere, we seemed to be surrounded by a low mechanical growl, growing ever louder and deeper, in complete contrast to the otherworldly delight of just a minute before. Like an apparition, Remi came into view in a wooden speedboat, as elegant and over-the-top as anything I'd ever seen. Joaquin and Lars didn't say a word, but their astonished wide-open eyes said it all. What a boat! Long, low, and gleaming, it was speed and beauty made real.

Some distance from the shore, Remi yelled over the rumble of the idling engine "Good evening, gentlemen. I think I'm about as close as I dare."

Lars shouted back, "I can bring Nick and Joaquin out to you. The dinghy is tied up on the other side of the island."

"Sounds good," Remi said, adjusting the throttle so the boat stayed more or less in one place. Even though it was some distance away, the sound the engine made was so deep it actually reverberated in my chest. Joaquin and I picked up our bags and hot-footed it to other side of the little island. We got in the dinghy and Lars started the outboard. We put-putted around the island, the contrast between the two boats so pronounced it was comical. As we neared the speedboat, Lars told Joaquin to put the bumpers out so dinghy wouldn't damage the floating perfection that was Remi's boat. He maneuvered the dinghy alongside and Remi held the gunwale and helped me and Joaquin aboard.

"I don't know what I was thinking," Remi said to Lars, "about building a bonfire. Tonight's the Midsummer celebration. There are bonfires all over the place. Good thing you gave me your coordinates."

"That's right," Lars said, "I was too preoccupied with Voslakians to think much about it. Maybe next year," he said wistfully, clueless as to how different his life would be a year from now, on another island, halfway around the world.

"I'll take these two to Signe," Remi said to Lars. "She asked you to stand by. We may need to rely on you for some help, if that's okay. I'll call you tomorrow," he said and waved. And like that, I had the answer to my question: Lars waved back and said he'd see us later. I had no idea what was going on, but waved anyway, hoping I'd see Lars later, if only to thank him for getting us out of harm's way. I was beginning to be uncomfortable about the fact that, without any ado, it appeared I was no longer in control of making my own decisions. Somebody was. But who? Signe? I had no idea. For the time being there was nothing I could do but just be a passive participant. Meanwhile, the magnificence of the speedboat had overwhelmed Joaquin into silent awe. No sooner had we sat down on the leather seats, than Remi pushed the throttle forward and the boat fairly stood up and ran across the water, emitting a constant powerful roar. Joaquin was sitting next to Remi. Remi looked at him and shouted, "That's the sound of 650 horsepower."

Joaquin smiled and tried to say something but no words came out. At the speed we were going I doubted whether he would have been heard anyway. We were in open water and although the seats were comfortable enough, between the roar of the massive engine, the wind and the chop of the boat on the water, it wasn't the most comfortable of rides. About all there was to do was to sit back, look around, and wait until we reached wherever we were going. After an hour or so, I began to think I was having an out of body experience. The longer we went, the worse it got until, finally, Remi slowed the engine a little and the boat eased down in the water, allowing a view ahead. I had seen plenty of pictures of Helsinki when I was on-line researching our trip. I immediately recognized the grand, neoclassical Helsinki Cathedral, its columns, pediments, and domes in the distance, rising majestically above the harbor and cityscape. Remi continued to slow the engine until we arrived at a public dock of sorts, with various boats of all sizes and types tied up at the water's edge. When Remi finally cut the engine, I involuntarily breathed a sigh of relief, loud enough to make my feelings known to anyone around. At that point, I didn't care who heard me.

We had tied up between a sailboat on one side and a small commercial fishing boat on the other. I looked at my watch. It was a little after six in the morning and a fisherman was already selling fish out of ice-filled wooden boxes, right on the bow of his boat to customers. The twenty-four-hour-a-day daylight seemed to affect ev-erything, including shopping. As I stepped out of Remi's boat, I realized I was step-ping onto granite steps that ringed the harbor on three sides. The steps rose from underwater to a large public plaza where an open-air market was set up. It seemed the architecture of the city was rising directly out of the ocean which, of course, it was. The plaza contained table after table, each displaying their wares—from fat bundles of ferny fresh dill, to bunches of cut wildflowers, to gleaming sides of salmon. Each table sported its own large red or orange canvas umbrella which not only cast shade, but colored the light filtering through so everyone and everything was bathed in an appealing warm reddish glow. I was lost in the scene when Remi's face appeared in front of mine, saying something I didn't understand.

"I'm sorry, what?" I responded, realizing the noise of the speedboat had affected my hearing.

"I said, do you want a cup of coffee?"

"To tell you the truth, I just realized how tired I am. Between the flight, the change in time, and now this round-the-clock daylight, I have no idea when was the last time I slept."

"You don't need coffee, then," Remi said chuckling. "Let's get you and Joaquin to your hotel. It's right across the plaza."

It was a mercifully short walk and, like seemingly everything else in Finland, the hotel was modern, attractive, and spotlessly clean. Remi lead the way to the reception desk. The clerk asked for our passports and airline tickets, giving them back along with the key card to our room.

Remi looked at the key cards and said "You're on the fourth floor with a view of the plaza and the Gulf of Finland. Two big beds which, if you don't mind my saying, looks like you both could use. I have business to attend to. Why don't we meet back here at what—noon? That'll give you a few hours to make up for the sleep you didn't get last night."

I looked at Joaquin and he nodded. "Sure," I said, "any longer than that and we might not wake up." I looked at my watch. "So, the local time is a little after seven a.m.?"

"That's right."

"Okay, then we'll see you at noon, right here. Thank you, Remi, for that, ahem, amazing ride."

"My pleasure. See you at noon. I'll let Signe know you're here and that we're on our way."

• • •

Okay, time to put the journal away. The voice over the intercom just announced the familiar instructions: "As we prepare to land at San Francisco International Airport, please fasten your seatbelt and return your seat back and tray table to their full upright and locked positions. The local time is ten minutes past four o'clock in the afternoon."

We'll pick this up later.

Above: There's a lot to look at in the international terminal of the San Francisco airport–so much so that it's easy to not pay attention and run into people, like I did. That said, I wonder what would have happened if I hadn't been looking up at what I thought might be boats floating across the ceiling. If I'd been paying attention, would I have avoided running into Mad? And then what would have happened–or not happened? They're not boats, by the way–they're supposed to bring to mind the way the Wright brothers built the first airplanes, by stretching fabric over the wings.

THE DISTINCTIVE FINNAIR TAIL LOGO, IN THE BLUE-AND-WHITE COLORS OF THE FINNISH FLAG.

Left: Map of a section of Northern California, north of San Francisco. The red arrow on the left points to the town of Sebastopol where Mad wanted to buy a house. The other red arrow points to Rutherford, in the middle of the Napa Valley, where Grandpa Nick and I live. The two small towns are less than forty miles apart. You can see where San Francisco is at the bottom of the map.

Chapter VIII

The Two-Toned Hairdo

June 27, 2013

San Francisco Airport, International Terminal, Air France Lounge

Day Seven of our week-long trip

It's Grandpa Nick again. I'm back and you're going to have to suspend your belief for this next twist. To quote the heavyweight boxer, Muhammad Ali, the chances of it happening were "slim to none–and Slim just left town;" the type of occurrence you'd say "only happens in books." Not only did it happen, but it made me start to feel like maybe fate was playing a role in this story, and I don't believe in fate. Here's how it went down.

Joaquin and I made it through customs without a hitch and were walking along the concourse, looking for the Air France lounge. Finnair didn't have their own lounge but did have an arrangement with Air France to allow their passengers to use their lounge. We wanted a place to sit down for a few minutes to figure out what we were doing next. Joaquin was behind me with a map of the airport on his phone, issuing directions–left, right, straight ahead–which I was more-or-less following blindly. I'll admit that after a 14-hour flight, I was a little soft in the head, but I found myself mesmerized by the woman walking in front of me. Or more precisely, mesmerized by her hair. It was white blond, cut to her shoulders. But the bottom couple of inches was a straight, black stripe, so she had this geometric, two-tone hair-do–white blond and black. Now I'm no more interested in other people's hair than anyone else but, between Joaquin's instructions and my infatuation with the two-tone hair-do, I ran into her when she abruptly stopped in front of me. And, because he was looking at his screen, Joaquin ran into me and wound up on his backside, looking up with a bewildered expression. I turned to the woman to apologize when we both realized we knew each other. Big time.

"*Nick?*"

"*Mad?*"

"Well, I'll be…"

"Old, by the looks of it," she said, laughing.

We hugged each other like the old friends we were who hadn't seen each other for more than forty years.

Joaquin got back on his feet. The bewildered look on his face hadn't changed, only now he wasn't comprehending what he was witnessing. He did, however, have more sense than Mad and I, motioning with his head that we should move to the side of the passageway, out of the human traffic, every member of which seemed to be in a hurry.

"You're not trying to catch a plane or anything, are you?" I asked her.

"No. Just got off one."

"Joaquin and I were going to hang in the lounge here for a bit and regroup," I said pointing to it.

"Air France–oo-lah-lah," Mad said enthusiastically. "I'll let you buy me a drink."

"It's a deal," I said.

•　　•　　•

"This, I take it, is Joaquin," Mad said once we were sitting down inside the lounge. As they shook hands, Joaquin said "I feel like I know you, kind of."

"Oh, do tell," she said.

"I just read Grandpa's book, or journal–the second one about Kauai. You're in it."

"I'll say I was in it. I had a leading role. Too bad he never let me read it."

"Come on, Mad, you know I promised G I wouldn't let anyone read it–at least not right away," I said.

"How long is 'right away?'"

"Forty-five years."

"Well, not to put too fine a point on it, I think that's now. The summer we spent on Kauai looking for Dagywn was in 1968 wasn't it? And, correct me if I'm wrong, but I believe it's presently 2013, which would make it…"

"Forty-five years," Joaquin said, apparently listening to the conversation even though he had turned his attention back to his phone.

"That's right," Mad said, winking at Joaquin. "I think it's time I got to read it."

"Yeah, Grandpa, you let me read it–and that was last year, before the waiting period was over."

"Okay you guys. You're right. As soon as we're home, I'll make a copy for Mad and get it to her. I guess I've lived up to my side of the agreement with G… finally. I think I got tired of doing the math."

Changing the subject, I said to Mad, "It's funny–any time I imagined running into you, I figured it would be in an airport, since I knew you traveled a lot with the World Bank."

"You were obviously right about the airport, but wrong about the World Bank. I quit, or retired, or whatever you want to call it," Mad said with some enthusiasm. "When I was still working for them, I traveled all the time–but I never ran into *you*," she said laughing.

"So, you're traveling for pleasure now?"

"Very much so. If things go according to plan, I'm going to buy a house." She went on to explain that she'd been divorced for ten years and was on her way to Sebastopol in Sonoma County to look for a house so she could be close to her stepson and his pregnant wife. Mad had not had children of her own, but thought of her stepson as her own and was genuinely fond of his wife. She was looking forward to being a grandmother.

"Well, I recommend it highly," I said. "I'm the president of this guy's fan club," I said, nudging Joaquin, who pretended not to notice.

"Where's home for you these days?" Mad asked.

"Rutherford. Remember Hattie's old summer place?"

"Sure. Kind of hard to forget."

"Well, that's where I am." I shook myself, flashing on what an unbelievable coincidence running into her was, and then blurted out, "I almost didn't recognize you without the dreads."

"What? You were there, Nick, when Melea gave me that buzz cut on the sailboat. Remember? Those dreads have been on the bottom of the ocean for a long time now."

"That's right. How could I forget that?"

"You missed the bright orange phase, when I was living in Paris. My female co-workers told me it was 'too carroty.' That's when I changed it to this. Do you like it?" she asked, swinging her hair left and right.

"Mesmerizing," I said.

"I guess we have to serve ourselves," Mad said, scanning the room. "Let's get something to drink and you can tell me what in the world you and Joaquin were doing wherever Air France took you."

"Finnair. We flew Finnair. They just share this lounge with Air France. We were in the Åland Islands, actually."

"Really? What in the world… ?"

"Well, you know."

"Yeah, as a matter of fact, I *do* know. But not the latest. Come on. Spill the beans."

Above: The Air France lounge, where Grandpa and I met with Mad, his long-lost friend from back in the day. She was part of the team that went looking for Dagywn in Kauai in 1968, so she knew all about what was going on–probably better than anybody. Some of the stuff we were talking about was pretty wild–so much so, that Grandpa joked about needing the "Cone of Silence," like the one Maxwell Smart and his boss, the Chief, used in the tv show from the 1960s, *Get Smart.*

THE CONE OF SILENCE, FROM THE 1960s T.V. SHOW *GET SMART,* WAS ADMITTEDLY SILLY, UNTIL YOU REALLY NEEDED ONE.

Chapter IX

Catching Mad Up

June 27, 2013

San Francisco Airport, International Terminal, Air France Lounge

Day Seven of our week-long trip, *continued*

Joaquin writing:

"So come on. I'm all ears," Mad prodded after we had drinks in front of us.

"You're the one who set this in motion, Joaquin. You first," Grandpa said.

I put my phone to sleep and turned to Mad. "It started last summer, when my friend Darren showed me a leather pouch filled with a lot of gold nuggets."

"Really?" Mad said, surprised.

"Yeah. His dad found it in their winery right where a barrel of wine had been."

"'Had been?' What happened to it?" Mad asked.

"Someone stole it. When I told Grandpa about the pouch of gold, he took me up to the attic and gave me one of his journals to read. I didn't have to read very far to get the connection."

"Which was?"

"Grandpa figured the gnomes were back at it–'procuring' supplies and leaving gold as payment. He wrote about it happening before."

"Then I got the idea of trying to get in touch with G by sending a message using the homing pigeons, like Grandpa and G used to do, from the second journal."

"Did it work?" Mad asked.

"Yeah, that's the amazing thing–it did. I didn't tell Grandpa what I was doing. I was sure he'd tell me it wouldn't work. But I found the dovecote, kind of hidden in an overgrown part of the garden, and a bunch of the pigeons were still living in it."

"A bunch of pigeons with excellent memories," Grandpa chimed in.

"Anyway, Doyle helped me and we sent a pigeon off with a message to G and the next day the pigeon came back–with a new message…"

"Doyle? Grandma Hattie's houseman?" Mad asked.

"Yeah. He lives with us now."

"'Us?'" Mad asked.

"Yeah. Well, I spend a lot of time at Grandpa's. You could say I have more than one family unit."

"Joaquin sends a pigeon off with a message and hears back after forty-plus years of me not hearing a word from them," Grandpa said, shaking his head.

"Yeah, it was definitely cool. G wrote back that he wanted us to come up and talk with him so we did."

"Up on Mt. St. Helena?" Mad asked.

"Yeah. We met all the guys. That's when G and Aalto asked us to go to the Åland Islands and get the rest of their peeps and bring 'em to California. That's what we've been doing."

"Aalto?" Mad asked.

"She's the wizardress–I guess she took over from Dagywn."

"Oh, that's right. I actually met her right after Dagywn decided she should take his place. Interesting," Mad said

"Have you ever been there–to Åland?" I asked Mad.

"The Åland Islands? No, but I've heard of them. They're between Finland and Sweden, aren't they?"

"Yeah, right there at the southern end of the Gulf of Bothnia, where it opens onto the Baltic. There's like 6,500 islands, but most of them aren't much more than a big rock poking out of the water.

"So that's what you've been doing… like right now?" Mad asked, incredulously.

"Yep–that and running for our lives."

"Really?" Mad said seriously.

"Really" I said, "but before we tell you about that, don't you find it odd that you were part of the last chapter of this venture, back in 1968 and nothing happening for 45 years, when the action starts up again, all of a sudden you're back on the scene? How does *that* happen?"

"I have absolutely no idea," Mad said, "It has the stink of fate about it, doesn't it?"

"It crossed my mind," Grandpa said.

"So what are you doing right now, in this lounge?" Mad asked.

"We're going to meet up with Lars, a cohort of ours, at a little after eight. He stayed behind to secure the tribe members inside their crates."

"Whoa, you lost me. *Crates?*"

"Forty-three of them, hand-built by Lars, one for each… *gnome,*" I said quietly, looking around to see if anyone heard me. "The three of us are here to receive the shipment. They're due to arrive tomorrow afternoon. Courtesy of DHL, if you can believe that."

"*Via DHL…?*" Mad asked, obviously having trouble believing it.

"You should see 'em. Each one has a totally customized interior."

"This is crazy."

"Yeah boy. But there's more. Tomorrow, after we get them out of their crates, we have to get them up to Mt. St. Helena."

"How?"

"Signe bought a bus–a 'lightly used' rock-and-roll tour bus, if there is such a thing. Lars got his international Class B license in Finland. He's cleared to drive the bus here in California, so that's what he's going to do. Drive forty-three gnomes up to Mt. St. Helena in a rock-and-roll tour bus. Makes perfect sense, doesn't it? But you asked what we're doing here in the Air France lounge. The short answer is we're killing time."

"Hold on a minute–I don't mean to interrupt. Is anyone else hungry? I could eat a skunk."

"I don't know if they serve skunk, but we passed an okay-looking buffet coming in. You want to give it a try?"

"Absolutely. You coming, Joaquin?" Mad said, getting up from her chair.

"Right behind you."

We all loaded up what we wanted onto trays and Grandpa said he'd feel more comfortable sitting somewhere with no one sitting close by. I looked around the lounge for some place more private than where we had been sitting and spotted a group of three chairs around a round table, way off in a corner. "Let's go over there."

"Do we need to lower the Cone of Silence, too?" Mad asked with a smile.

"If we had one, I'd use it," Grandpa said half-seriously.

As Mad chomped down on an about-to-fall-apart focaccia sandwich, Grandpa said, "I see you've moved on from your 'white food only' days."

"Yes, I've expanded my horizons. You're one of the few people who'd remember that."

"One of the many things I remember from that summer… but that was then–this is now and 'now' has too many moving parts–it's making me nervous," Grandpa said.

"I can see that," Mad said, "but, frankly, *nervous* sounds like an appropriate response, Nick. If you'll let me, maybe I can help. But first give me a little more of the back story."

"You mean like the part where we had to run for our lives?" I said.

"Yeah, what was that about?"

"Voslakians."

"Do you mind?" Grandpa interjected, "Let me bring Mad up to speed first and then you can tell her about the Voslakians."

Above: Standard gold bars (the kind the United States keeps at the Fort Knox Gold Bullion Depository). They weigh approximately 27 pounds each. They are made by pouring molten gold into bar-shaped molds and are required to be at least 99.5% pure. Because weight is more important than size, there is no standardized size for gold bars, but most are approximately 10 inches long, 3.25 inches wide, and 1.5 inches thick—a little smaller than the common clay brick used in construction – and a whole lot heavier. Think of it: just three of them weigh almost a hundred pounds. *Bottom right:* The gnomes have been mining gold for a very long time. Here's how Swedish artist Olaus Magnus thought it looked. From his book, *Historia de Gentibus Septentrionalibus*, published in 1555. That's a gnome mining on the left.

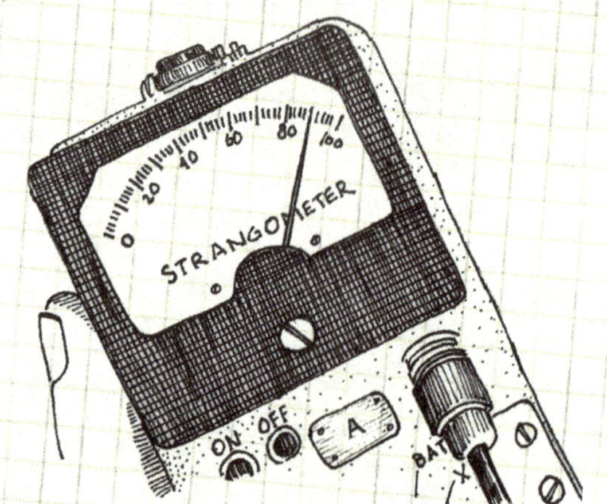

I'M FAIRLY SURE THE SO-CALLED "STRANGE-O-METER" WAS JUST SOMETHING GRANDPA AND MAD MADE UP WHEN THEY WERE TEENAGERS, BUT IF IT WAS ACTUALLY REAL, IT WOULD PROBABLY LOOK LIKE THIS. GRANDPA DREW THE PICTURE.

Chapter X

How Far Does Your 'Strange-O-Meter' Go?

June 27, 2013

San Francisco Airport, International Terminal, Air France Lounge

Day Seven of our week-long trip, *continued*

Grandpa Nick writing:

"Are you sure you don't have to be anywhere?" I asked Mad. "This may take a while."

"I told you, nobody even knows I'm here, so I'm free to do as I please–which feels great, by the way."

"I'm sure it does. I envy you, but I don't have a choice whether to see this thing through or not. I made a commitment, so I need to quit whining and get on with it."

"You can whine a little more if you want," Mad said sarcastically.

Joaquin looked up at her and smiled.

"No, I'm done. It's unseemly. Okay, here's how it went down. Are you ready?"

"Lead on, Macduff," Mad said, quoting Shakespeare.

"The plan was to meet Signe first thing when we arrived on Åland. That was on the 21st, but she was a no-show, which bummed me out big time. She sent Lars in her place, basically to tell me to cool my jets. Did I tell you she's the real head of the tribe?"

"No, I thought Gob was," Mad said.

"No. Let's see, how can I say this? Gob's an inside joke for outside consumption. He's a decoy, meant to draw attention away from the real power."

"Okay… I guess. And who's Lars–besides a carpenter and bus driver?"

"Lars just graduated from architecture school. He's trying to find a job and living with his widowed great aunt on Åland while he's looking."

"What's his connection with Signe?"

I looked at Joaquin, who rolled his eyes. "Let's see how short I can make this. Lars's great-aunt's sister was coming for a visit from Oregon. Because of the upcoming visit, his great-aunt asked Lars to build a new outhouse, which he did. While he was digging the hole, he accidentally came face-to-face with Signe, because the hole he was digging was right next to the gnomes' cave, or more specifically, Signe's bedroom."

Mad turned to Joaquin, eyebrows raised, and asked, "He's not making this up?"

"Nope. Just wait; it gets weirder."

I proceeded to explain to Mad about how Lars's great-aunt's sister, whose name is Grete, was a real piece of work who, once she found out about the gnomes living next door, hatched a plan to turn their underground home into a tourist attraction–with tunnels and windows dug into the hillside so you could see what the "'wee folk" were up to. She wanted to call it "Wee World"–can you imagine? I also told her how the whole thing took off like wildfire and how Grete even got the town's mayor to buy into the idea, with everyone certain they were going to get rich in no time.

"What happened?"

"Signe is what you might call "hyper-capable." I wasn't surprised that she already had plans and back-up plans in place for extreme emergencies. She swung into action and started issuing orders, including to Lars, who had quickly became a friend. According to him, the plan she chose was to 'self-kidnap' the tribe."

"What's that supposed to mean?"

"Basically disappear themselves and blame it on someone else. There was obviously no way the gnomes were going to let themselves get made into some kind of a carnival side show. Signe knew she had to get everyone and everything out of their underground home in a hurry, which is what she was working on anyway–and what Joaquin and I were supposed to help with–namely the upcoming move to California. The project changed completely when it had to be carried out with the urgency it demanded. Instead of being able to put everything into motion slowly and deliberately, it all had to be sped up. Big time. And that worried Signe. She knew carrying out plans quickly and under stress was how mistakes were made and she simply didn't allow mistakes–not made by herself, or others."

"I'm not trying to be flip, but why didn't they just book a bunch of staterooms on an ocean liner and sail to America? They could have gotten on board in the middle of the night and stayed hidden in their rooms until they arrived here." Mad said.

"That could have worked. And, lord knows, it would have been a lot easier than what we did, but you're forgetting one thing."

"What's that?"

"Their gold," I said leaning in, barely above a whisper, "which, in certain circles, is a known quantity–like the stuff legends are made of, you know?"

"Oh, that's right."

"And as you also are no doubt aware it's impossible to own that much gold without someone, somewhere wanting to take it from you. Even before the idea of the gnomes being made into a tourist attraction was being threatened, Signe had spent a great deal of time working out the safest possible way to move their gold to California. It's Signe's opinion–and I agree with her–that their gold was at the greatest risk when it was being moved from one place to the other. She thought the tribe, along with their gold, would be safe if she floated the rumor that the whole tribe had been kidnapped. Anyone privy to the rumor would probably assume their gold had also been stolen because, well, who wants to kidnap a bunch of gnomes without their gold?"

"But why did they have to physically move it? There are all sorts of ways any amount of gold can be transferred from one place to another without physically having to move it–believe me, I know. I did it more than once at my old job at the bank," Mad said.

"No doubt, but the gnomes have this thing about 'their' gold. They want *their* gold and not someone else's. Every single little bit of their gold was mined by one gnome or another, stretching back millennia. The idea of swapping their gold for an equal amount of someone else's gold would be like giving up a child. And I'm not exaggerating."

"Okay, I get it, but that's a serious logistical problem. I don't know how much they have, but gold is heavy! 27.4 pounds per standard bar. That adds up in a hurry."

"Don't I know. It was a huge problem. Hats off to Signe. She had a good plan in place, but the scope of it nearly did us in."

"Well, you're both here now, so I guess it's safe to say you made it. Did the gold make it?"

"We'll see," I said.

"You mean it's not here yet?"

"Nope. First Lars comes, followed by the gnomes and then, a few days later, the gold. You picked the perfect time to show up, Mad—just in time for the action."

"And we haven't even gotten to the Voslakians yet," Joaquin piped in.

"Yeah, that's been scary and very strange," I said.

"As if everything you've told me so far isn't about a hundred-and-ten on the Strange-O-Meter."

I laughed. "How far does your 'Strange-O-Meter' go?"

"Only to 100. You already broke it."

"Do you want me to keep going?"

"Are you *kidding*?" Mad said.

How Hawala Works

"Hawala" is the Arabic word for "transaction" or "trust." Mad explained to me that it's basically a bank-less banking system that's been used worldwide for more than a thousand years. During the 8th century, traders on the Silk Road got tired of being repeatedly robbed and were in need of an alternative for cash to pay for goods. They turned to hawala—a simple system for transferring money from one individual to another, anywhere in the world, based on trust. How it works is diagrammed below:

STEP 1

I'M MR. GREEN. I'M IN SAN FRANCISCO AND I WANT TO SEND $5000 TO MY GRANDFATHER IN HELSINKI, FINLAND. I GO TO MY LOCAL HAWALADAR, MR. RED, AND GIVE HIM THE MONEY AND TELL HIM WHERE I WANT IT SENT AND TO WHOM. MR. RED TAKES MY MONEY AND GIVES ME A SECRET CODE, WHICH I WILL SHARE WITH MY GRANDFATHER. HE'LL NEED IT TO PROVE HE'S WHO HE SAYS HE IS AND GET THE MONEY IN HELSINKI.

STEP 2

MR. RED, THE HAWALADAR IN SAN FRANISCO, CONTACTS MR. YELLOW, THE HAWALADAR IN HELSINKI. HE TELLS MR. YELLOW HOW MUCH MONEY HE HAS RECEIVED FROM ME, WHO IS GOING TO PICK IT UP IN HELSINKI, AND GIVES MR. YELLOW THE SECRET CODE MY GRANDFATHER WILL USE TO PROVE HE IS WHO HE SAYS HE IS.

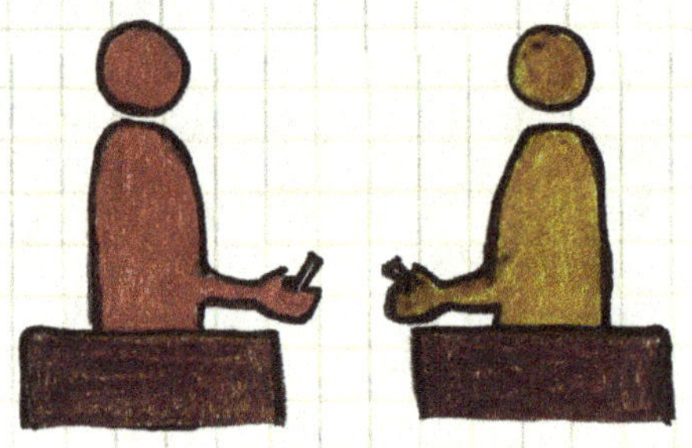

STEP 3

I (MR. GREEN) TELL MY GRANDFATHER (MR. BLUE) THE SECRET CODE THE HAWALADAR GAVE ME AND HOW MUCH MONEY I SENT. I TELL HIM WHERE TO GO IN HELSINKI TO PICK UP THE MONEY.

STEP 4

MY GRANDFATHER, MR. BLUE, GOES TO SEE MR. YELLOW, THE HAWALADAR IN HELSINKI. HE GIVES HIM THE SECRET CODE AND RECEIVES THE MONEY. THE TWO HAWALADARS, MR. RED AND MR. YELLOW, WILL SETTLE THEIR ACCOUNTS SEPARATELY.

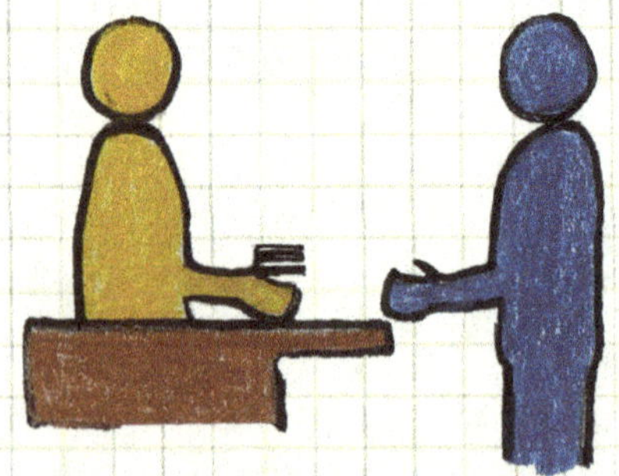

Chapter XI

Enter the Voslakians

June 27, 2013

San Francisco Airport, International Terminal, Air France Lounge

Day Seven of our week-long trip, *continued*

Grandpa Nick here:

"Like I said, the fact that it was Lars who met me at the graveyard instead of Signe pissed me off–so much so that I felt like I had to make it up to Lars with a beer. We went back to the hotel where Joaquin and I were staying. At some point in our conversation at the hotel bar, Lars excused himself and went to the bathroom. When he came back, I could tell that something was wrong. I asked him if everything was okay, but I could tell it wasn't; he was actually shaking."

"He asked me if I knew anything about Voslakia, which I'd never even heard of. Joaquin had joined us, and Lars explained to us both that the last thing Signe said to him before she disappeared was to be sure to be on the lookout for any Voslakians. Lars didn't know much about them either, other than they had a reputation for being criminal with a penchant for all kinds of violence."

"Now that I think about it, I *have* heard about them," Mad said. "Voslakia was part of the Soviet Union, right?"

"Yes, but they've always been a breed apart. Since Russia broke up, they've been officially independent. Extreme violence and aggravated mayhem seem to be part of their national heritage, along with free-range corruption. It's a bad combination. They joke that their national motto is "Everyone has their price." Nobody likes them–everyone's just afraid of them. Lars said that they'd just as soon do you bodily harm as talk to you."

"Charming," Mad said. "What do they have to do with Signe?"

I told Mad about the gnomes' long and sad history with the Voslakians and how, even though they hadn't lived there for more than two hundred years, the gnomes still feared them. Then I told her the worst part: about how Lars was sure he'd seen a Voslakian at the graveyard and then again in a hotel bathroom.

"He was completely freaked out," I told Mad, "He said we'd have to leave right that minute."

"Where'd you go?" Mad asked.

"A toy cabin on a toy island," Joaquin said.

"Actually, that's accurate–Lars's great-aunt owns a very small island with a very small cabin in the Åland archipelago. As isolated as it was, I agreed with Lars that it was a good place to hide out and figure out what to do next. Once we got settled, he told me he had the name and number of a friend of Signe's she said to call in case of an emergency. It didn't take us long to agree we were, in fact, in the middle of an emergency and we should give this friend a call, which we did."

"So who was this friend of Signe's?" Mad asked.

"No one I'd heard of. His name is Remi. Remi Wingrove."

"*The* Remi Wingrove?" Mad said incredulously."

"You *know* him?"

"Everyone in the international banking community knows Remi Wingrove. He's probably the top *hawaladar* in the world. I've actually met him. And my-oh-my, there's nothin' wrong with Remi Wingrove."

"What do you mean?"

"I mean he put the 'some' in handsome. Big time," Mad said.

"Hmmm… he did look a little like Omar Sharif," I offered.

"A little?" Mad asked. "More like his twin brother."

"Who's Omar Sharif?" Joaquin asked.

"An actor," I said, "way before your time."

"A very good-looking actor," Mad added.

"What's a 'hawaladar,' or however you pronounce it?" Joaquin asked.

"You got it right," Mad said, "a hawaladar is someone who practices the hawala system–an old-school way of banking without a bank–very simple and complex at the same time, if that makes sense. It was started to protect traders from being robbed of their cash, something that happened a lot of in the 8th century along the Silk Road. Basically it's a worldwide system of moving money without actually moving it—it's all built on trust. The fact that it's still around today gives you an idea of how well it works. Here, give me that napkin and I'll show you."

Mad drew a simple diagram involving customer A who wanted to get money to customer B, and how A used hawaladar X to initiate the transfer and hawaladar Y, who dispersed the funds to customer B. That's my interpretation of Mad's diagram on page 74.

"No one knows how many hawaladars there are in the world," Mad continued, "but there are a lot. It's used mainly in India, parts of the Middle East and Africa, but you can find a hawaladar virtually anywhere in the world. As large as the halawa system is, you have to be someone truly exceptional to rise to the top. Remi Wingrove is that person. I've never heard a bad word about him."

"You ought to see his boat," Joaquin said with genuine enthusiasm. It's a 1931 Gar Wood Baby Gar. I took a picture of it with my phone to send to my friend, Darren. Take a look. It's sick."

"I'll say it is," Mad said, looking at Joaquin's phone.

"My kidneys still haven't recovered," I said.

"You rode in it?" Mad asked.

"Yeah, from Lars's little island—we pounded our way to Helsinki," I said, exaggerating a bit.

"How'd that happen?" Mad asked.

"Remi lives in Sweden, on the coast, not that far from Lars's island. He came and picked us up. The idea was to get us to Helsinki as quickly as possible to meet with Signe without being noticed by the Voslakians. Not that anyone might notice the arrival of a 33-foot, 650-horsepower vintage wooden speedboat that's worth probably a million dollars."

"You sound ticked off, Nick," Mad said.

"I'm not really. I appreciate Remi's help but, frankly, it was a tough trip—at least for me—and I was majorly jetlagged; not a good combination. He kindly got us a hotel room in Helsinki and suggested we get a nap in before meeting with Signe. I think we both looked as if we'd been rode hard and put up wet, as they say."

"What's the history between Signe and Remi?" Mad asked.

"I may have offended Signe when I asked her the same question, but you have to admit, they're an unlikely pair. From what she told me, they've helped each other out of some sticky situations over the years. Apparently, Signe's relationship with Remi started with Remi's great-grandfather, who started the family in the hawala business back when. Not surprisingly, Remi has his ear to the ground in all kinds of places, including some dark ones. He was the one who tipped Signe off to the Voslakian's plans to help themselves to the gnomes' gold. Like I said, the Voslakians have left the gnomes alone for the last couple of hundred years, so they had receded some on Signe's radar."

"Who knew the gnomes were going to move their gold?" Mad asked.

"Only a very select, trusted few, but there was a weak link—one Signe hadn't taken into account. She's still kicking herself for it."

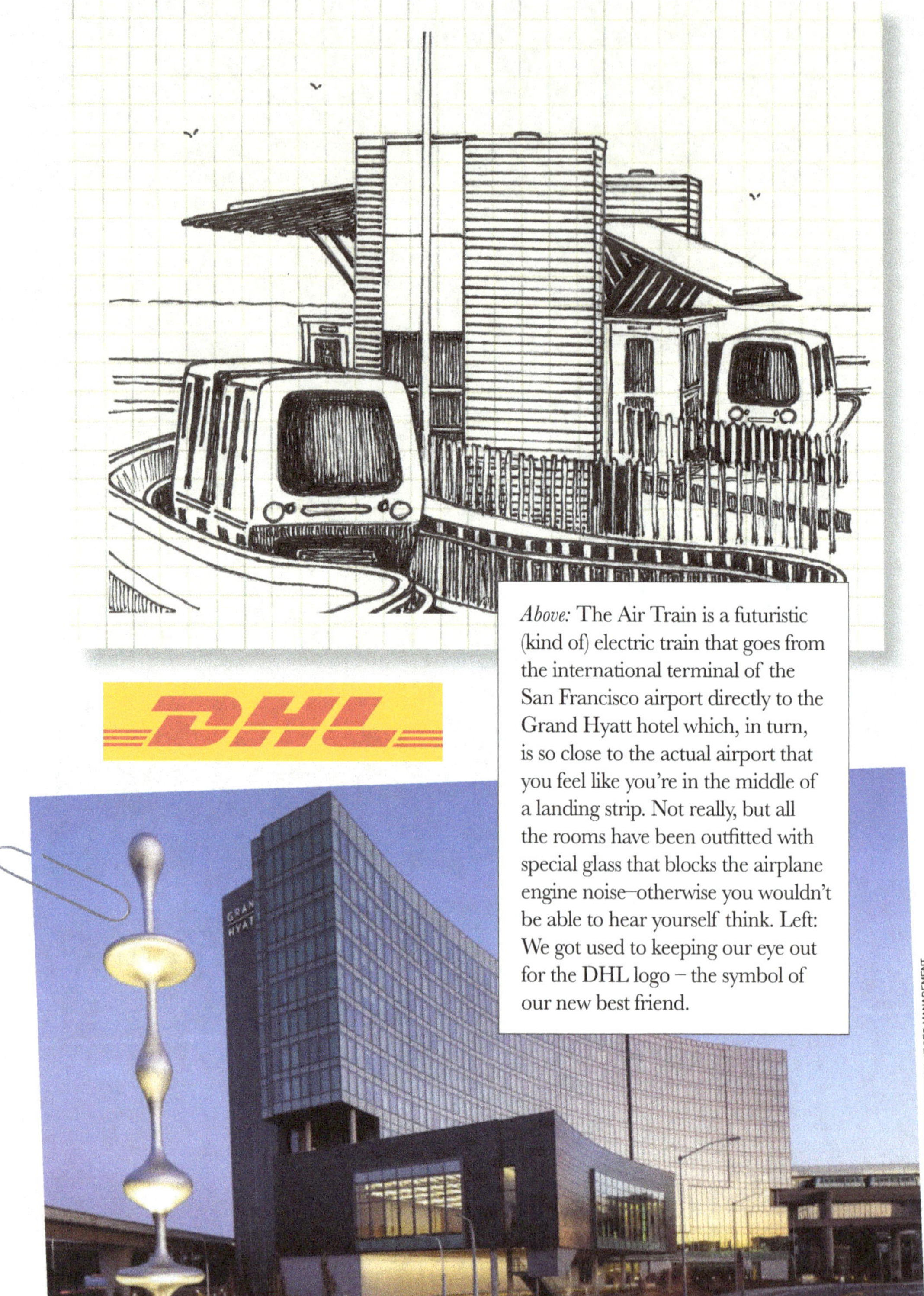

Above: The Air Train is a futuristic (kind of) electric train that goes from the international terminal of the San Francisco airport directly to the Grand Hyatt hotel which, in turn, is so close to the actual airport that you feel like you're in the middle of a landing strip. Not really, but all the rooms have been outfitted with special glass that blocks the airplane engine noise—otherwise you wouldn't be able to hear yourself think. Left: We got used to keeping our eye out for the DHL logo – the symbol of our new best friend.

Chapter XII

Bad Boris and the Weak Link

June 27, 2013

Grand Hyatt hotel, San Francisco Airport

Day Seven of our week-long trip, *continued*

Grandpa Nick writing:

"So who was this weak link?" Mad asked.

"More like *what*–if you can believe it, it was a crow–a crow with a misplaced grudge. You remember how the gnomes use the earth's crow population to communicate around the world? Well, for the first time ever, there was a breach of trust between one of the crows and the gnomes. The crow with a grudge was flying the last leg of a message from Aalto to Signe about the upcoming move. Once the crow delivered the message to Signe, he turned around and repeated the information to Bad Boris. And that set some bad juju in motion."

"'Bad Boris,' *really?*" Mad asked, raising her eyebrows.

"I think he prefers 'Boris the Bad,' but 'Bad Boris' seems to have stuck. He's the self-proclaimed leader of the Voslakians. By all accounts he is, in fact, very bad. He's also very short, which wouldn't matter one way or the other, except there are rumors that there's a gnome somewhere in Boris' family tree, which could explain his hatred of the gnomes."

"The plot thickens," Mad said. "What in the world could have induced that crow to violate hundreds of years of trust?" Mad asked.

"A lie and a long memory, basically. Signe is still kicking herself for not seeing it coming. It goes back to the 1700s, when the gnomes were still living in Voslakia and Signe was just a kid. She was out target practicing with her slingshot and ran across a baby crow who'd fallen out of its nest. She was carrying it home, hoping someone knew how to revive it. The mother crow came back to the nest just as Signe was leaving, carrying the dead crow, her sling-shot sticking out of her back pocket. The mother crow put two and two together, mistakenly, and started a hatred of Signe that's lasted from one generation of this crow family to the next. The other crows in the community figured out what really happened, but they were never able to convince the aggrieved crow family that Signe was trying to help the baby crow, not kill it. The opportunity for revenge just happened to surface in this one crow—who's name is Croaker, by the way."

"Croaker?"

"Yeah. Crows don't really have names—not that other crows use. Just like humans, they can tell who's who by their voices. Remi named this one because of his distinctive, low croak."

"How'd Signe figure out she'd been betrayed by this Croaker?"

"Remi told her."

"How'd he know?" Mad asked.

"Would it surprise you he speaks Crow?"

"No, I guess not. Rich, handsome, and a multi-talented know-it-all. I can see how all that might be annoying," Mad said.

"Tell me about it," I said. "Apparently one of *his* crow friends told him there were rumors flying around, literally, that one of their own was working for both the gnomes and Bad Boris and Remi told Signe. She's been staying a few steps ahead of Croaker ever since, but it's taken all her guile to pull it off."

"So she hasn't confronted Croaker yet?" Mad asked.

"No. She's thinking that down the road, she might be able to turn his treachery to her advantage. Generally speaking, I think it's a bad idea to cross Signe," I said.

"I think you're right. What time are you supposed to meet Lars?" Mad asked.

"A little after eight," I said, looking at my watch. "It's only a quarter to six. Joaquin and I were going to check in at the hotel first and then meet Lars. Did I hear an offer of help a while back?"

"You did."

"Well?"

"You know I'm not just ornamental, as Tutu used to say. Count me in."

"Cool. Thanks Mad. We can put our feet up at the hotel for a bit and then meet Lars at the warehouse Signe rented—it's not far from here. We need to make sure everything is copacetic—that the keys work, the electricity is on, you know. And Lars needs to check out the bus, which is supposed to be parked in the warehouse.

Mad leaned in and said in a whisper "What about the gold?"

"Signe was going to have the gold delivered at the same time as the gnomes, but she decided it was too much. The plan now is to get the gnomes settled on Mt. St. Helena and then come back next Wednesday. Signe, Aalto and G will come with us. We'll accept the delivery and then have it forwarded to Mt. St. Helena using Brinks's armored trucks."

"It sounds easy when you say it like that," Mad said with a smile.

"Truth is, I don't think there's going to be anything easy about it. Is anyone else tired of sitting?" I asked.

There was a simultaneous "I am" from both Mad and Joaquin so we decided to take the so-called "Air Train" to the hotel and regroup. Mad wound up getting a room adjoining our two-room suite. In the elevator going up to our rooms, we decided to take a break for an hour and then meet in the lobby.

• • •

"Doyle sends his regards," I said to Mad an hour later. We were in the back of a cab. Joaquin was sitting in front, plugged into the game on his phone with one earbud in and one out so he wouldn't miss anything. I gave the cab driver the address of the warehouse.

"How is the old boy?" Mad asked.

"He's doing okay. He's looking forward to seeing you."

"Well, I'm looking forward to seeing him. Is that in our plans?"

"Of course, but first we've got to get through the next few days. I don't know how Signe does it. I'm verging on 'overwhelm.'"

"Well you've got Joaquin and me now. We'll keep you on track, won't we Joaquin?"

"Right on," he said, turning to look at Mad in the back seat, giving her a thumbs-up.

We were making our way through an office park where all the buildings and landscaping looked the same—bland, bland, and blander. It was a late summer afternoon, but the fog was already in, obscuring the sun, the wind whipping up, blowing scraps of paper through the air, making the scene feel abandoned and lonely. Somehow it felt like the last place in the world you'd unload a tribe of gnomes, not to mention an unfathomable fortune in gold.

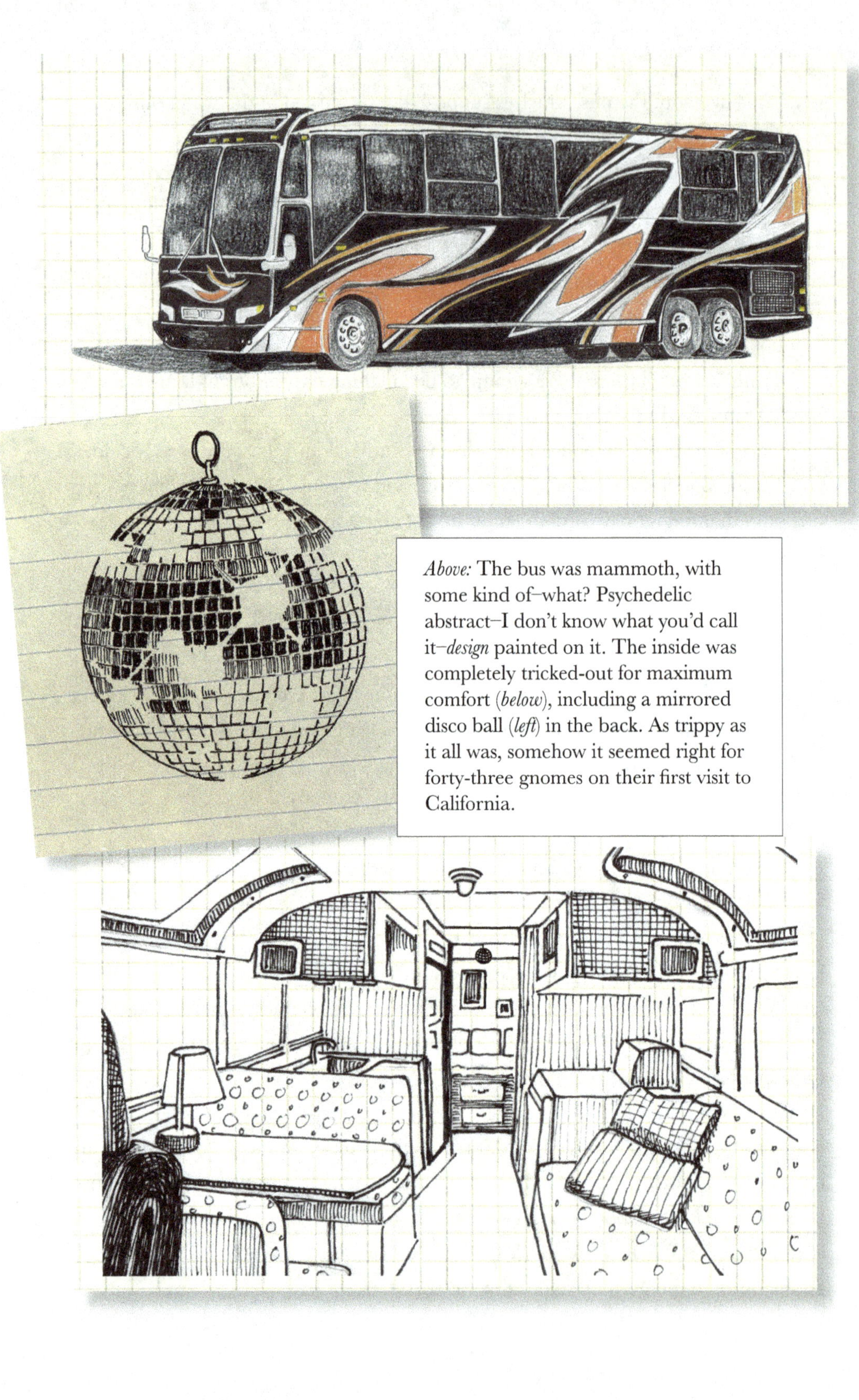

Above: The bus was mammoth, with some kind of–what? Psychedelic abstract–I don't know what you'd call it–*design* painted on it. The inside was completely tricked-out for maximum comfort (*below*), including a mirrored disco ball (*left*) in the back. As trippy as it all was, somehow it seemed right for forty-three gnomes on their first visit to California.

Chapter XIII

Shag Carpet and Toilet Paper

June 27, 2013

Millbrae Industrial Park, Millbrae, California

Day Seven of our week-long trip, *continued*

Grandpa Nick writing:

We stopped at the address I had given the cab driver: one of the countless, nearly identical pre-fab metal buildings with side-by-side corrugated steel roll-up doors. There wasn't a single person anywhere in sight, but I picked up this threatening vibe somehow. The whole industrial park, or whatever it was called, creeped me out.

"Are you okay?" Mad asked as I opened the front door to the warehouse.

"A little jumpy," I said.

The warehouse was completely empty except for a large bus with a vaguely psychedelic, sparkly paint job parked right inside one of the roll-up doors.

"Rad," Joaquin said when he saw it. "Is it open?"

"It should be. Go check. See if the keys are in it," I said.

"On it," Joaquin said.

"I'm going to check out the bathroom," Mad said.

I stood there by the front door and took the place in. *So far so good* I thought to myself–the warehouse was as advertised, in terms of size, the keys worked, the door opened, and the electricity was on. I found the heater thermostat and cranked it up. At the same time as the gas flame whooshed into life in the overhead heater a strange voice said my name loudly. I jumped about a foot straight up in the air. Heart pounding, I turned around and Lars was standing right in front of me.

"Jeez Lars, you scared the hell out of me."

"Sorry. I thought you heard me come in," he said.

"No matter," I said, shaking his hand. "I'm glad you're here. Everything okay?"

"Yeah. That's a long trip, though. Feels good to be up and walking around. Cool bus," he said, looking over my shoulder to where it was parked.

"We just got here. Joaquin's checking it out. Go take a look."

"Toilet paper," Mad yelled from the other side of the warehouse.

"Toilet paper?"

"You need to buy toilet paper. There's only two rolls. Without putting too fine a point on it, I'm guessing 43 gnomes confined in crates for a day or two are going to need it."

"I think you're right. That could have been a disaster."

"Aren't you glad you brought me along?"

"Totally."

"I take it Lars arrived?" she asked.

"He's here. I'll introduce you."

We walked over to the bus and I introduced Lars to Mad and we all scoped out the interior. The 1970s-theme continued inside, with shag carpets and crushed velvet upholstery, including a small mirrored disco ball at the back of the bus. I doubted whether any of it would matter one way or the other to the gnomes; they were only going to be in it for a few hours.

"Why don't you give it the once over, Lars, and make sure the gas tanks are full. Will you check to see that both roll-up doors work, too? After that, we can go back to the hotel and do nothing for a bit–kind of like the calm before the storm. I already got you a room."

"Thanks. It won't take long to check out the bus. Did the rental company deliver the floor jack?"

"Yes–it's on the other side of the bus. I'll call us a cab."

"I already got a rental car," Lars said. "I need to find a place to buy some cordless drills for us to unscrew the crates once they're here. I figured you and Joaquin could help me with that. Then I have to pick up Matti at the air freight office, remember? I don't want him to have to hang out in his cage any longer than necessary."

"Oh man, I *did* forget. We don't want to forget Matti, do we? That would be a hard one to explain all around. Do you want me to get him a room, too?"

"No, it's okay. As long as my room has a couple of beds," Lars said. "He's probably going to be a little–how do you say?–*discombobulated*–is that correct? He might need the company."

"Yes, I think you're right. Good call. I'll make sure you've got a room with two beds."

"Who in the world is Matti?" Mad asked.

"Matti is one of the gnomes. He has claustrophobia. Just the thought of being enclosed in a wooden crate was too much for him. He flying here disguised as an English sheepdog–in a travel carrier he can see out of."

"You're not kidding, are you?" Mad said.

"Nope," Grandpa said.

"I'm speechless," Mad said, shaking her head.

I turned off the warehouse lights and the heater and locked the doors. Lars drove off on his errands and the three of us got a cab back to the hotel. On the way there, I asked the cab driver to stop at a supermarket. A few minutes later, I asked him to open the trunk to accommodate the huge 36-roll package of toilet paper I had just purchased. I would have tried to explain, but nothing I could think of made any sense. I sure as heck couldn't tell the truth, right? So I let him close the trunk and think what he wanted.

Above: Grandpa and I collected all kinds of stuff on our short, intense trip. He left it to me to make some sense of it all by making them into—I'm not sure what to call them—collages? Assemblages? Whatever they are, I hope they help visualize what we went through, which was pretty wild. *Left:* Corgi dogs are known for being particulary sensitive about their height, so let 'em be the way they are—just the way they were born. That's Fatboy Long over there; he says "don't make me bite you."

Chapter XIV

Awkward Questions

June 27, 2013

Grand Hyatt hotel, San Francisco Airport

Day Seven of our week-long trip, *continued*

Joaquin writing:

Grandpa left it up to me to organize this book–his journal, my journal, his writing, and my writing, some of my sketches, his paintings and drawings–in a way that hopefully makes sense. So I need to interject something here. It was a little strange, but what in this story isn't? I couldn't figure out why Mad was asking me about it and not just asking Grandpa herself. I think I figured it out. If I'm right, I'll tell you later.

Once we got back to the hotel, Grandpa invited Mad to our suite for what he called a "nightcap." He called Lars in his room and invited him and Matti, as well. Grandpa decided to take a quick shower before anyone arrived, but considering Mad's room was right next to ours, she was over in a flash. That left the two of us in the living room of our suite. Out of the blue, she asked me about Chuy–whether or not he was still around?

"You mean Uncle Chuy?" I asked.

"Oh, that's right. I knew he was your uncle–I just forgot."

"He's still around. He doesn't live that far from us."

"How's he doing?" Mad asked.

"Okay. His wife died about a year ago. To tell you the truth, we don't see him that much."

"Why not?"

"I don't know. I tried to find out last summer. I actually went and talked to him and it was like some big mystery or something. I asked Grandpa about it, and he was just as vague."

"What? Like they had a fight?"

"Something like that. You should ask Grandpa."

"I will," she said, just as Grandpa came into the room.

"You will what?" he asked.

"Ask you for that glass of wine you promised."

"Coming right up."

Just then there was a knock on the door. I opened it and it was Lars, by himself.

"Hi Lars," Grandpa said, "Where's Matti?"

"In the room. He said he's happy on his own," Lars said.

"What's he doing?" Mad asked.

"Watching a cooking show on television."

Grandpa did a double take, asking "What, is he hungry?"

"No—I ordered him room service—oatmeal, an apple, and a bunch of mixed nuts. And a beer," Lars said. "He just wants to chill and watch television. I don't blame him after what he's been through the last twenty-four hours."

"Was it that bad?" I asked.

"No. Just long," Lars answered, "although he did have company—a standard poodle and a corgi."

"You don't say," Grandpa said.

"Matti said they almost didn't let the corgi on the flight," Lars said.

"Why not?" Mad asked.

"Apparently when his owner dropped him off at the air freight office in Helsinki, the clerk said the corgi's cage didn't meet their specifications."

"Why not?" I asked.

"He told the owner that the dog had to be able to stand up in the cage or else they couldn't take him. The owner told the clerk that those were fighting words because the corgi *was* standing up. The corgi told Matti if he hadn't have been in the cage he would have bit the clerk."

"I don't blame him," Mad said, "although it definitely wouldn't have helped his situation. Speaking of 'situations,' tell me what happened after Remi took you to Helsinki."

"A lot," Grandpa said, looking at me.

"Yeah. We haven't even told you about going to see the Baron Edmond yet," I said, "or 'Fast Eddy,' as Signe called him."

"Wait a minute, wait a minute," Mad said. "You met with Baron Edmond?"

"At his townhouse in Paris. And, oh yeah, we got there in Remi's private jet," I said. "It's a Gulfstream V, just like Dr. Dre's."

"Well, that's good to know," Mad said with some sarcasm. "There's not a chance that you're just a little envious of Remi, are you, Nick?"

"Not a chance," he said, rolling his eyes.

"Well, you don't need to be a forensic accountant to figure what the three of them–the Baron, Remi, and Signe–have in common," Mad said. "It's money. A lot of money. I mean, a *really* lot of money."

"Yep, and that's not all," I said.

"It's definitely *not all*," Grandpa said. "In fact there's so much, I think you're better off if you read what happened instead of us telling you, if you're not too tired."

"No, I can definitely stay awake for this," she said, taking our two journals.

"One is Joaquin's and one is mine. You'll figure out the sequence of our entries–they're in chronological order. You should start on page 93 of my journal. It starts with Remi dropping us off at the hotel in Helsinki."

"Got it. What time are we meeting tomorrow? I'll give these back to you then," Mad said.

"Count me out," Lars said, "I already have my marching orders. I'm going to sleep in while I can. And if Matti follows his normal pattern, he'll sleep all day tomorrow. Let's say I meet you guys in the lobby downstairs at noon?"

"Sounds good, Lars. Get a good night's sleep. Mad, we don't have to meet the DHL shipment until 1 o'clock at the warehouse. After that, I expect it's going to be a circus. Probably a long one. So you tell me: what time?"

"Late breakfast–10?" Mad asked.

Grandpa looked at me to see if it was okay. I said "sure," and that's how we left it.

Like I said, I thought there was more to her questions about Uncle Chuy than she was letting on. The fact that she dodged asking Grandpa about Uncle Chuy reinforced my suspicions.

Above: Signe's office in the ice-skate factory was pretty much over-the-top: a French technique called *treillage* that used trelliswork painted white on the walls, black-and-white checkerboard floor, and big landscape paintings done in the French Rococo style, to say nothing of multiple crystal chandeliers. "Nothing succeeds like excess," Signe said about it with a chuckle. And, oh, did I mention homemade cookies?

Chapter XV

Tea and Cookies in the Ice Skate Factory

June 22, 2013

Helsinki hotel and *Erinomainen Nopea Luistimet* (the ice-skate factory)
Helsinki, Finland

Page 93 of my journal
Day Two of our week-long trip

Grandpa Nick writing:
Joaquin and I took the elevator up to our room on the 10th floor. It was attractive in a kind of anonymous way–crisp, modern and monochromatic. The windows were, thankfully, outfitted with blackout shades. I debated for about two seconds whether or not to pull them– afraid we wouldn't wake up if the room were dark– but said the heck with it and pulled them down. Three minutes later, we were both asleep.

Longer than a nap, but shorter than a night's sleep, whatever it was, was kind of strange, but definitely better than nothing. I'm not sure how chipper we looked, but we managed to be down in the lobby at 12 o'clock sharp, just as Remi was walking up. Even though he was casually dressed, it was impossible not to notice he looked like a million bucks. And I'm sure that was an understatement. "Better?" he asked.

"Better," I said.

"Let's get a cab," he said. "It's too long of a walk."

We got into a waiting cab in the front of the hotel. Joaquin and I sat in the back with Remi up front. He said something, presumably in Finn, to the driver and we were off.

From the back seat, Joaquin asked, "Just for the record, Remi, what kind of a boat do you have? I have to tell my friend, Darren."

"It's one of yours–it's American. A 1931 Gar Wood Baby Gar. You can tell Darren it's 33 feet long, has a new Rolls Royce 650-horsepower, 12-cylinder engine, and has a top speed of over 100 miles per hour."

"Wow," Joaquin said.

Remi laughed. "You probably didn't notice."

"Notice what?" Joaquin asked.

"That's the name of the boat–'Wow.'"

We all laughed.

"So where are we going?" I asked.

"It's a little hard to explain," Remi said. "It won't take long to get there. It will be easier for you and Joaquin to just see it."

We left the city center and entered what in America would be called a light industrial area. In a few minutes we arrived in front on a nondescript three-story brick building that looked like all the other buildings around it, with three rows of identical windows, all of which had been more-or-less whitewashed on the inside. Above the equally nondescript gray steel double doors were an unadorned sign that read *"Erinomainen Nopea Luistimet,"* spelled out in fading paint.

"What does it mean?" I asked, pointing to the sign.

Pushing a small button next to the door, Remi looked up at the sign and said "roughly, 'Swift Skates,' as in ice-skates. Finns invented them, you know. About 5000 years ago."

"For real?" I said, trying to tell if he was serious. None of this was making much sense.

"I'll let Signe explain," Remi said.

There was a buzzing sound and Remi pushed one of the doors open. We all walked into what looked like a semi-abandoned large factory that made… ice-skates? I had no idea. The equipment looked like it hadn't made anything in a long time. I wondered how much weirder this was going to get. It was strange enough that Joaquin took his earbuds out and started looking around with some intent.

"This way," Remi motioned. We passed row after row of generic-looking ma-chines. As we approached what I suspected was the office–a separate room with windows, but shades completely drawn on the inside–Joaquin elbowed me and mo-tioned with his head off to one corner where dozens of new looking wooden crates, all the same size–about twice as big as a refrigerator box–were neatly organized. All of them were sporting big, fresh labels from the international shipping company DHL, emblazoned with "Priority One" in red letters, along with prominent "This

Side Up" designations, seemingly on every side of the crates.

Strange, I thought. Joaquin apparently felt the same way.

Remi knocked on the shaded glass office door.

Nothing happened for about a minute, then there was what sounded like locks unlocking and finally the door eased open slowly. At first it appeared that there was no one on the other side of the door and then all three of us looked down; sure enough, there was Signe. Looking back on that first meeting, I now realize I was expecting a female version of Gob and his rustic co-horts–with all their layered clothing and clumsy bonhomie. Signe was the exact opposite: stylishly dressed in a lavender-gray sweater set and black trousers, wearing a single strand of pearls and simple pearl earrings, she was the picture of understated European sophistication, only in miniature. Her salt-and-pepper hair was short on the sides, longer and wavily brushed back on the top. Her face showed the effects of time, but it was open and friendly, complemented by her manner, which was the essence of casual charm.

"Welcome, welcome. Come in," she said, bowing slightly at the waist and sweeping her arm in the direction of the room. "You've caught me practicing staying awake during the day and I must say, I'm not quite sure how you do it," she said chuckling to herself. The room was as much of a surprise as Signe herself. Understand we had just walked across a dingy factory floor, filled with old, grimy manufacturing equipment. The contrast between the two rooms couldn't have been more complete: the high-ceilinged room we had just walked into was all light, airy and sparkling. It wasn't huge, but it wasn't small, either. I couldn't help but do a 360-degree turn-around to take it all in. My impression was one of a lot of white with various shades of green and sky blue, and a lot of rainbow glints coming from an incredible array of crystal chandeliers hanging from the ceiling, at different heights. All four walls were covered with treillage–a French trick using lattice arranged to fool one's eye into seeing depth when what you're looking at is actually flat. In between the treillage panels were mirrors and large romantic landscape paintings filled with puffy clouds, soaring birds, trees, flowers, rolling meadows, and grazing sheep. The ceiling, not surprisingly, was painted sky blue with scattered clouds that I swear were moving. Taken together it was a lively, bright, slightly surreal scene.

"Beats living in a cave, don't you think?" Signe asked with a mischievous grin. "My friend Armi Ratia–she founded Marimekko, famous for its Finnish designs–

says 'beautiful things make life more bearable.' I agree, don't you? Besides, as nice as our cave was, it was still a cave; this makes for a pleasant change, especially during our long, dark winters.

"I'm Signe, by the way. You must be Nick," she said turning towards me, her arm extended. After shaking my hand and making direct eye contact, she walked to Joaquin and said "And you must be Joaquin. Very nice to meet you both. You've come a long way—about halfway around the world by my calculation. I apologize for missing our meeting in Eckerö but there have been unforeseen developments of the most worrisome kind. As I'm sure you agree, time is of the essence, so if you don't mind, I'm going to just start in and explain the situation without belaboring it. If there's anything you don't understand, or something that you think I've overlooked, please speak up. If there's anything you want to eat or drink, just let me know. There's coffee, tea, juice and water. I also made some cookies this morning—cookies help difficult discussions, don't they?" she said, looking around at all of us smiling.

"So, I'm going to start things off and answer two questions you're probably asking yourselves: Where are we? And why are we here?

"First off, we're in Helsinki, Finland, obviously, but more specifically, we're in what the English call a 'bolt hole'—a place where you can bolt to when you need to escape and hide. I bought this factory building just after Gob and the boys left on their exploratory journey back in 1879. Without them around I thought it could serve as a 'safe house,' if you will, in case we ever found ourselves threatened and in need of a place to run. Oddly, after all these years of not needing to use it, just as we were readying ourselves to relocate to our new home in America, we find ourselves under attack and on two different fronts. It certainly emphasizes the fact that one must never let one's guard down—*ever!* Just for the record, no one, except for the other gnomes and you three, know of the existence of this place. So far, we've been lucky our sworn enemies, the Voslakians, know nothing of it and it must stay that way—I can't emphasize that enough.

"Each member of the tribe has their own room here. To make sure they would be comfortable in case we had to be here for an extended period of time, everyone was allowed complete freedom in fitting out the spaces however they liked. I mean, look at my space—nothing like a little French Rococo to perk one's mood up, eh? Nick and Joaquin, when you have time, you should take a tour of some of our tribe members' rooms—you'll see everything from a rustic log cabin to a Danish Modern suite. For a bunch of gnomes who've been living underground for centuries, their interior design skills are quite impressive.

"So that's where we are—hiding out in a bolt hole. And why are we here? Well, that's rather more complicated. Before I continue, cookie anyone?" she said holding up the plate, looking around the table.

Below: That's the Duke of Wellington, front and center in the painting of the Battle of Waterloo, which took place in 1815. Although it was fought in Belgium, the fight was between the French army, led by Napoleon Bonaparte, and the British, with the Duke of Wellington commanding a coalition force, aided by a Prussian army under the command of Field Marshal von Blücher. The battle was a decisive one, ending Napoleon's reign and ushering in an era of European peace that lasted until World War I. If it hadn't been for the Baron's family, however, things might have turned out very differently–in essence the British didn't have the necessary capital to fund the war and relied on the Baron's family for a huge influx of gold bullion to continue their military efforts. The Baron's family, in turn, relied on the gnomes to deliver the bullion across that all-important "last mile." The means the gnomes employed to accomplish the delivery have remained a secret to this day, but I'm guessing it had something to do with tunnels.

Chapter XVI

"Balls" said the Baron

June 22, 2013

Erinomainen Nopea Luistimet (the ice-skate factory)
Helsinki, Finland

Day Two of our week-long trip, *continued*

Grandpa Nick writing:
"Where was I?" said Signe distractedly, putting the plate of cookies down. "Oh yes, the 'Why are we here?' question. All right, first a little background. It started with Lars digging the new outhouse for his great-aunt and our, literally, running into each other when he dug into my bedroom. What are the chances of that happening, eh? Anyway, it did and, luckily for all involved, he turned out to be an honorable young man and we have become quite good friends. If it hadn't been for his efforts I, and the rest of my tribe members, would have been part of an underground freak show by now, open to the paying public, mind you.

"Abandoning our cave was a tricky proposition as we were literally under Lars's great-aunt's and her sister's noses. Even though Lars had blessedly interceded on our behalf and derailed the theme park project, there was no way those two old biddies were going to give up so easily. Luckily, in preparation for our move to California, I had started the process of relocating our gold weeks earlier so there wasn't much left to do on that front. No sooner had we relocated here, the dreaded–and I do mean 'dreaded'–Voslakians raised their big, ugly heads for the first time in a long time.

"We lived in Voslakia more than 200 hundred years ago. Every year we were there things got worse. There's nothing original about making a group of outsiders–like us gnomes–into the enemy, blaming us for everything that went wrong.

Once they found out about our gold, though, they were merciless in their attempts to put their hands on it. It made living in Voslakia impossible. We were able to avoid being captured and tortured, but the possibility of extreme violence was too much so we left and relocated to the Åland Islands. We thought we'd live there forever—which we would have if the members of the church near our cave hadn't finally raised enough money to replace their bell in the tower and started ringing it constantly. As you may be aware, church bells and gnomes simply don't go together. Something had to go and it was us. Which is why Gob left in 1879, in search of a new home—one without church bells!"

"Back to the Voslakians," I said, "So after all those years, they just suddenly reappeared in your lives?"

"Yes, but only because that crow broke our confidence. I've gone over it many, many times and I don't think there was anything I could have done to avoid it," Signe said sadly.

"What happened?" Joaquin asked.

"As you know, we rely on the worldwide network of crows to send messages anywhere we need to. You're aware, aren't you, that crows have an actual language?" Signe asked no one in particular.

"As a matter of fact, I do," I said, "I watched a television program on it. It was about a professor at the University of California at Berkeley—fascinating stuff. The professor was able to identify 56 distinct sounds that represented individual words."

"The professor must not have been trying very hard—there are many more words in the language of crow than 56!" Signe said. "Of course, being able to communicate with animals is inherent to us; it's just something we do naturally."

Remi half raised his hand and said quietly "I also speak crow. There aren't many, but some of us Roma have made it a specialty. Over the years, being able to communicate with the crows has come in very handy. I was aware, of course, of the long-standing relationship between the gnome folk and the crows, as well as the degree of trust that existed between them. But, as the saying goes, that trust is only as strong as the weakest link and Signe and her tribe were betrayed by one bad crow."

Signe continued the story, "The crow—who Remi calls Croaker—divulged to Bad Boris the contents of a message between Aalto and me. The message contained details regarding our impending move, including the transfer of our gold to a new location. That single act of betrayal gave the Voslakians enough information to make a series of plans, all of which are meant to harm us and steal our gold."

"Roma?" Joaquin asked.

"The actual name of our tribe," Remi said. "Throughout history, we've been referred to, pejoratively, as 'gypsies.' We prefer 'Roma.'"

"Got it," Joaquin said.

I put the whole subject of Croaker and the Voslakians on hold for the moment and, at risk of seeming rude, asked Signe, "So, if you'll forgive me, you haven't told us exactly why we're here."

"Right—you're quite right to keep me focused. To put it as succinctly as possible, you're here to help get us out of here—all forty-three of us—and on our way to our new home in California. The forty-three of us and, of course, our gold. We made a dramatic modification to our gold and it's improved our situation immensely. But it still represents a problem because, well, we have so much of it."

"If I may, what was this 'dramatic modification' you made?"

"Well, one day I was talking to the Baron about the pros and cons of keeping one's wealth in gold…"

"Excuse me," I interjected, *"the Baron?"*

"Yes, the Baron. We go back a long way—to 1815 when some of our folks lent him a hand when his great-grandfather funded the Duke of Wellington's efforts against Napoleon at the Battle of Waterloo. His grandfather's agents hit a snag navigating that crucial last mile trying to reach the Duke with the gold and we were able to step in and save the day, rather handily, if I do say so myself. No one quite knows the ins and outs of gold like his family—except, perhaps, we gnomes and Remi here. But, yes, *the Baron.* As I said, his family and our tribe have been friends for a long time. He's been helping us in this relocation endeavor. A genius, that one.

"So the Baron and I were talking about gold and some of its drawbacks. Of course it's better to have it than not have it, but, let's face it, as a commodity, gold is very heavy, takes up a lot of room, and can't be moved easily or quickly. And for us gnomes, given our size, it presents even more of a problem. The Baron thought about it and said one word that changed everything."

"What was it?" I asked.

"'Balls,'" Signe said.

Right: The Baron's family coat of arms, which I only saw on the Baron's black velvet slippers. *Middle right:* At the Baron's suggestion, all of the gnome gold was melted down and formed into balls about the size of a grapefruit. Each was stamped with a unique series of runes. If it hadn't been for this innovation, it's likely that none of what happened in this story could have taken place.

An Australian athlete who shipped himself home half-way around the world c.o.d., tells in this story how it felt inside the crate.

By REG SPIERS

ADELAIDE, Australia Nov. 10 (XANA)—I am the first man to air-freight himself halfway across the world —and I hope I'm the last.

Sealed inside a five-foot-long packing case, I flew the 10,000 miles from London to Perth, Australia, in the cargo hold of an air India Boeing 707. Altogether, I was 63 hours without food or water, but I was comfortable nearly all the time. It was pitch black inside the freight compartment, but this did not worry me either.

The real danger was that I might be offloaded and kept for a later plane at any of the stops along the way. Also, there was the danger that the cargo hold might not be pressurized or heated, in which case I would have frozen or suffocated to death.

Air India, which has taken the whole adventure very graciously, tells me now I am lucky to be alive, but my plan seemed fool-proof right from the start, and so it proved to be.

I am 22-years-old, and quite a good javelin thrower in my native Australia. This year, I was determined to qualify for the Tokyo Olympics, and I seemed to be a certainty for the Australian team until I injured an arm and failed to make the team. However, I was told that if I regained top form, I might still be given a chance at Tokyo.

It was then autumn in Australia—the seasons are upside-down in the southern hemisphere—and the sports season was over, so I decided to go to London and train with the British javelin throwers.

Last May, I left my wife Catherine, and my 2-year-old baby, Joanne, right here in Adelaide, my home town, and worked my way to England in a freighter. Unfortunately, my arm was still weak, and I couldn't throw the javelin very far at all.

My original idea had been to get my wife and baby across to Europe, but climate

SOLID GOLD BALL WITH RUNE MARKINGS.

Above left: Newspaper clipping from 1964 describing Mr. Spiers's air journey in a cargo box. *Left:* The wooden crate Reg Spiers had built to ship himself from England back to his home in Australia. Hearing the story on the radio gave Signe the idea of doing the same thing to transport her people to California. Their size made it somewhat easier, but it was still a major undertaking.

102

Chapter XVII

Gold Fever

June 22, 2013

Erinomainen Nopea Luistimet (the ice skate factory)
Helsinki, Finland

Day Two of our week-long trip, *continued*

Grandpa Nick writing:

"As I was about to say, he's the one who came up with the idea of shaping our gold into balls. I'd like to lay claim to it, but it was his idea," Signe said.

"Balls? I don't understand," I said.

"He said to forget forming our gold into ingots–you know, those brick-shaped blocks everyone seems to use for gold–shape it into something more manageable, he said, something you can roll rather than lift. Like I said, he's very clever. It took a bit of an effort, even for us, but we melted down all of our gold ingots and re-shaped them into balls, just big enough so we can lift them without too much effort. It was my idea to construct a track, rather like one of your Uplander roller-coasters, as I believe you call them, for rolling the gold from one place to the other–lickety-split, no sweat–you just have to remember to keep your fingers out of the way! I can't tell you how this has changed the relationship we have with our gold. As a tribe, we've moved several times in the millennium we've been in existence. And each time, the difficulty of moving our gold determined how quickly we could relocate. Being able to roll the gold has made all the difference in the world.

"Case in point, when we came under threat from Grete and her amusement park gang, I didn't think she'd actually succeed but, just to be safe, I decided to move the last of our gold away from our cave as quickly as possible. Many years ago I bought a boathouse on Torpvägen, the road down the hill from our cave. We converted it from a boathouse to a warehouse and then dug a tunnel connecting our cave to the warehouse, just to make sure we had a subterranean, hidden exit in case we ever needed it. In addition to providing entry and exit, the tunnel also contains the track I told you about, which makes very quick work of rolling the gold from the cave to the waterfront warehouse."

"Is that what those big boxes we saw in the other room are for?" Joaquin asked.

"No, those filled with gold would be so heavy that it would cause all sorts of problems. Those boxes are for us."

"What?!" Joaquin said, more loudly than he intended.

"Listen men, the trick to surviving is not to get caught. And not getting caught means not attracting attention to yourself. For the most part, we gnomes are home-bodies–we don't particularly like gallivanting about. But when we do have to travel from one place to the other, it's fraught with problems–especially that part about not drawing attention to one's self. Of course, if the distance isn't far, we simply travel by night; that's when we're up and about anyway. But if it's any distance we need to travel, that's a different story. I occasionally listen in to what you Uplanders are up to on what you call a 'transistor radio.' And I like some of your music, espe-cially those big band numbers. Well, purely by chance one night, I was outside our cave, enjoying a full moon, listening to my radio, enjoying a pipeful when I heard a story about an Uplander who sent himself in a box from England to Australia, via airplane. Took him three days, but he did it. I figured if he could do it, so could we, because–no offense– just about anything you can do we can do better.

"This idea had never occurred to me before and it, literally, opened whole new worlds to us. It took some help from Remi, but I eventually discovered DHL and started, using his telephone, a conversation with one of their representatives in Hel-sinki, by the name of Minna. She and I quickly became friends, partially because, let's face it, I'm fairly certain we've made her a lot of commissions. That's okay by me because she's always delivered as promised. Anything we wanted picked up at one place and delivered to another, she was able to make happen. It was Minna and her company that got us shipped in boxes from our warehouse to here, all without anyone taking notice. And, if things go according to plan, it's how we're going to get from here to California."

"Are the Voslakians aware of any of this?" I asked.

"Only that we're moving, not how we're getting there or where we're headed," she answered.

"How can you be sure"

"Because I used Remi's phone to set it all up–not the crows," Signe said.

"There's some comfort in that, I guess, but to be perfectly honest, Signe, I'm scared of those guys–the Voslakians–scared for myself and scared for Joaquin, scared for all of us–you, Lars, and Remi included. If the Voslakians are as ruthless as you say they are… well, I didn't sign up for that. I agreed to get you and the remaining tribe members, along with your gold, to California, or more specifically, to Mt. St. Helena. That's it. I'm sorry, but the presence of Voslakians changes the situation for me."

"I understand," Signe said seriously. "In the Old Times we had allies we could reach out to, like the giant trolls. We'd tell them what we needed, they'd name their price, and then they'd make a quick and ugly end to whatever the problem was, including the Voslakians. It was never a permanent solution–violence never is–but it allowed us to survive long enough to make our next decision. Now there's only one giant troll left–Lucinda–and she's in Iceland. Last time we saw her, she said she was never going anywhere again where the Uplanders don't believe she exists–said it was bad for her health. Granted, we've had some strange reports that there may be one or two living in, of all places, northern Idaho in the United States, but we've never been able to confirm if that's true or not. Either way, it doesn't do us much good them being so far away.

"Back then, if the trolls weren't available, we'd hire a clan of faeries and they'd enlist a dozen or so squirrels and once word got out, there'd be a line of gnomes who'd pay to watch it all go down. The faeries and squirrels versus the Voslakians– it was part warfare and part theater. Those were some memorable battles, surprisingly fierce, actually. But the faeries seem to have scattered to the four corners; I don't think I could get more than two or three of them together in one spot these days–and as far as those crazy squirrels go, no one except the faeries could control them. Anyway, how'd we get started on this? It's all past history. We're going to have to take a completely different approach; we're going to have to outsmart the Voslakians, period. Frankly, it shouldn't be that hard."

"What are you thinking?" Remi asked.

"I'm thinking we need to consult the Baron. There's too much at risk here, across the board."

"Do you want me to get him on the phone?"

"Only to tell him we're coming to see him, don't you think? This isn't a telephone conversation. We need to see him in person," Signe said.

"Who shall I say is coming?" Remi asked.

"All of us–Nick, Joaquin, you, and me. We all have a stake in this, one way or the other. Tell him we'll be there–when? Will you fly us?"

"Of course. I can have the plane brought here, to Malmi, which shouldn't take more than two hours and, from there, it's only three hours or so to Le Bourget. I'll call him now and tell him to expect us around seven this evening. Okay?"

"Thank you, Remi," Signe said before turning back to me, "I know you're going to have to give this some thought, Nick. I respect that and whatever decision you ultimately make. But before you make your final decision, let's all talk with the Baron. And let me leave you with something that may influence your decision," she said.

"What's that?" I asked.

"Gold fever. You may have heard of it and thought that it was some kind of a made-up thing. But let me assure you, it's for real–at least for you Uplanders it's real; we gnome folk have been around vast amounts of gold for so long we're immune to it. In the Uplander world, however, the more gold there is and the closer it is, the more likely a breakout of gold fever will occur."

"What are the symptoms?" Joaquin asked.

"Makes you crazy," Signe said. "Makes you lose your mind and take stupid chances–ones that don't make any sense at all. You may doubt me, but I can almost guarantee an outbreak amongst those Voslakians. And it's going to ruin any chance they might have had putting their hands on our gold. Mark my words."

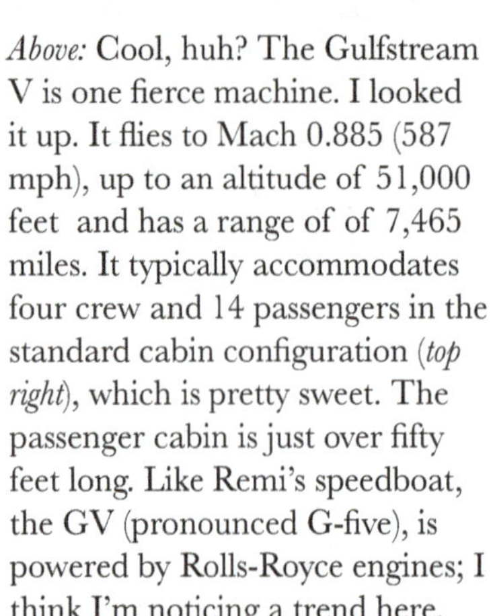

Above: Cool, huh? The Gulfstream V is one fierce machine. I looked it up. It flies to Mach 0.885 (587 mph), up to an altitude of 51,000 feet and has a range of of 7,465 miles. It typically accommodates four crew and 14 passengers in the standard cabin configuration (*top right*), which is pretty sweet. The passenger cabin is just over fifty feet long. Like Remi's speedboat, the GV (pronounced G-five), is powered by Rolls-Royce engines; I think I'm noticing a trend here.

Above: The façade of the Baron's townhouse or, *hôtel particulier,* as the French say, was impressive but nowhere near as—*WHOA!*—its interiors *(left).* I don't really know how to describe them except to say that, truly, they looked like something from a different world.

Chapter XVIII

Grim Facts

June 22, 2013

The Baron's *hôtel particulier*
Paris, France

Day Two of our week-long trip, *continued*

Grandpa Nick writing:
Remi ordered us a cab to get from the ice skate factory to our hotel to pick up our passports and then on to the Malmi airport, north of the city center, Helsinki's airport for private aircraft. In the cab I thought about what Signe said about gold fever—about it causing stupidity and mistakes. I had little doubt that what she said was true, but mistakes weren't what was worrying me. What I cared about was the violence the Voslakians might inflict on any or all of us, which seemed like a very real possibility. My gut reaction was there was no way I was going to be able to reconcile being part of what Signe called their "relocation endeavor."

Meanwhile, what in the world was I doing getting on a private jet with Joaquin to fly to Paris and meet with a Baron? This was crazy. I wondered whether my extreme tiredness was affecting my ability to make decisions. I suspected the continuous 24-hour-a-day sunlight was taking a toll on my internal clock. When Remi said he'd tell the Baron we'd be there by six, I realized I had no idea what time of day it was, even whether it was a.m. or p.m. or, worse, what day of the week it was. I wondered whether or not I'd be able to sleep on the flight to Paris—a question, it turns out, I didn't have much control over. The next thing I have much memory of is the plane jerking to a stop and finding out from Joaquin we were in Paris. I hoped I hadn't been snoring.

"It was like a full-on attack of narcolepsy," Joaquin said.

"What was?" I asked.

"You."

"Me?"

"Yeah, one minute you were awake and the next you were sound asleep. Lights out, Helsinki."

"Here in this chair?"

"Yep."

"Well, at least I made it to my seat before being hit with the sleep stick."

I looked around at my surroundings. It was a cocoon of tasteful, understated luxury, everything in shades of cream and beige with accents of chrome. The oversized leather chairs–which could be swiveled in a complete circle–looked like they should be in someone's fancy living room, not on a plane. Remi and Signe were deep in conversation at the front of the plane, but looked up and nodded with a smile. Man, I hoped I hadn't drooled while I was asleep. Without any delay we disembarked and were greeted at the bottom of the steps by a customs official who checked our passports, asked a few quick questions and then motioned us to some kind of long, black car, doors open in anticipation of our arrival. I couldn't help but notice that the chauffeur's expression didn't change as he held the door open for Signe, so I guessed that he was employed by the Baron and had met her before. Signe accepted his offer of a hand getting up into the car, which she managed with considerable grace.

Once we were settled, the driver took off, following the signs to the "*City Centre.*" Given the time of day the traffic was surprisingly light, with most of it going the opposite direction, commuters anxious to get home. We made our way along the *Rive Gauche*–the "Left" bank of the River Seine–to the 7th arrondissement–a district sometimes simply called "*le Faubourg,*" by most accounts the most prestigious neighborhood in Paris since the aristocracy started moving in in the 17th century. Hardly surprising for the Baron's family, who had roots in international banking going back to the 1700s.

We slowed in front of one of the many classic pale limestone *façades*, three stories tall, rows of French doors (with the drapes pulled shut), each set of doors fronted with a narrow black wrought iron balcony with shiny brass finials–a traditional, formal exterior that didn't share what might be happening inside to anyone who might be looking from the outside. The double, solid wood, black-painted gates in the center of the building opened noiselessly and we drove

through into an interior cobbled courtyard, with a large, simple limestone fountain splashing gently at its center. It wasn't hard to imagine horses watering at its
edge in a not-so-distant past.

Dressed identically in what I guessed were the uniforms of the house–plain
black jackets, dark gray trousers, white shirt, black silk tie and jazzy, golden yellow
brocade vests with brass buttons–two young men opened the doors on either side
of the car, while a third swept his arm and said "This way, please. The Baron is
waiting for you in the library."

From the moment we stepped into the interior of the Baron's *hôtel particulier*–or
townhouse, if you will–there was so much to take in that it could only be described
as a friend of mine once put it, "a dazzling display of luxe on the loose." Everywhere you looked there was layer on layer of rich colors and textures. What could
have simply been too much proved that excess could somehow tame itself into a
harmonious, appealing whole. Muted, diffuse lighting, a crackling fire in an ornate-
ly-carved black marble fireplace, Oriental rugs, wonderful landscape paintings, one
hanging above another, polished wood paneling, glints of gilt frames and crystal
objects, flowers artfully arranged in ornate porcelain vases and everywhere the
gentle scent of what? Iris? It could have been intimidating but, instead, the effect
was one of lived-in comfort and, if such a grand room can be called such a thing,
it was cozy.

Seated next to the fire, in a gold-framed, tiger-striped chair was the Baron himself, looking every bit the conductor of this elaborately-staged visual feast. High
forehead, pure white hair swept straight back, clad in black–from turtleneck to
trousers, to velvet slippers, embroidered with what I guessed was the Baron's family
crest. It was as if someone had called central casting and requested the quintessen-
tial aging European aristocrat. There was a silver-topped cane propped next to his
chair which, I guessed, was why he didn't stand up to welcome us. Both Joaquin
and I halted at the entrance to the library, trying to absorb the scene, a little overwhelmed, while Signe practically bounced across the room saying, "There you are.
It's been too long, Eddy. You're lookin' good," she said, holding his hand, straining
on tiptoe to give him a peck on the cheek.

"Not so bad yourself, Signe, especially for someone–what?–not a day over 300?"
the Baron retorted.

"Something like that," Signe said with a dismissive wave of her hand, "still upright and stable, which, apparently, is more than can be said of you–what's with the

cane?" The Baron shrugged silently, rolling his eyes. "Well, meet my new friends. You know Remi, of course," Signe said, Remi winking at the Baron and bowing his head. "And this is Nick Sinclair and his grandson, Joaquin, come all the way from California to help in our endeavor. Nick, Joaquin, meet Baron Edmund. Better known to some of us as Fast Eddie–for his sailboats and racehorses, of course."

Joaquin and I shook hands with the Baron and exchanged pleasantries. He urged us to make ourselves comfortable, which was easy to do in a room designed to practically embrace its occupants in comfort.

"To what do I owe the pleasure?" the Baron asked no one in particular.

Because Signe had just stated that Joaquin and I were going "to help in their endeavor" I felt the need to state the situation more accurately–so that it included my misgivings. "If you'll allow me to clarify my grandson's and my involvement, Baron. From the beginning I looked at this–I'm not sure what to call it –*Project? Mission?*–from a purely logistical point of view. I thought we could be of practical assistance in getting Signe's people and their fortune safely to California. I can assure you, life-and-death concerns never entered my mind, as they now have with the presence of the Voslakians. The logistical side of this was going to be hard enough but, in all honesty, I would never have considered us becoming involved if there were any kind of physical risk to either of us. The degree of danger we now face was never part of the equation."

"Understood," the Baron nodded. "But let me share a grim fact with you. I've watched the Voslakians and their horrible behavior my entire adult life and I can assure you if they meant you any harm, you'd already be in the hospital–or, more likely, the cemetery."

Shot puts and cassoulet. Talk about a weird combination! Good thing Grandpa tipped me off that cassoulet was basically "beans and wieners"–which sounds a lot less intimidating. Whatever you call it, it was good. I think the Baron was trying to impress Grandpa, so he broke out one of his wines–a Chateau Lafite, which seemed to make everyone happy, so I guess it was good. Before lunch, Remi got on his cell phone and made arrangements to buy just about every shot put in Europe–well, maybe not every one, but a lot of them–like 8,869 to be exact. At 16 pounds each, that's a total of 141,904 pounds. Signe decided that four shot puts to a crate would be about the limit of what two gnomes could lift– about 64 pounds–which made 2,217 crates! And they all had to be shipped from all over the place, via DHL, to Åland, highest priority. The cost must have been huge.

CHATEAU LAFITE, IN PAUILLAC, ALMOST ON THE COAST OF SOUTHWESTERN FRANCE.
IT IS IN THE HAUT-MEDOC REGION, HOME TO SOME OF THE FINEST WINES ON THE PLANET.

Chapter XIX

Beans and Wieners at Fast Eddy's

June 22, 2013

The Baron's *hôtel particulier*
Paris, France

Day Two of our week-long trip, *continued*

Grandpa Nick writing:

"You're right to be concerned about your safety, but in this case, violence isn't going to be the Voslakians first response–greed is. I know these miscreants well and how they think," the Baron said. "You're much more useful to them alive and unharmed than you would be harmed or, god forbid, worse. They think by watching your actions, you and Joaquin are going to lead them to the gnomes' gold, and you can't do that if you're dead. Sorry to be so blunt, but we're in an extreme situation here and I'm simply telling it like it is," the Baron said seriously.

"And my guess is, they've already caught gold fever," Signe said.

"Oh, I'm sure they have. We'll make that work to our advantage," the Baron said, "and in so doing, avoid any violence."

"How?" I asked, not at all convinced.

"Deception," the Baron said. "We manipulate the situation, pointing them in the direction of a 'discovery' that will lead them away from the gold and, more importantly, away from all of you. One critical question first: How big did you make the gold balls, Signe."

"The exact circumference?" Signe asked.

"No, just approximately."

"Like this," she said, holding her hands in a sphere shape a little bigger than a large grapefruit.

"Wonderful," the Baron said, "We're in business."

"What are you thinking?" Remi asked.

"Shot puts," the Baron answered.

"Shot puts?" Remi asked, disbelief in his voice.

"Shot puts," the Baron reiterated. "We're going to throw the Voslakians off the trail of the gold with shot puts and give you some time to get packed up and gone without them breathing down your necks. Look, it's not that complicated. We're just going to put them on the trail of something else to look for. First we have to make sure they are aware of our plan to deceive them. Once they 'uncover' our plan they'll be very pleased with themselves and their skills of detection. They'll feel like masters of the universe. By playing to their egos, we practically guarantee that they'll never suspect our actual plan—they'll be too busy congratulating themselves."

"I'm sorry, but I'm missing something. We're going to get them to steal shot puts instead of the gold?" I asked.

"It's a classic double-double cross," the Baron said.

"That hurts my head," I said, my frustration with the whole situation starting to show.

"No, it's simple," he said, rising carefully from the chair. Using his walking stick, he went over to an ornate desk and produced a piece of paper and an old-fashioned fountain pen. Seating himself at the desk, he said "Look, here it is by the numbers. Where is the gold now, Signe?"

"We moved all of it from our cave in Åland to the warehouse there. Lars helped us set up an assembly line and we built wooden boxes sturdy enough for the gold balls. They should be all packed by the end of the week and shipped to the ice skate factory," Signe replied.

"How many balls to a box?" the Baron asked.

"Four—any more than that and we wouldn't be able to lift them. Each crate weighs approximately 30 kilos. It takes two of our men to maneuver one."

"30 kilos?" I asked, risking sounding stupid.

"Over 60 pounds," Remi said.

"Okay, here's what we do," the Baron said:

"One—We produce a fake plan on paper we intentionally let the Voslakians steal.

"Two—The plan will say that we intend to disguise the gold balls by painting them black, to resemble shot puts and that's how the outside of the crates will be labeled.

"Three–We will provide them with their location and when we intend to have them picked up and shipped so they can plan their theft accordingly."

"You think that's going to work?" I asked.

"Like I said, if we secretly let the Voslakians discover our plan they're going to feel so confident that they'll never suspect a further ruse. Plus, as Signe has pointed out, they're all afflicted with gold fever, which will be clouding their judgement."

"Oh, I don't know, you guys. How are the Voslakians going to find the fake plan?" I asked.

"They're on to you, aren't they?" the Baron asked me.

"They were when we first arrived in Åland, but we gave them the slip when we stayed on Lars's island and Remi got us to Helsinki," I said.

"Well, we'll get you a hotel room and it will be easy enough to make them aware of your whereabouts. All you have to do is put the plan in the safe in your hotel room and disappear for a few hours. I guarantee you it will be gone by the time you get back. Signe, does the rogue crow–what's his name? Crooker?–know he's been uncovered?"

"No. His name is Croaker and I thought we might be able to put his deceptive ways to good use without him knowing I'm using him. I've left him alone for the time being."

"Well, here's your opportunity: Use him to get a message to Remi about what hotel Nick and Joaquin are staying in and that Nick's put a written copy of the plan in the safe in his room."

"Why me?" I asked. Instead of walking away from the project, here I was being pulled way further in.

"This is no-risk, Nick. Just put the plan in the safe and get out of the hotel for a few hours. The one thing you should do, though, is make a note of what number you leave the dial of the safe on. They might just take a photo of the plan instead of actually taking it. They'll never think they need to leave the combination dial in the same position as they found it–okay? If the dial's been turned, we know they've opened the safe and taken a photograph of our plan."

No risk, I thought to myself. Why did those two words worry me? Maybe because I didn't believe the Baron. And why was he assuming I'd go through with his plan? For the moment, I bit my tongue.

"Are you willing to sacrifice four balls of gold to this venture, Signe?" the Baron asked.

"Why? What are you thinking?" Signe responded.

"Just in case the Voslakians check to see if the contents really are gold balls, we need to spray paint four of them black and put them on top of the first crate so they can scratch through the paint and see the gold underneath. I think it's worth the cost, Signe. Do you agree?

"I hate giving the Voslakians anything, but I think this qualifies as 'insurance' that the entire plan works. So, yes, let's do it."

"Who knows what color shot puts are?" the Baron asked.

Without hesitating, Remi said "they come in all colors, but standard ones are either a metallic iron-gray color or black."

"Let's go with black," the Baron said, "it covers better. We're going to need a great number of shot puts. Of course, the Voslakians don't know exactly how much gold you have, but whatever we put in front of them should be impressive. Do you think you'll be able to get that many?"

Signe turned to Remi and asked "What do you think?"

"I think we're going to find out," he said, standing up, removing his cell phone from his pocket. "Let me see what I can do," he said, leaving the room.

"If we can fill the warehouse with boxes of real shot puts, I think it's safe to say that the Voslakians will show up in no time to confirm that they're there. My guess is they'll scratch through the paint on one of the balls to see that they are, in fact, gold. I just hope they choose the box we want them to. We should be able to position it so it's their first choice. If the gold test is successful, they'll be back to steal the rest of the boxes faster than you can say 'Helsinki.' After that, how long it takes for them to figure out they've been duped I can't say, but Signe, you and your people have got to get in motion as soon as the Voslakians take the bait. Once they've figured out what's happened, they're going to be on the war path."

"Yes, of course. Our departure gets set in motion as soon as the Voslakians check out the warehouse."

Just as she said the words, Remi came back into the library and explained that there were plenty of shot puts out there, but that they were in locations all over Europe, from Norway to Poland. "It's going to take some doing," Remi said somewhat dejectedly.

"Do you have a list of the sources?"

"Yes, of course."

"And how many we're ordering from each?"

"Yes."

"Then all I need to do is turn over the information to Minna at DHL and she can set it up. Everything is going to need to be shipped at the highest level of priority to our warehouse," Signe said.

"There's not going to be a shot put left in Europe," Remi mused, "good thing there are no Olympic games this year."

"So who do you talk to about food around here, Eddie? I'm feeling peckish. And I bet my traveling companions are as well," Signe said.

"We can't have that, can we? Let's go see what Madam Cochet has to offer. Of course, there's always cassoulet–it's been cooking since just after the war ended. As it's eaten, she replenishes the pot with the necessary ingredients and it just keeps cooking. It's been a 70-plus year reminder of what we all went through. Extraordinary, actually. Nothing quite like it anywhere."

Joaquin leaned towards me and whispered out of the side of his mouth, "What's cassoulet?"

"Beans and wieners."

"Good to know," he said.

The Baron grabbed his cane and led us down one hallway and then another, finally reaching a large kitchen with massive dark beams in the ceiling and dozens of all different-sized shiny copper pans hanging down. The kitchen was warm and smelled good, an altogether welcoming and pleasant place. The Baron introduced us to Madam Cochet, a compact, elderly woman with gray hair neatly double-braided over the top of her head. If you ask me, she could have been anyone's French grandmother. We sat on stools at a large, square wooden island in the middle of the kitchen. We all decided to have the cassoulet and Madam Cochet instructed us to serve ourselves from the very large pot on the stove. She put several long, skinny loaves of bread on the table, along with a wooden bowl filled with greens of all kinds. The Baron opened a bottle of wine, explaining it was from his own winery, Château Lafite, vintage 1998.

"Wow." Not the most sophisticated response, but I couldn't help myself–either for the wine or the vintage.

"Yes, well, I'm trying to impress you, you see. I understand you have your own family winery in California."

"I do. But I know when to stand back and let others do what they do best. I'm not that involved in the day-to-day running of the winery. We do, however, make some wonderful wines but not, I think, on a par with your Lafite."

"I think you're being modest, Nick, but thank you for the compliment. *Bon appétit* everyone," he said, raising his glass, "Here's to getting safely to the new."

"Safely to the new," we all repeated.

. . .

Joaquin here. I didn't say anything in that meeting in the Baron's library because I was having trouble believing what I was hearing. They all struck me as good, smart people, but I had serious doubts about their abilities, collectively, to actually pull off the plan. Somehow the whole spray-painting of gold balls, talking crows, and shipping gnomes halfway around the world in crates all sounded a little what? Amateurish? I'm not trying to be disrespectful, but it reminded me of some of the crazy plans Darren and I used to come up with when we were in the third grade. That was it. It was like a bunch of third graders were in charge. The plan just didn't seem professional. As we were being driven back to Remi's plane, I wondered if there was anything I could do to improve our odds for success. I wasn't sure, but I was certain that I'd have to raise a red flag and let Grandpa know what I was thinking. But not right now; right now, it was taking everything I had just to keep my eyes open. I turned and looked at Grandpa who was sitting next to me; his eyes were blinking way too much, too. We were both dead on our feet. Whatever we were going to talk about was going to have to wait until we both got some sleep.

Right: Slices of tomato and cucumber on rye bread with some mild, white cheese is a popular breakfast in Finland, along with very strong coffee. *Middle right:* It seemed unlikely the Voslakians had the ability to track our whereabouts through our passports, but just in case, we decided to stay somewhere our passports wouldn't be needed, which is how we wound up at Signe's secret hideout–the old ice-skate factory, on the outskirts of Helsinki. The equipment, still on the factory floor, looked very much like the old postcard I found *(bottom)*.

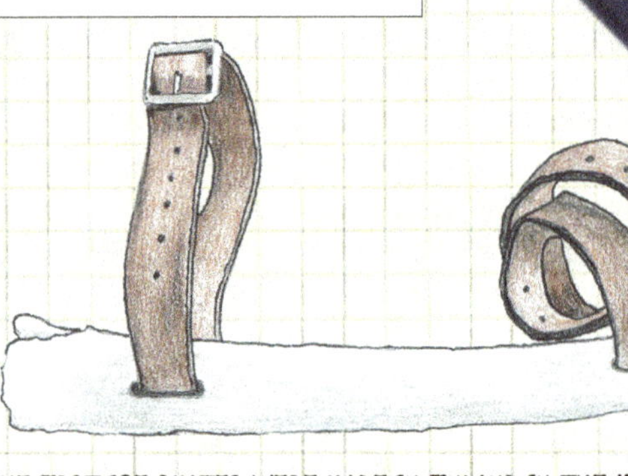

Chapter XX

Sitting Ducks?

June 23, 2013

Helsinki hotels and *Erinomainen Nopea Luistimet* (the ice skate factory)
Helsinki, Finland

Day Three of our week-long trip

Joaquin writing:

The next several hours went by in a fog. I'm pretty sure everyone slept on the flight from Paris to Helsinki and that we were basically zombies on the cab trip from the airport to the hotel. I was more than happy when Grandpa asked me to pull down those black-out shades in our room and to get some sleep somewhere that wasn't moving.

The next morning, we went to some windowless room downstairs, in what must have been the hotel basement, where the complimentary breakfast was served. The smell of coffee was strong and it seemed like most of the folks were eating sliced tomatoes and cucumbers and some kind of pale cheese on skinny slices of dark bread—an interesting choice for breakfast. I dished up some scrambled eggs and bacon from a row of covered chafing dishes and toasted a couple pieces of bread in a toaster the hotel had provided on the buffet table. Grandpa just had coffee.

"You find what you wanted?" he asked me.

"Everything but the Froot Loops," I said as seriously as I could.

"Really?"

"Grandpa! As if…"

"Well, you never know," he said taking a sip of coffee, "Man, this is strong enough to walk into your mouth. But it's good, especially with the hot milk. You want some?"

"No, I'll pass. But you should have some tomatoes and cucumbers."

"What?"

"It's what everyone else seems to be eating. Don't you want to fit in?"

"I'll pass this time. Listen Joaquin—and don't freak out—but I'm thinking we should go home. In all the commotion yesterday—flying to Paris, meeting the Baron, and being so damn tired—I didn't get to ask the question I really wanted to, namely, what was stopping the Voslakians from just popping us in the gourd if and when they felt like it. I mean, I get that there's a plan in place, but I can't see how it protects us, other than hoping the Voslakians' greed is going to override their history of violence. I guess that's a possibility, but maybe not. And I don't feel like taking that chance and finding out too late that we're in deep trouble."

I thought about what he said which, actually, wasn't far off from what I was already thinking—about it all being kind of an "amateur hour" effort.

"I'm not looking to get beat-up or worse, but if we go home now, what are we going to tell G?" I asked.

"The truth. That it was too dangerous."

I was quiet again, trying to think through the options. "Is there anything we can do to make it less dangerous?" I asked.

"Yeah. Go home," Grandpa said.

"There's gotta be something we can do other than just give up. Do you think the Voslakians even know where we are?"

"You mean specifically where we are this minute?" Grandpa asked.

"In this hotel, yeah," I answered.

"I doubt it. But they might. And they *will* know when Signe deliberately uses Croaker to get a message to Remi revealing our whereabouts to the Voslakians, to get them to steal the fake plan. That's *if* it goes down the way the Baron laid it out."

"If the Voslakians don't know where we are right now and won't know until Signe tells Remi via the rogue crow, then we're safe for the time being, right?"

"Supposedly," Grandpa said.

"For how long?" I asked.

"Until all the shot puts arrive and everything can be arranged for the big deception at the warehouse in Eckerö. I'm guessing two or three days."

"How in the world would they know where we are when we've given them the slip?" I asked him.

"Because we used our passports to check into the hotel. I'm thinking it's possible they have access to whatever database keeps track of that kind of stuff."

"Like how?"

I could tell Grandpa was starting to get exasperated by my questions, but I needed to know what he was thinking. "Oh, I don't know. But I'm guessing it's possible. They're probably way more technologically advanced than we think," he answered.

"Okay. Then let's stay somewhere where we don't need passports."

"Like where?"

"Like Signe's factory–there's plenty of room there, right?"

This time it was Grandpa's turn to be quiet. "All right. Let's take this 24 hours at a time. I'm willing to do that," he said, surprising me. "I'll call Remi and tell him we're going to stay at the factory. Tomorrow morning we'll reevaluate the situation and see where we stand. He drained the last of his coffee and said "Let's get our stuff and get out of here."

We walked over to the futuristic-looking elevators, contained in clear glass tubes. The effect was weird, watching people levitate up and gliding down to a gentle stop. Once in our room, it didn't take long to pack up, because neither of us had unpacked much. We got into an elevator car going down that already had a few people in it. I glanced over Grandpa's shoulder to the elevator right next to us, on our right. There was no mistaking the two Voslakian men in the car, stopping on the floor we had just left. My blood ran cold and I got so lightheaded, I reached out and grabbed the rail that went around the elevator car. Grandpa looked at me but probably thought I was freaked out about the glass walls. So much for us being "safe" for three or four days, but if I told him what I'd seen, we'd be on the next flight home. Maybe I shouldn't have, but I decided not to say anything–and I didn't feel good about it. Any of it. By the time the elevator opened onto the lobby of the hotel, though, I had an idea.

"I know," I said. "Let's deliberately throw them off our trail, just in case, you know, they *are* able to track our passports."

"What are you thinking?" Grandpa asked.

"I saw another hotel across the street–the Hotel Kämp. Why don't we check in and just not stay there and go the factory?"

"Kind of a waste of money," Grandpa said.

"Is this the time to worry about that?" I asked. "Aren't the gnomes paying for all this? I mean, it definitely seems like they can afford buying us a little insurance.

Besides, we need a hotel room with a safe so we can put the plan in it for the Voslakians to steal, or photograph, or whatever they're going to do with it."

Grandpa thought for a minute and then said "All right. Let's do it."

We walked across the street, checked into the hotel and then walked back out again and hailed a cab. There was no way to tell if it would work or not, but it made me feel a little better that we'd done something to throw the creeps off our trail. As we settled into the back seat of the cab, Grandpa looked at me with kind of a panicked look on his face and said "Do you have any idea where the factory is?"

I thought fast and remembered I took a photo with my phone of the sign outside Signe's factory because the name on it was so weird. I scrolled through the photos quickly and showed it to the driver and said "This is where we want to go." The cab driver took a look at the photo and, in perfect, if accented, English, said "This is a first—an ice-skate factory in the middle of summer."

I didn't know what to say so I just asked if he knew where it was.

"No, but I can Google it. There can't be more than one, right?" he said, smiling.

"I doubt it," I said.

"You took a picture of the shot-put factory sign? What for?" Grandpa asked.

"So I could show Darren—*Erinomainen Nopea Luistimet*—that's about as foreign as it gets. It's a good thing I did because I have no idea where we were."

"I think we just lucked out," Grandpa said.

"Yeah, and I think I'll delete it. Since we're being cautious now, I wouldn't want it falling into the wrong hands," I said, moving the photo to the trash on my phone.

After about a ten-minute, cross-town trip, Grandpa and I were standing on the sidewalk outside *Erinomainen Nopea Luistimet*, luggage in hand. Grandpa checked the door knob; not surprisingly it was locked. I pushed the doorbell and looked up. As I expected, there were two cameras above the front door, one pointing left and one pointing right. Hopefully whoever was monitoring them knew who we were or it was likely we'd never get in.

We waited for what felt like an eternity when the door finally buzzed and Grandpa pushed it open. The main part of the factory, where all the machines were, was just as empty and eerily silent as the last time we were there. All of a sudden, from seemingly out of nowhere, Signe appeared in front of us, not quite looking herself. I couldn't quite tell what was different until I realized we had woken her up. Even though they were living above ground, they were still following their traditional awake-sleep pattern—the exact opposite of us "Uplanders."

Dressed in a long, bright red robe she said, "Well, well, I wasn't expecting you two. What's happening? Is everything all right?"

"Yes and no–and sorry for waking you up," Grandpa said.

"No, no–nothing to worry about. I gave up trying to sleep at night, like you do. It just wasn't working for me. Come in, come in. Tell me what's going on" Signe said, ushering us into her fancy room. We took seats at her big table and I started in. "Grandpa and I were talking, Signe, and he feels like we didn't really figure out the problem of the Voslakians yesterday when we were at the Baron's. I guess I agree with him. We're feeling a little like sitting ducks."

"That's one I haven't heard before, but I get what you're saying. What are you thinking?"

"Only that we thought it was best not to stay somewhere where we needed our passports to check in–which is why we're here. We're thinking it's possible that the Voslakians have access to a database that can tell them our whereabouts by means of our passports," I said.

"Do you have any reason to believe this to be true?" she asked.

"It's just a hunch," I said, not wanting to reveal the fact that I'd seen two of them in the elevator at the hotel–at least not in front of Grandpa.

"Well, I put considerable store in hunches," Signe said, "so I say let's assume the worst. Am I correct that you're thinking of staying here?"

"If you have room," Grandpa said.

"You're welcome to stay here. We even have a few Uplander-sized rooms. And for the record, I agree–we *didn't* do a good job of thinking through your safety yesterday. As skilled as he is at developing strategies, sometimes there can be 'holes' in the Baron's thinking, given his–what shall I say? His *unique situation.* Accept my apologies for our being less than thorough. The Baron has the means to be cavalier in ways most people don't. When you've had some level of protection your entire life, it's easy to take your safety for granted. We'll address your concerns presently, but first, let's get you settled," Signe said and then hesitated, finally aksing "Have you had any sleep yet? No offense, but you both look a little ragged."

"Did we get enough last night?" I asked, looking at Grandpa. I know it sounded like a stupid question, but I truly didn't know.

"Almost, but I didn't come here to sleep–I'm ready to do something. We can get settled later," he said.

Left: If you ask me, being inside of a English sheep dog costume would be just as bad as being inside one of the gnomes's travel crates, but I'm not claustrophobic, so what do I know? I will say Hilma, the seamtress, did a masterful job of making Matti look like a real dog. We checked into the Hotel Kämp *(below)* but didn't stay there, hopefully throwing the Voslakians off our trail. *Bottom:* Matti made the trip from Finland to California in the cargo hold of the plane in a big dog crate. Apparently he had a corgi and a standard poodle to keep him company on the trip.

Chapter XXI

Lucky 13

June 23, 2013

Erinomainen Nopea Luistimet (the ice-skate factory)
Helsinki, Finland

Day Three of our week-long trip, *continued*

Joaquin writing:
Signe seated herself at the head of the long table in a chair that had been outfitted with what could only be called a "booster seat." Grandpa sat to her right and I sat on her left.

"All right then. Let's get cracking. The next step, as far as I see it, is to get the fake plan in the hands of the Voslakians. So how are we going to do that now that you don't have a hotel room?" Signe asked.

"We do, actually," I said. "We went across the street to another hotel and checked in there. We made sure the room had a safe. It's basically the same plan as we talked about with the Baron, only we won't be staying in the room."

"Good," Signe said, "What's the name of the hotel?"

"Hotel Kämp."

"Okay," Signe said, writing the name down on a small tablet of paper. "Back to the real plan," she said, laying her hands flat on either side of the tablet. "But before we start, I've been told I can be overly 'businesslike' when I discuss these things but, from experience, I find it best to just stick to the facts and present the information in the most logical way I can, so please don't take offense at my delivery. If all goes according to plan, there will be time for niceties later. So, onward: I heard from Remi this morning. In addition to saying he'd deliver the Baron's decoy plan to me today, he'd also spoken with Minna at DHL. She said all but one of the shot-put manufacturers were going to be able to fill our orders and she'd already made the arrangements to have them all shipped, Priority One, to our warehouse in Eckerö. I know it sounds absurd to have the heaviest imaginable cargo shipped at the highest–and most expensive–priority, but that's the way it has to be. So, the first order of business is," she said, continuing to write on the tablet, "to make sure the shot puts are where they need to be in the warehouse, ready to be stolen by the Voslakians. That's number one. Oh, and by the way, before I forget, I wanted to make sure you didn't think that we're a bunch of backward-looking Luddites here. We're perfectly aware of cell phones and computers, emails and texts and all the various electronic wizardry at work today. It's just that we, collectively, have made the decision not to avail ourselves of it. That's not some kind of a value judgement, it's a practical one. All things digital leave trails and we'd just as soon not lead anyone to us. It's that simple. Can you understand our position?"

"Considering we're here because we may have unintentionally left our own 'digital trail,' we understand," Grandpa said, looking at me for confirmation. I nodded, but it made me think. Could the gnomes–or anyone for that matter–live in today's world and resist technology completely? I remembered the part of Grandpa's second journal when Dagywn admitted to watching *As the World Turns* every day on television. And Signe, herself, said just the other day how much she enjoyed listening to her 'transistor' radio, as did Gob, to follow 'his boys,' the San Francisco Giants baseball team. My guess was that they weren't going to be able to hold off against the outside world for very long, but this definitely wasn't the time to discuss it one way or the other.

"Good," Signe said, "On to number two: we have to switch out the top four shot puts in the first box and replace them with the four real gold balls painted black– our decoy box. We'll handle that at our end. As soon as I know all the shot puts are in place, including the four decoy gold balls, I'll let you know and you can put the plan in the safe in your hotel room. What's the room number?"

We both said "514" at the same time.

"Next is for me to send a message to Remi, via Croaker, with all the information I want the Voslakians to know, including that you and Joaquin have agreed to help us and that I have provided you with a detailed plan. And that I've advised you to put it in your room safe for safe-keeping in room number 514 at the Hotel Kämp. You did say that you haven't stayed there, right?'

"That's right. We came straight here after we checked in," Grandpa said.

"You should go today and each buy a suitcase and some clothes to take there and put in the room. A completely empty room might cause suspicion. It's important that they believe you've been staying there. Once the Voslakians have had a chance to read the fake plan, I don't think it's going to take long for them to act on it—I'm guessing they'll be at the warehouse in Eckerö in no time.

"I didn't discuss it in Paris yesterday, but I thought of this last night and I think it's a necessary step. I'm going to have all the real gold balls painted black. It's one more layer of deception that could become critical. We'll also make our own labels with a fake shot put company logo on it and put them on all the boxes. That way if any of the boxes of real gold get opened in transit—say, intentionally by a customs agent or, gods forbid, accidentally, the contents will, by all appearances, conform with the label. It's a major undertaking, but I'm committed to doing it. I think we better ask Lars to help on that."

"What do you want him to do?" I asked.

"I need him to track down what's called a painting tent, like what's used in an auto body shop—or so I'm told. It's used in conjunction with a paint sprayer, which we're also going to need to paint the gold balls as quickly as possible. After they're painted, they'll need to be packed back in their boxes, labels put on the outside, including the shipping labels and bills of lading, ready to be picked up and shipped to California."

"Who's moving them from the warehouse to here?" Grandpa asked.

"DHL," Signe answered. "They're the only ones I trust. Most of the gold is already here; there's only a few boxes left at the warehouse in Eckerö. I broke it down to a bunch of small shipments instead of one big one, which would have attracted too much attention. Of course DHL has no idea it's our gold they're handling; they just think it's a ridiculous number of small, very heavy crates being transported a very short distance. It's a good thing Minna is discreet."

"Did you say most of the gold is already here?" I asked.

"Yes," Signe answered. "Hidden. For the time being."

I wanted to ask where, but I figured that would be pushing it—besides, I didn't need to know. But I was curious. I guessed there were rooms in the ice-skate factory I didn't know about.

"So you're going to set up the paint tent here to spray the gold?" I asked.

"Yes—you haven't seen it yet, but this place is very large; there's plenty of room," Signe said, confirming my suspicions.

"Does Minna know you're a…?" Grandpa asked.

"A little old gnome crone?" Signe asked, before Grandpa could finish his sentence.

"I wasn't going to put it that way, but yes," he said.

"No. I've either gotten Remi to intercede on my behalf or talked to her on Remi's phone. I think it's in her best interest to know as little about her best customer as possible. She's a smart one, so I'm sure she has some suspicions, but like I said, she's the soul of discretion."

"Got it," Grandpa said.

"And the real shot puts will stay in the warehouse in Eckerö?" I asked, just to make sure I was following Signe's plan. "Until the Voslakians steal them thinking they're the gold balls painted black, right?"

"Yes. And on the day we leave for California, I've arranged for two different pick-ups here—the first one for the gold and the second for all of us. I want to see the gold being loaded up and put on the DHL trucks with my own eyes. Once that's done, we'll be in our traveling crates and ready to go at the same time as the Voslakians are, most likely, stealing the shot puts. I've asked Lars to be here that day to attach the lids to our traveling crates just before we are loaded up and taken to the airport. As the Baron was quick to point out, it's essential that all 42 of our crates and all the gold are in transit to California before the Voslakians discover they've been duped. And here's where the two of you come in: I need you to keep the warehouse in Eckerö under observation—surreptitiously, of course— and confirm that the Voslakians have, indeed, stolen the shot puts. I suppose it's possible, for one reason or another, that they won't steal them, but I think that's highly unlikely. So after you've seen the Voslakians remove the shotputs from the warehouse, you'll have to get yourselves, as quickly as possible, from Eckerö to the Åland airport and from there to Helsinki to catch your flight to San Francisco. It's a logistical nightmare, but we've got to know whether the Voslakians have swallowed the hook. Or not.

"As far as Lars goes, after he's finished sealing us in our crates and supervising our being picked up by DHL, he needs to go to Finnair's air cargo facility and drop off one more item."

"One more item? What?" Grandpa asked.

"Matti," Signe said.

"Who's Matti?" Grandpa asked.

"One of us. It so happens he's claustrophobic. He can't go in an enclosed crate," Signe said.

"Then how's he going to get to California?"

"In a cage."

"*A cage?*" I asked.

"A dog cage. He's going to be disguised as a dog. Hilma, our seamstress, has already made the dog suit for him. He's going as an Old English Sheepdog."

With that, Grandpa put a fist to his mouth and tried to stifle his laughter, which made me laugh. At first, Signe looked a little horrified and then she started to laugh, too. With all the tension over the past few days some kind of a release wasn't surprising. We recovered after a minute or two and got back to business, having added one more surreal layer to an already bizarre enterprise.

"Just out of curiosity," I asked, "what if the Voslakians figure out the ruse and don't pick up the shot puts, what then?

"At that point there won't be much anyone can do because we'll all be on our way to California, including our gold. Knock on wood," Signe said, strangely knocking her head first and then the table. Grandpa and I followed suit because, 'when in Rome…' but it felt a little foolish. "As the Baron said, the goal of the fake plan is simply to buy us enough time to safely leave the country—along with our gold. I suppose it's possible that they could follow us to California but they'd need access to a great deal of information that isn't readily available. And even if they did get access to the information, by the time they figure out where the gold has gone, we'll already be burrowed into Mt. St. Helena and there's virtually no way they can trace us that far. I'm certain of that."

I'd read enough spy novels to know that when characters say things like "virtually no way" it seems to always invite trouble. Somehow, though, I didn't think that making that point was going to make much difference one way or the other, so I let it go and simply asked, "What do you want us to do now?"

"Find Into. He's Master of the House and he'll get you set up with accommodations. After that, go buy those suitcases and clothes and take them over to the Hotel Kämp. As props, they won't be needed right away, but you might as well get it done while you've got the time." Signe said.

"Where do we find Into?" Grandpa asked.

"Just go in the back, down the hall," she motioned over her shoulder, "you'll find him. There aren't that many of us here. I'm going to talk with Remi about having

Lars set up the painting tent and getting the rest of the supplies he needs. I'm thinking we'd better keep Lars close by for the next few days; he should stay here, too. Will you tell Into there'll be three of you Uplanders staying with us?"

"You got it. Let's go, Grandpa," I said and we left Signe intently writing notes to herself.

"Big plans for such small people," Grandpa said quietly.

I just nodded, glad for the moment that we were staying and helping, but I definitely had some big doubts about things going according to plan. I'm definitely not always right, but this time, oh boy, was I—things definitely didn't go according to plan.

1. Eckerö, where much of this story takes place, is on the far western edge of the Åland archipelago. The inset drawing, at right, shows a small corner of Eckerö and how close all the sites in this book are to each other.

2. Lars's great-aunt, Hilma's, house where Lars built the new outhouse.

3. Part of the gnomes' cave (specifically Signe's bedroom) was right next to the outhouse and, technically, on Hilma's property.

4. *Torpfjärdens Båthamn*, the bird-watching area.

5. The green-roofed boathouse converted to a warehouse. The tunnel from the gnome cave to the warehouse went straight between numbers "3" and "5," as shown by the dotted red line.

6. The dock where we tied up Remi's fishing boat so we could spy on the warehouse.

Chapter XXII

Google Maps

June 23, 2013

Helsinki hotel and *Erinomainen Nopea Luistimet* (the ice skate factory)
Helsinki, Finland

Day Three of our week-long trip, *continued*

Joaquin writing:
Grandpa and I walked down a long, very plain hallway, as Signe had instructed, and knocked on the solid wooden door at the end. It opened slowly and, when there was nothing to see at eye level, we both looked down and saw a fairly young-looking male gnome, dressed in blue jeans and a white t-shirt–different from Signe's high style, but also a complete departure from the look we had come to expect from the rustic, multi-layered look that Gob and his gang wore. It was all a little confusing.

"Hello there," he said in a pleasant voice. "Signe told me you were on your way–Nick and Joaquin, right? I'm Into. Pleased to meet you," he said, holding out his hand. We both shook hands with him and he opened the door wider and we entered a large, well-lit room, filled with several rows of identical large, low wooden tables, all arranged symmetrically, all covered with piles of papers of varying depths, pencils and pens, tape, staplers and paper clips–in short, all the stuff a normal office would have–except all the furniture was about half the size we were used to. The room had a busy air about it, with a handful of gnomes seriously pursuing whatever it was they were pursuing. I'm not sure what I expected exactly, but it wasn't this; by the look on Grandpa's face, it wasn't what he expected, either.

"Surprised?" Into asked.

"Yeah, a little," I said.

"Most of the gnomes have more traditional jobs, like mining and engineering, but like any group that's been around for a long time, we've developed an organization that supports our daily life–"the back of the house," I believe you Uplanders call it. Our impending move to California has added much to our work," Into said, making a sweeping motion with his hand. "We make sure everything runs smoothly, no matter where we are."

No disrespect intended, but I was having trouble imagining exactly what type of work they were up to. I mean, practically the entire world didn't even believe they existed so, to my thinking, wouldn't that mean they could do whatever they wanted–without filling out any paperwork? Like the discussion about technology, I knew this was a subject for some other time, so I let it go.

"Signe said you were going to be staying with us, yes?" Into asked.

"That's right. We're not sure for how long though," Grandpa said, obviously leaving that "24 hours at a time," option open, at least in his mind. As far as I could tell by our discussion with Signe it seemed like we were committed to see this through until the end, no matter what kind of danger we were in. Instead of making an issue out of it, I could take the "24 hours at a time" approach, too. "Signe wanted us to let you know that Lars would also be staying," I said.

"No problem," Into said, "We've got plenty of room. After we purchased this building and modified it for our use, I've got to admit that I thought adding Uplander rooms was a bit much, but Signe seems to have a sixth sense about these things. Although, just for the record, you're our first Uplander guests. Follow me."

We followed Into down another nondescript hallway, this one lined with pale wooden doors, each adorned with a brass number. We got to number three and Into opened the door to a large, high-ceilinged bright room, sparsely furnished with contemporary Scandinavian furniture, everything in subtle shades, with accents here and there of very bright, intense colors–hot pink, chrome yellow, turquoise and chartreuse. Hanging from the ceiling was a collection of three spiky, modern-looking chandeliers, turning and sparkling like stars or sunlight on the water.

"Cool," I said, looking the room over.

"Just like uptown, but not as crowded," Grandpa said, clearly impressed.

"One room with two beds–is that okay with you?" Into asked.

Grandpa and I both said "sure" at the same time. Truth be told, neither of us was quite sure what to make of the Scandinavian gnomes' presenting us with a surprise at practically every turn. Who knew if it was intentional or not, but so far the gnomes were successful at not conforming to any preconceived notion we had about who they were, how they lived, or anything else about them. Which leads to another topic to add to my "later" list: I wondered if Grandpa had the same difficulty in imagining Gob and the gang living this way–all modern and sophisticated–truly about the exact opposite of the old-fashioned, anachronistic way they lived on Mt. St. Helena. Maybe by being apart for so long the two groups had just drifted in different directions? Or maybe Gob and the guy gang had been operating on their own for so long they had simply developed their own style. Whatever it was, the two groups had certainly diverged–like in opposite directions. I couldn't help but wonder how it would work out when they were all together again. Like I said–I filed it under "discussions for later."

"Is Lars arriving today?" Into asked.

"I believe that's correct," Grandpa said.

"Well, I'll make sure the room next door is ready for him. Just so you know, there are black-out shades on the windows to help you sleep and you'll probably need these," he said, holding two small plastic bags in his open palm.

"What are those?" Grandpa asked.

"Ear plugs. We'll be up and about while you're sleeping and I'm afraid we're not the quietest folks around. Take them. Just in case," Into said.

"Thanks, Into," I said.

"Will you be needing anything else?" Into inquired.

"Maybe so. I'm thinking that it might be a good idea if we had a look at the warehouse in Eckerö before the plan goes into effect, so we know what to expect. Signe has asked Joaquin and me to surveil the warehouse after the trap has been set, so to speak, and to report on what the Voslakians do. I'm thinking we should know the lay of the land and what we're getting ourselves into, you know?" Grandpa said.

"Indeed," Into said.

"Can you book us a flight there as soon as possible?" Grandpa asked. "How much time will it take in total to get from here to the warehouse in Eckerö?"

"From the airport here I understand it only takes about an hour to fly from Helsinki to Åland. Once you land at the Mariehamn Airport in Åland, getting to the warehouse in Eckerö is a short distance. If you hired a taxi, it would probably be only 30 minutes, maybe less, to get there. If you look up the Church of St.

Lawrence in Eckerö on Google Maps on your phone, in the satellite mode, I can show you."

Bingo. I knew it, I thought to myself. *The gnomes had entered the digital world after all.*

"I think the best thing is to ask the taxi driver to drop you at the *Torpfjärdens Båthamn* on the road called *Torpvägen*–see here?" Into said, enlarging the map on my phone to show where we were going.

"*Torpfjärdens Båthamn?*" I asked, mispronouncing it badly.

"It's a popular bird-watching spot. Your cab driver will definitely know where it is," Into said.

"Where do we go once we get there?" Grandpa asked.

"Basically, when you get there, you're there. It's a boathouse we modified into a warehouse. It's right next to the bird-watching area. There are several boathouses around it–all of them painted red–but ours is the only one with a green roof; all the others have either dark gray or metallic silver roofs. It doesn't have what you Uplanders call an "address" or a name on it, but you can't miss it."

"All righty then," I said. "I assume the warehouse is locked, right? How do we get inside?"

"Good that you asked. Since we always get inside via the tunnel, there's no way to unlock the doors from the outside, but there's a hatch under the warehouse that's never locked, basically because no one but us knows it's there."

"How do you get to the hatch? You don't have to swim, do you?" I asked.

"No. There's a small rowboat tied up to the pier; if you get in the boat and row under the warehouse, you'll see the hatch door above you. The hatch opens down, not up. Once it's open, you'll see a pull-down ladder. Once it's down, tie the rowboat to the ladder and go up the ladder and through the hatch into the warehouse. The switch for the lights is next to the double doors, on the dockside of the warehouse. It's all pretty obvious."

I wouldn't class myself as a big worrier, but the fact that Into just described a situation that involved a row boat, a hatch door under a warehouse and a pull-down ladder definitely worried me. And the fact that he said it was all "pretty obvious" only increased that worry.

"And there's no key for the front door we could use?" Grandpa asked, obviously having similar thoughts.

"No. Sorry. Like I said, there's only one set of doors that go to the outside and they only lock from the inside.

"As complicated as all this sounds, I think we have to go and check it out, don't you?" Grandpa said, looking at me.

One of the things I liked about Grandpa was that it wasn't unusual for him to ask my opinion–and ask it like it mattered.

"Yep," I said.

"And Joaquin…" Into said quietly, leaning towards me.

"Yes."

"Don't tell Signe I Googled the warehouse location," he said with a wink.

Above left: The *Knight Rider* t-shirt I bought as a joke for my friend Darren. *Above:* The famous department store, Stockmann (where I found the t-shirt), in downtown Helsinki. *Left:* Grandpa and I made a pretty good meal for all hands, if I do say so myself: salmon with *beurre blanc*, asparagus, and new potatoes–and a strawberry Pavlova for dessert. We tricked out the two long tables with wildflowers and lots of votive candles. It looked–and tasted–great.

GRANDPA'S SALMON WITH BEURRE BLANC (ABOVE) AND THE STRAWBERRY PAVLOVA (RIGHT).

Chapter XXIII

Salmon and New Potatoes for 47

June 24, 2013

Erinomainen Nopea Luistimet (the ice skate factory)
Helsinki, Finland

Day Four of our week-long trip

Joaquin writing:

The next morning, as we were getting ready to leave our room at the factory, Grandpa and I almost stepped on a big envelope with our names on it, on the floor in front of the door. I opened it. Inside there was a blue folder containing the fake plan written by the Baron. I handed it to Grandpa, who read it quickly, and then put it in his over-the-shoulder messenger bag. The factory was silent as we left, all the gnomes presumably sleeping. Once outside, I figured out how to call a cab on my phone. We didn't wait more than a few minutes before it showed up. Even though it was a short wait, I was able to do a little online searching and it appeared the big department store, Stockmann, was going be the best place to get some suitcases and a bunch of new clothes, so that's where I told the driver to take us. It seemed a little strange to be buying stuff that you didn't need, but what didn't seem strange these days? Stockmann department store was practically in the middle of Helsinki, not that far from the landmark Helsinki Cathedral. It was a huge store. Once we got inside, Grandpa and I decided to split up and meet in an hour back at the entry to the store.

We both took off to the departments most likely to have what we were each looking for. I made a stop at the luggage department first and scored a cool backpack that I could use for school next year. Next was the clothing department where

I decided I might as well get some stuff I'd actually wear, so I took more time than I expected picking enough to fill the backpack. Looking through some shirts, I ran across a David Hasselhoff *Knight Rider* t-shirt. I bought it for Darren as a joke. He'd kill me, but there was a picture of KITT, the talking car, also on it, which made it even better.

I was a little late, but as it turned out, so was Grandpa as he'd decided the same thing I had, namely to buy stuff he'd wear. Being practical must run in the family. We moved out of the way of the other shoppers coming and going and put our purchases down. I got out my phone and after doing a quick search for the Hotel Kämp, realized it was just down the street. Once we got outside, we could see it from where we were standing. Even though we were packing a lot, we decided to hoof it the couple of blocks it took to get there. We were both huffing by the time we got to our unused room.

"So we've got to make it look real, right?" I asked.

"Yeah," Grandpa replied.

"Which means we have to get rid of all the packaging and hangers and stuff and make it look like we brought it from home."

"I don't think we have to put too fine a point on it, but better safe than sorry. We didn't come all this way to screw up on a some detail. Put all the packaging and stuff on top of the bed and we'll throw it away somewhere—not in this room—just in case the Voslakians are more thorough than I think they are."

We created a scene that looked as natural as possible. Grandpa put the blue folder with the fake plans in the safe, closed it, and spun the dial. Then, just to make sure it worked, he opened it and closed and locked it again. He then took a picture of the dial so we'd have a record of how he left it, just like the Baron suggested. Satisfied with our work, we gathered up the trash and went in search of someplace to toss it, winding up in the basement where there were plenty of dumpsters.

So far, our trip to Finland had been back-to-back intense activity. Outside the Hotel Kämp, Grandpa mentioned that Signe needed to give Lars time to spray paint the gold balls, so there was nothing we needed to do right at the moment. We decided checking the warehouse in Eckerö could wait until tomorrow morning.

Standing outside the Hotel Kämp, we realized we were in the only part of Helsinki where we kind of knew our way around. Grandpa suggested we go back to where Remi had docked his boat. Was it just yesterday? Or the day before? I couldn't tell—this 24-hour-a-day sunlight was messing with me. Anyway, Grandpa wanted to see the outdoor market we walked through—whatever day it was.

It turned out to be only a few blocks away and, like it was the other day, the big plaza was bustling with people and vendors, offering everything from reindeer hides to wildflowers, and everything in-between, all of it under a canopy of red and orange umbrellas. We were taking it all in when Grandpa turned to me and said "I've got an idea."

"What's that?" I asked.

"How about we cook for the clan tonight?"

If you've read the other journals, you know my grandfather is a good cook, so I didn't think it was a strange thing to suggest until I thought about it: did he actually want to cook dinner for forty-three people—no, make that forty-five including the two of us? No, forty-six including Lars. Maybe we should invite Remi? It's hard to get Grandpa to change his mind once he gets an idea, so we wound up buying two big sides of salmon, a small bushel of new potatoes, and several bunches of fresh dill. He kept asking if anyone had any cloudberries, whatever they were, but the answer was always the same: not until mid-July. So we bought a bucketful of beautiful strawberries instead. Everything else we needed we got at the indoor market right next to the outdoor market. By the time we were done, we were loaded down. We grabbed one of the cabs that were lined up outside the plaza and made it back to the factory; this time I had the address already written down on a piece of paper in my wallet.

To tell you the truth, I'm getting to be a good cook, myself. Once we got back to the factory Grandpa wrote a note telling Signe we were making dinner for the group and stuck it in her door, not wanting to wake her up. I offered my services as sous-chef to Grandpa, to which he said "I couldn't do it without you."

I guess it shouldn't come as a surprise that the gnomes' factory was equipped with the equivalent of a commercial kitchen—all brightly lit stainless steel and completely outfitted with everything you'd need to prepare a meal for, well, forty-six (or forty-seven) people. And, yes, everything was about at the height of a kitchen you'd expect to find in a grammer school classroom. I wondered if they had the same set-up in their cave back in Eckerö? I'm not sure why, but I had a hard time imagining the same gleaming, modern kitchen in a cave.

Into, who'd been up late working, stuck his head in to see what was going on. Grandpa's attention was on removing the tough skins on the bottom half of the asparagus spears using a vegetable peeler, but managed to look up and tell Into we were cooking dinner for the group and pointed to a large bag which contained several bunches of wildflowers. "Would you please tell whoever is in charge of setting the table they're welcome to use them however they like, along with as many of the votives as they want–they're in the bag next to the flowers."

"Well, you've asked the right person because that's my responsibility–at least tonight it is–it's a rotating chore. What are we having?" Into asked.

"Chef's Surprise," Grandpa answered. "You'll see soon enough. And, Joaquin, will you call Remi and see if he wants to come?"

"What time?" I asked.

"Since we're here in the factory, I figured we'd follow 'house rules' and eat at midnight."

That kind of surprised me, but it made sense, too. In order to pull it off, though, there was no way I was going to make it without a nap sometime this afternoon, that's for sure. Grandpa too.

Into was hanging back, looking a little uncertain of himself, but finally said "Do I assume you're going to want wine, and for it to be paired with the dinner? If you do, those duties fall to me as well–but on a permanent basis. Are you sure you don't want to tell me what you're making?"

"Of course, when you put it like that," Grandpa said, "salmon with a *beurre blanc* flavored with lemon and dill, steamed new potatoes and asparagus."

"A perfect summer meal," Into said. "What would you say to a Château Grenouilles Grand Cru?"

"That's a Chablis, isn't it?" Grandpa asked.

"Yes," Into replied, "better than the Montrachet, I think, which would be too buttery and big for the *beurre blanc*. Better the flinty acidity of a Chablis. It's been described as 'racy and elegant.'"

"Who am I to say no to racy elegance?" Grandpa said with a smile, whisking the *beurre blanc* sauce.

So forty-seven for dinner it was, along with the Château Grenouilles Grand Cru–which was, by general agreement, an inspired pairing. Into was pleased.

Before dinner, Signe made a point of lining everyone up and introducing us to them, one by one. There was no way I was going to remember everyone's name, but it made us all feel closer. As it turned out, Grandpa (and I) came through with a very tasty meal, seemingly enjoyed by all, including Lars and Remi. Also present in the room, but deliberately overlooked, was the specter of the upcoming move.

In just a few days all of this would be gone, replaced by a new and foreign world. And everyone knew plenty could go wrong in getting from Point A to Point B—very wrong when the Voslakians were factored in.

Instead, everyone turned their attention to what was directly in front of them and it was fun. Looking down the long tables filled with dozens and dozens of flickering votive candles, the bouquets of summer wildflowers, and a lot of happy faces and spontaneous laughter, it was easy, for the moment, to forget the difficulties we all knew might lay ahead. Preparing the meal for them all was totally the right thing to do.

Way to go, Grandpa.

Oh yeah. The gnomes went totally nuts for the strawberry Pavlova—a big meringue filled with vanilla ice cream and sliced berries. What's not to like?The

Right: The rowboat was right where Into said it would be, tied up to the wharf across from the warehouse—even the oars were there. *Below middle:* The view from up the hill, above where Lars's great-aunt lives, overlooking where the Gulf of Bothnia meets the Baltic Sea. The warehouse is at the bottom of the hill, hidden by the trees. *Bottom:* Signe and the members of her tribe cleverly remodeled the boathouse, converting it into a warehouse, including a shed-roofed extension off the back end that connected directly with the tunnel. The tunnel, in turn, ran up the hill, connecting to the gnomes' cave. She later had a rolling track installed inside the tunnel to move all the gold balls from the cave to the warehouse, and then had them transported to the ice skate factory in Helsinki.

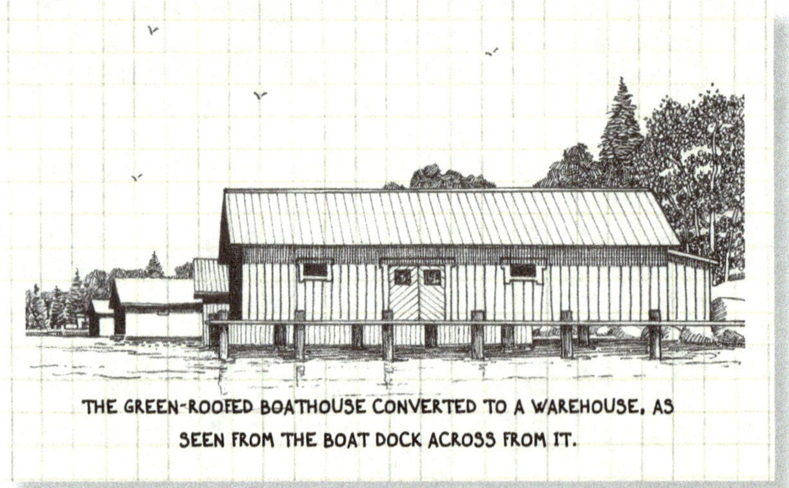

THE GREEN-ROOFED BOATHOUSE CONVERTED TO A WAREHOUSE, AS SEEN FROM THE BOAT DOCK ACROSS FROM IT.

Chapter XXIV

Green Roof

June 25, 2013

Erinomainen Nopea Luistimet (the ice-skate factory) and the warehouse in Eckerö
Helsinki, Finland and Eckerö, Åland Islands

Day Five of our week-long trip

Joaquin writing:
Even though all the food had been eaten, including seconds on the dessert, no one
appeared to be in any hurry to leave the table when Grandpa and I got up and excused ourselves at 1:30 in the morning. The next morning, the kitchen and dining
room were spotless; only the wildflower bouquets were left on the tables. And once
again all was quiet in the factory as we closed the front door behind us and called
for a cab to take us to the airport.

Getting to Eckerö was just as Into said it would be: a short, one-hour flight from
Helsinki to Åland and, once we landed, a thirty minute cab ride to the bird-watching spot. The road abruptly ended in a cul-de-sac, wide enough to turn the cab
around. After paying him, the cab driver took off back up the road and Grandpa
and I both stood there for a minute taking it all in. Looking towards the water (I'm
guessing it was the Gulf of Bothnia) there was a broad, marshy area ringed by trees
that I figured was the bird-watching area. The uphill side of the road was bordered
with lush green grasses and plenty of pine, spruce, and birch trees, as well as a surprising number of oaks and maples. It was a leafy, peaceful scene, complimented
by a cool, briny sea breeze and the gentle lapping of small waves on the shore. With
the exception of two old guys fishing off the end of a weathered wooden pier on the
far side of the boathouses, there was nothing going on, except for the birds–there
were plenty of birds. I saw teals, an osprey, terns and several that were completely

new to me. No doubt about it, the Åland Islands were a pleasant place to be.

"There's the warehouse," I said, pointing the only building around with a green roof. It was at the end of a row of similar-looking boathouses, all of which were exactly the same shade of weathered rusty red.

As we walked towards it, we could see the gnome's building was bigger than the neighboring boathouses. Tacked on to the end of the warehouse, closest to the road, was a small shed-roofed extension that looked partially dug into the bank. *Must be where the tunnel from the cave connects to the warehouse,* I thought. The pilings of the other boat houses held them two or three feet above the surface of the water. Because it was built into the steep embankment, the gnomes' warehouse and adjacent dock were maybe six or seven feet above the water.

We walked down to the end of the dock and back. "Just about what I expected. About a hundred feet long." Grandpa said, apparently having counted his steps.

"And there's the rowboat Lars said would be there," I said, pointing to a small boat tied to a piling at the end of the dock.

"So that's how we're going to get inside the warehouse?" Grandpa asked, waving at the fishermen who, not surprisingly, were watching our every move. I couldn't help but wonder how anyone within sight was going to react to the parade of DHL delivery vans about to descend on the warehouse.

"I guess so. There's only the one set of double-doors and, like Into said, they're locked with no way of opening them from the outside," I said.

"Well, there's no time like the present," Grandpa said, pulling the rowboat closer to the dock. "Let's give this a go." After undoing the line, I waved at the fishermen, too; *might as well keep it friendly and normal-like for as long as possible,* I thought. I used the ladder at the end of dock to step into the bow end and got down on my knees, facing forward. I held the rowboat next to the ladder while Grandpa got in. He put the oars in the oarlocks and maneuvered us under the warehouse. Once we were under the hatch it wasn't hard to pull the ladder down to the level of the rowboat. We were plainly visible to the fishermen, so *if this bottom-up entrance to the warehouse was supposed to be some big secret, it sure as heck wasn't any more,* I thought to myself. I turned around and looked at Grandpa who nodded for me to go up, which I did, pushing the hatch open when I got to the top. I pulled myself up and into the warehouse and then leaned over the opening and watched while Grandpa stowed the oars and tied the boat snug to the ladder. He climbed up the ladder and pulled himself into the warehouse just like I had. He was spry for an old guy.

We both got on our feet and high-fived each other and slapped the dust off our clothes, the noise of which echoed in the cavernous space. It was dimly lit, with raw, unpainted wood floors, walls and ceiling. There was a row of milky skylights along the ridgeline of the ceiling that probably kept out as much light as they let in.

The space was empty except for an elevated channel, at about knee height, made from copper tubing, just the right width and depth to hold a softball-sized ball. It was an odd-looking apparatus, snaking along one side of the warehouse—one end of it disappearing through a curtain of what looked like black rubber strips and the other end stopped at what looked like a conveyor belt made out of hundreds of metal skateboard wheels. I went over to look at the curtain made out of strips of black rubber and, sure enough, it covered the entrance to the cave. The opening was about five feet tall; if I bent over, I could walk in. I wanted to see where it went and what the gnomes' cave looked like, but this didn't seem like the time to go exploring.

Like I said, the conveyor belt picked up where the channel made of copper tubes left off, running on other side of the warehouse, ending more or less in front of the double-doors to the outside. There were two free-standing sections of conveyor belt on wheels next to the doors, as well. I was getting a picture of how the parts fit together—the gold balls were rolled from inside the cave and packed into waiting boxes on the conveyor belt. The boxes were then rolled directly into the back of waiting vans with the help of the two rolling sections of conveyor belt. The whole thing was designed to eliminate the need to carry the boxes which, as Signe noted, two gnomes could lift—but not without effort. It wasn't sophisticated—it was more like "homemade"—but considering the warehouse was empty, it obviously worked. Now, all that was missing were the 8,869 shot puts which were, no doubt, on their way. It was heartening that the events of the day had gone off as planned and the situation in Eckerö was just as Into had described it. What was about to happen next, though, I wasn't so sure about.

Grandpa and I were standing in front of the double doors that led outside, wanting to see how they opened.

"They lock from the inside, all right," he said to me, "but there's no mechanism for unlocking them—you need a key. I assume Signe knows where it is."

"You're right. She does. And so do I," said a low voice behind us. Grandpa and I both turned around, some kind of noise emitting from our mouths—something between a squeal and a gasp.

Right: Remi's fishing boat was everything his Gar Wood speedboat wasn't–plain and practical–which was just fine with me and Grandpa. We needed somewhere inconspicuous where we could watch the warehouse without being noticed. The fact that it had a "head" on it (that's a toilet for you landlubbers), made it all the better. *Bottom:* The thin spit of land where the dock was (where we docked Remi's fishing boat), was probably wide enough for a car, but there was no place to turn around, so most everyone stopped at the cul-de-sac, a little way up the road, about opposite the warehouse (you can see it on the map on page 136). We could just see a corner of the cul-de-sac from our lookout–enough to see Bad Boris and his henchmen make a mess of parking their cars before running down the dock to the warehouse, expecting to walk away with a fortune in gold.

Chapter XXV

A Soupçon of Luck

June 25, 2013

The warehouse with the green roof
Eckerö, Åland Islands

Day Five of our week-long trip, *continued*

Joaquin writing:
"Jeez, Ahti, where'd you come from?" I said, my heart racing. I remembered the red-haired gnome's name from last night's dinner. Like I said, there was no way I could remember all their names, but Ahti was easy–he was the only one with red hair.

"Hi Ahti," Grandpa said, shaking his hand. "You scared the stuffing out of us."

"Sorry about that. I didn't expect you to be here. Signe wanted me and Pentti to supervise the last shipment of the gold to the factory this morning. We also have to take the shipping labels off the shot-put boxes, whenever they arrive. There'll be a few more of us tomorrow so we can get it done faster."

"How'd you get here so early?" Grandpa asked.

"We figured out how to hitch rides on the planes that go between Helsinki and Åland–in the luggage holds. We're good at not being seen," Ahti said.

"So I noticed," Grandpa said.

"How do you get to the airport?" I asked.

"We call it the double-decker–I get on Pentti's shoulders and put on a long Uplander coat. All anyone sees are Pentti's feet and my head. It's fooled every cab driver so far."

"Where *is* Pentti?" Grandpa asked.

"Back in the cave–probably taking a nap. That was some dinner last night–

some party–thanks to both of you. It was delicious," Ahti said.

"The pleasure was ours," Grandpa said. "Glad you enjoyed it."

"So what are you doing here?" Ahti asked.

"After the shot puts are delivered, Signe wants me and Grandpa to see wheth-er the Voslakians actually take them. We thought we'd better check it out–just so there're no surprises, you know?" I said.

"They're supposed to start arriving this afternoon, right?"

"Yes. And the rest of them tomorrow morning," I said.

"I just hope we can get this done before the Uplanders who live around here get too curious," Ahti said.

"Do you think they will?" Grandpa asked.

"Wouldn't you?" Ahti asked. "First, I don't know how many–but a lot–of DHL vans have come down this road in the last few weeks and packed up 2,217 boxes of our gold and now, probably an equal number of vans will be doing the same thing in reverse–delivering box after box of the shot puts to the warehouse and then–maybe–the Voslakians will take them all away again? Ålanders tend not to interfere in other people's business, but that doesn't stop them from wanting to know what's going on. I don't know–I'm a gnome. What do *you* think?"

"I think you're right," Grandpa said. "Do you have any suggestions?"

"Not really. Signe told DHL to space out the gold pick-ups by about thirty min-utes, and that's what they did. I guess it went off okay. At least no nosy neighbors wanted to know what was going on. She told DHL to do just the opposite for the shot-put deliveries–to gang all them together like a parade–one this afternoon and one tomorrow morning, so they could start and finish as quickly as possible. If the Voslakians try to cart them off later and somebody starts asking questions, that's their problem, not ours, right?"

"That's the presumption," Grandpa said, not too convincingly.

"After the shot puts are delivered, Signe's going make the Voslakians aware of the fake plan in your fake hotel room and that's going to tip them off that we've supposedly disguised all of our gold to look like black shot puts and they're here in the warehouse just waiting for them to steal–is that correct?" Ahti asked.

"Correct. And Joaquin and I will be hiding somewhere to see what actually goes down and you and the rest of the gnomes will already be on your way to California. Don't forget, the whole purpose of this scheme is simply to buy you the time to get gone from here. The Voslakians can't take revenge for being duped because they don't know where you're going," Grandpa said.

"All the same, I'm going to be wishing for a soupçon of luck," Ahti said. "I think we all should. And you need to find a place for a lookout, don't you?"

"Somewhere with a clear view of the warehouse," Grandpa said, "I figured some place with tall grass and a few granite boulders would work."

"How long do you think the lookout is going to last?" Ahti asked.

"No way of telling," Grandpa said.

"If you have to wait for very long, hiding out in the tall grass may not be the best choice, especially if you need a glass of water or if nature calls," Ahti said. "Let me show you something," he said, reaching for an old key hanging on a rusted hook next to the double doors. The key was at eye level–his eye level. I doubt I would have never spotted it. "Remi has a fishing boat in Grissleham, across the way in Sweden. We can make sure it gets here in time."

"You're not talking about his speedboat are you?" I asked.

Ahti laughed and said "No, no, it's a real fishing boat. It's small enough that we could tie it up to that dock over there with the other boats," he said pointing to the rough wooden dock where the old guys were fishing. "You'll have a clear view of the warehouse *and* some creature comforts, even a small stove to make coffee."

Grandpa and I looked at each other and, without saying anything, decided it was a good solution. "How do we make that happen, Ahti?" Grandpa asked.

"Do either of you have Into's number?" Ahti asked.

"He gave it to me at dinner last night," Grandpa said.

"If you don't mind," Ahti said, holding out his hand. "Could borrow your phone? I'll call him and see how to do this."

"Sure," Grandpa said, handing him his phone.

Ahti walked off into the warehouse, dialing Remi's number. I could tell it wasn't the first time he'd used a cell phone–more evidence that the gnomes had entered the digital world, albeit secretly–a secret that everyone seemingly knew.

Ahti walked back and gave Grandpa his phone, saying, "Remi's going to have his son bring it over. Pentti and I will be here; we'll make sure it gets tied up so there's a clear line of sight to the warehouse."

"What's the name of it," Grandpa asked. "It wouldn't be so good if Joaquin and I were hanging out on someone else's boat."

"*Vellamo*," Ahti said. "She's a sea goddess. A very beautiful one."

"Okay, *Vellamo* it is. Thanks for arranging that, Ahti. It's a good solution,"

Grandpa said.

"Just so you know," Ahti said, "I'm leaving these doors unlocked. DHL knows they'll be unlocked and where to place the boxes of shot puts. We'll leave them unlocked to make it easy for the Voslakians to come inside and do whatever they're going to do. Signe thinks they'll be so blinded by gold fever they won't think it's strange that the doors are unlocked."

"She's probably right," Grandpa said. "So how long do you think you'll be here?"

"Until the last of the shot puts have been delivered and we've taken off all the tags, and stickers, and bills of lading from the boxes. As soon as we're finished, Signe told us to hightail it back to Helsinki so we can all leave."

"As soon as we see what the Voslakians do, we'll be right behind you. Where have you been staying?" Grandpa asked.

"Here, up the hill in our cave. We left a lot of our old stuff when we moved to the factory, including our old beds. It's okay. We just have to make sure Lars's great-aunt and her sister don't catch sight of us–those are a couple of wicked women!"

"So I hear," Grandpa said.

Right: Signe was right—the amount of work that had gone into each of the gnomes' travel crates was hard to believe. I think there must have been some competitiveness going on, with each gnome trying to outdo the other. The Victorian one even had a gnome-sized, upright piano in it! The accent was definitely on "cozy" in almost all of them — not a surprise considering that traveling in a wooden crate couldn't be all that comfortable. My guess was that most of the time they were in transit, they'd be asleep—at least I know that's what I'd do if I were stuck inside a box for that long, no matter what it looked like. I couldn't help but wonder what they were going to do with the crates once they reached California? *Top right:* The log cabin theme. *Below:* The Victorian look.

Chapter XXVI

The Pace Quickens

June 25, 2013

Erinomainen Nopea Luistimet (the ice skate factory)
Helsinki, Finland

Day Five of our week-long trip, *continued*

Grandpa Nick writing:

Once we got back to Helsinki we decided we couldn't wait until midnight—or later—to eat when the gnomes did. A burger and fries sounded good to both of us. It didn't take long for Joaquin to use his phone to find a place—Friends & Brgrs. It had a bunch of good reviews and was in the part of town we were familiar with. Turned out it was a good choice and, by the time we finished, we were both stuffed. I told Joaquin it was okay to take on a little extra because we needed to "lay down a base," for all the action that was about to happen. Turns out I was right.

We cabbed it back to the factory and, after we buzzed, it was Into who let us in.

"You're up early," I said to him.

"The pace is quickening," he said.

"We were just at the warehouse and talked with Ahti. He said some of the shot puts would be delivered this afternoon and the last of them tomorrow morning," I said.

"Yes. They'll should all be delivered there by 10 o'clock tomorrow. If that goes as planned, it means we depart the day after tomorrow—first the gold, then us. Lars will be done painting the gold balls black today which, if everyone pitches in, means we can get them all boxed up and ready to go tomorrow. Oh, and Signe wants to talk with you when she gets up—something about you being the consignee for the travel crates when they arrive in San Francisco. Has she talked to you about that?"

"Not yet," Grandpa said. "Is there anything that needs being done right now?"

"Let's go in the back and see," Into said. "Signe told everyone that they could take eight things with them and suddenly everyone's emotionally attached to every single thing they own. Maybe we can help move things along."

The hallway between the gnomes' rooms was a blur of activity, with indecision the overriding emotion. Individual gnomes would walk out of their rooms carrying a rocking chair or a painting and then suddenly turn around and put it back. There were audible sounds of frustration—groans, moans, and yelps. Into clapped his hands and said, "Ladies and gentlemen, boys and girls. I know this is hard, but we're not moving to a wasteland. Concentrate on what's truly unique or of great personal meaning to you. There's no need to be over-dramatic about what you leave behind—I guarantee you we'll find a suitable replacement once we settle on Mt. St. Helena. If you want some help getting what you've chosen into your travel crate, Nick and Joaquin have offered to help. So make your choices and let's get going."

We spent the next couple of hours helping everyone get their favorite, can't-live-without-it possessions into their travel crates. In the process, we got to take a look at their individual rooms and Signe was right—the rooms showed some serious talent. A few of the travel crates were more-or-less anonymous and plain, but there were many more, the owners of which had gone all out creating fantastic surroundings for themselves. One of my favorites recreated the look of a rustic log cabin, complete with stacked log walls, a stone fireplace with a flickering fake fire, multi-colored braided rugs and alpine landscape paintings. The other looked like a Victorian library, with a floor to ceiling bookcase on one wall, wainscoting and floral patterned wallpaper on the others, olive green velvet curtains, a chandelier dripping with crystals and an Oriental rug with an intricate design. When we started helping carry their possessions, it didn't come as a surprise that many of them had outfitted their travel crates to be a compact version of their rooms in the factory. I guess there's no place like home, even if it's in a crate, right?

Lars appeared as we were finishing up with the loading. It looked like the paint sprayer had broken loose and sprayed him and the better part of his four helpers with black paint. They were so tired they didn't stick around long, leaving in search of a hot shower, but not before Into reminded Lars to make sure everything was in order with the dog cage Matti would be using to make the trip. Lars responded with a wave over his back as he walked away.

Signe appeared in the staging area, checking to see that everyone had kept to the eight-item limit.

"Are you having dinner with us?" she asked.

"No, I think we're going to turn in early tonight," I said, "your schedule is rough on us Uplanders."

"Don't make me call you a wuss, Nick," Signe said, winking at Joaquin. "I was going to talk to you at dinner about what you need to do regarding signing for all this once it gets to San Francisco," she said motioning her hand at the travel crates, "but it can wait until tomorrow morning. I'll write it out for you–you'll need to see Minna at DHL. They have an office at the airport. I'll let her know you're coming."

As we were about to say our goodnights, Remi showed up. Into was right: The pace was definitely quickening. I thanked him for letting us use his fishing boat as a lookout, which he dismissed as no big deal. His cell phone rang and after answering it, handed it to Signe, saying "The Baron wants to talk to you."

There was definitely what I call a "dense-and-tense" vibe in the air. The full scope of just what a high-stakes, complex venture we had gotten ourselves involved in was becoming increasingly real. It was unsettling. And if I'd known what was about to come next, it would have been even more unsettling.

It was a bummer that Ahti and Pentti didn't remove the packing slips from inside the boxes of shot puts, but it was an honest mistake, considering their lack of experience with the outside world. That one sheet of paper contained a lot of information: Apparently payment for the shot puts and their shipping was coming from Remi's bank in Stockholm. They were being shipped to a fictitious person at the warehouse in Eckerö with the unimaginative name of "John Smith." I wonder who thought of that? And the shipping cost was almost as much as the price of the shot puts themselves, which put the price of just one order of 144 shot puts at almost $23,000 American dollars, or about $160 for each one.

INTER - SPORT

Mynstersvej 23, kld 1834
Frederiksberg Denmark

70 28 17 66

Packing Slip

Order #3985

Order date: 6/22/2013
Shipping: Customer to arrange

Bill to:
Remi Wingrove
c/o Swedbank AB
105 34
Stockholm, Sweden

Ship to:
John Smith
53 Torpvägen
Eckerö 22270
Åland Islands

Qty	SKU	Description	Price	Ext. Price
144	842001	Champion Kuglestød	€74.16	€10,679.04

Sub total	€10,679.04
Shipping cost	€8,684.51
Total	€19,363.55

Notes from the sender: No need for signature. If no answer, leave on dock at front door.

Chapter XXVII

Telltale Packing Slips?

June 26, 2013

Erinomainen Nopea Luistimet (the ice skate factory) and the warehouse with the green roof

Helsinki, Finland and Eckerö, Åland Islands

Day Six of our week-long trip

Joaquin writing:

Grandpa and I were up early the next morning. Apparently Into wasn't sleeping much these days because he was still up when we went into the kitchen to make ourselves a cup of coffee before leaving for lookout duty at the warehouse.

"Good morning. I was just going to put a note under your door," Into said.

"Good morning to you, Into. What's the word?" Grandpa asked.

"The word is it's almost time to go. The last of the shot puts should be delivered about the time you get to the warehouse, so our departure is within sight," he said seriously. "Signe will make sure Croaker the crow knows the name of your hotel and room number and that the fake plan is in the safe in your room. He'll leak the information to the Voslakians. Once they've accessed the safe and read the fake plan, they'll show up at our warehouse in Eckerö to assess whether the gold is there or not—or at least that's what we expect to happen. If we're right, I don't think it will be more than an hour or two before they show up. They've been waiting for hundreds of years for this opportunity. If they don't show at the warehouse by tomorrow morning at this time—so twenty-four hours from now—leave anyway and start your trip back to California. But before you do, it's important that you stop by the DHL office at the Helsinki airport and meet with Minna. She's expecting you. As consignee of the shipment of the crates, you're going to need the correct paperwork in San Francisco. You don't need to worry about Matti; Lars is in charge of dropping him off at the Finnair air freight office and picking him up in San Francisco. And then you'll all meet up at the new warehouse in–where is it? Millbrae, California?"

"Yes, Millbrae. It's right next to the San Francisco airport. So we shouldn't plan on coming back here, right?" I asked.

"No, this is it." Into said.

"Okay," Grandpa said, looking at me, "This is not a drill. We've got our work cut out for us."

We went back to our room to make sure we had all our belongings and then called for a cab to the airport. Sitting in the back seat, Grandpa asked "Are you keeping a list of things we need to remember?"

"I can if you want me to," I said.

"Please. Write down to call the Hotel Kämp and have them send us our new clothes–I just realized we're not going back there before we leave. I bought some stuff I'd like to keep; I don't want to just leave it behind, do you?"

"No way," I said, thinking mostly about the David Hasselhoff t-shirt I bought as a joke for Darren. I wrote a note to myself on my phone.

Less than two hours later we were at *Torpfjärdens Båthamn,* the birdwatching spot, backpacks and satchels in hand. The parade of back-to-back DHL delivery vans must have already taken place because there was no one in sight, not even any fishermen on the pier. We walked past the warehouse and then onto the dock where the *Vellamo* was tied up. She was a purely utilitarian, old school fishing boat, the exact opposite of Remi's speedboat. Below decks there were two single bunks, a two-burner gas stove and a rudimentary head. There was a pair of powerful binoculars on top of one of the bunks. *Remi is one of those people who thinks of everything,* I thought to myself.

The next couple of hours we did what we could to pass the time. We were less than a hundred feet across from the warehouse so we didn't need the binoculars, but they came in handy for checking out the birds, of which there were plenty. And then, very inauspiciously, it started. An old Volvo sedan pulled up and parked on the road close to the warehouse, not on the dock next to it. Nothing happened for a few minutes and then the driver's side door opened and the driver got out. No doubt about it–Neanderthal forehead. He walked down to the end of the dock and then back to the double doors. He looked left and right and then pushed the right-hand door open and went inside.

"I don' know," Grandpa whispered.

"Don't know what?" I asked.

"If leaving the doors open was a good idea—it doesn't seem 'right' to me. Seems like it could tip off the Voslakians that something fishy is going on."

"Well, it definitely made it easy for our Voslakian advance man to take a look at the goods," I said.

"Too easy, if you ask me," Grandpa said, just as the Voslakian appeared in the doorway with a shot put in each hand, awkwardly trying to close the door behind him. He did his best at running down the dock to the Volvo, slammed the door and sped off, spitting gravel in a cloud of dust.

"He's taking those shot puts back to someone higher up to check them out, don't you think?" Grandpa asked me.

"Probably," I said. "If he had any pull he would have just gotten on his cell phone and told his peeps to get down here on the double. I think you're right—he took the balls back to Mr. Big. I sure hope he took the right ones."

"I don't think it's going to take very long to find out. Even if he picked up real shot puts and took them to wherever he did, whoever is in charge will want to double-check to make sure they're not leaving a fortune of gold behind by mistake."

Grandpa was right. It was just a little over an hour before the action started again: six cars drove up on the dock, doors all swinging open at the same time. First into the warehouse was a very short Voslakian, dripping with attitude, who couldn't have been anyone other than Bad Boris himself. There was no seeing inside the warehouse, even with both doors wide open, but there was a huge racket, lots of yelling and knocking about. Everyone piled out as quickly as they had stormed in. Once they were back outside on the dock, Bad Boris and the original advance man got into a major stand-off in front of the rest of the guys. Bad Boris was screaming at the scout, who raised both of his hands next to his head, as if to say "How was I to know?" Whatever it was he said, all it got him was "idiot" screamed at him in a very thick accent and a smack to the side of the head by Boris. What happened next was an almost comical effort to back six cars off the dock and onto the road at the same time.

"What do you think?" Grandpa asked.

"Obviously I don't speak whatever that was, but there's no mistaking the word 'idiot,' not to mention a smack upside the head," I said.

Grandpa laughed and said "Should we go take a look?"

"Why not?"

The scene inside the warehouse was mayhem–there were broken wooden crates and packing material everywhere and hundreds of shot puts strewn across the floor.

"Do you think they made off with the four gold balls?" I asked.

"Probably," Grandpa said. "I think the trick might have fooled the first guy, but Bad Boris saw through it. Leaving the doors unlocked *was* a mistake. Boris had to know if the gold was really in the warehouse, the gnomes would never have left it unguarded with the door open. I don't know – maybe it had the desired effect. Maybe the ruse, even if it didn't really work, bought Signe and company some time. Let's hope it was enough," Grandpa said, leaning over and picking up a piece of paper.

"What's that?" I asked.

"A packing slip from Inter-Sport in Copenhagen, Denmark," Grandpa said, "for 144 '*Champion kuglestød*.' I'm guessing '*kuglestød*' means shot put."

"Yep. I just looked up the translation."

"That's not good," Grandpa said. "Ahti and Pentti removed all the shipping labels and stuff from the outside of the boxes, but they didn't realize there were packing slips *inside* the boxes. It says here on the packing slip that the shipping was to be arranged by the customer. How hard would it be for Bad Boris to call Inter-Sport in Copenhagen and ask what company picked up the delivery? And once he finds out it was DHL, it wouldn't take much to figure out the location of the office that made the arrangements, would it?"

"Not at all," I said.

"We need to warn Minna!"

Above: The DHL offices at the Helsinki airport, where Minna worked, were busy places, totally in the open—not exactly the place where you'd expect some high-level international intrigue to be going down. That was, in fact, exactly what was happening. *Left:* It's hard to believe that something as small as a flash drive could cause as much trouble as it did. The ability to store huge amounts of information is only matched by how quickly the transfer, from one device to another, can be accomplished. *Below:* Small parcels are loaded into larger, custom-fitted containers (on conveyor belt) that fit perfectly inside the cargo hold of the jet. Larger crates are loaded in the center of the hold.

Chapter XXVIII

Minna Bears the Brunt

June 26, 2013

Helsinki International Airport
Helsinki, Finland

Day Six of our week-long trip, *continued*

Joaquin writing:
Grandpa called Remi and got Minna's number and told him why he was concerned. He then called Minna and introduced himself and apologized for being the bearer of bad news, but he had to warn her.

"What are you warning me about?" she asked.

"I'm not sure, but I'm fairly certain a group of bad actors is going to figure out Signe used your DHL office to make all these shipments, including the ones to California," Grandpa said.

"Well, all the California shipments are en route, so it's too late now for anyone to do anything," Minna said.

"But they could try and intercept the shipment once it arrives in California, couldn't they?" Grandpa asked.

"I suppose," Minna said, "but to access that information they'd need some serious hacking skills," Minna said. "Are they that sophisticated?"

"I have no idea, Minna. I just know they're bad people up to no good. And you need to protect yourself. Joaquin and I were on our way to see you anyway–about the paperwork for me being the consignee for the crates," Grandpa said.

"I've got it right here, all ready for you," Minna said.

"We'll be there as fast as we can. Meanwhile, can you alert your security that you may be in trouble—have them be on the lookout for some Neanderthal-looking creeps?"

Minna laughed. "Where were they last Saturday night when I went out dancing? But sure. I'm not sure what good it will do, but I'll let them know."

Apparently Minna didn't warn security or they didn't take her seriously because by the time we arrived at the DHL office at the Helsinki Airport, security personnel were in the process of untying her from her chair and removing a wide piece of tape from across her mouth.

"I should have listened to what you were saying," she said, rubbing her wrists. "All things considered, it could have been a lot worse. They wanted information from the computer, not from me. They probably thought I didn't know anything."

"Did they access your computer," I asked.

"Yeah. They brought a thumb drive with them and downloaded a lot," Minna said.

"I'm sorry you had to go through that," Grandpa said, "Can we do anything for you?"

"Yes, you can sign these papers you came for so I can go home," she said.

"I can do that," Grandpa said.

"Let me make a copy of your passport so I can attach it to our file," she said, handing Grandpa a stack of papers. "The top sheet has names, contact information, reference numbers, addresses, you name it—all the information you'll need to accept the crates in California. You'd better get going, hadn't you?" she said looking at her watch, "The crates will be in the air shortly."

"You mean they aren't already?"

"The first shipment is in the air; the second one—the forty-three crates—is loaded and the plane will be taking off at 4:20."

"Will the Voslakians have access to all that information now?" Grandpa asked.

"I think you'll have to assume that," Minna said, "I wouldn't underestimate them like I just did."

"One more question," Grandpa said, "What language did they speak?"

"Something Slavic—like Russian, but different. What was it?" she asked.

"Voslakian. Did they speak any English?" Grandpa asked.

"Yes, the one downloading the information did. Mr. Chatty, actually."

"How so?"

"He said sixty percent of the young people in his country were unemployed.

'This will give them something to do' he said, holding up the thumb drive."

"Thanks Minna. And, again, I'm sorry you had to go through that," Grandpa said.

"Thanks for trying to warn me," she said with a weak smile.

Once we were outside the office I asked Grandpa why he wanted to know if they spoke English.

"Because I'm trying to figure out how comfortable they'd be traveling to California."

"Do you think…" but before I could finish, Grandpa said "Yeah, I do and we have to get a move on," he said, looking at his watch. "We've got open tickets and if we get going–and there're some seats–we can catch the Finnair's 4:20 flight to San Francisco. Let's go!"

We hustled, but it just didn't happen. We wound up spending the night at a hotel near the airport. Missing the flight, combined with Minna getting roughed up and the Voslakians not falling for the fake gold balls trick didn't put either one of us in the best of moods. It made me wonder again about how good our plans were from the beginning.

Grandpa made reservations for the first flight out the next morning, which meant we had to get up at like four o'clock. Neither one of us said much until we boarded the plane at 6:15 and even then it wasn't much more than a sigh of relief tinged with a sense of defeat.

As you can tell by the vintage postcards, there are certain sites in and around San Francisco that have been perennial favorites with tourists and newcomers for a long time. *Right top:* The Golden Gate Bridge, considered one of the most beautiful bridges in the world, was completed in 1937. *Below middle:* Lands End, just west and south of the Golden Gate Bridge, is a park where the western United States meets the Pacific Ocean. *Below bottom:* Muir Woods, a few miles north of San Francisco, is a national park featuring a large forest of old-growth, coastal redwood trees, located on the slopes of Mt. Tamalpais.

1063. Lands End, between Fort Point and Cliff House, San Francisco, Cal.

Chapter XXIX

Do You Know What Day It Is?

June 28, 2013

Helsinki, Finland and Eckerö, Aland Islands
Twin Crafts Market restaurant, Grand Hyatt hotel
San Francisco International Airport, California

Joaquin writing:
The three of us, Mad, Grandpa, and I, were sitting in the hotel restaurant. Mad looked over the top of her coffee cup and asked "Do either one of you know what day it is?"

"I don't," I said flat out. It was the truth–I had no idea.

"No fair looking at your phone," she said, just as Grandpa was about to pull the phone out of his pocket.

"You know what? I actually don't," he said. "I know there's a whole lot about to go down today, but I can't tell you the date. Or what day of the week it is."

"I finished reading what you've been up to for the last seven days, so I'm not surprised. And just in case anyone else asks, it's the 28th and today is Friday. And you're right, Nick, a whole lot *is* about to go down," Mad said with certainty. "Are you guys ready for this?"

"It depends on what your definition of 'this' is, but we're as ready as we're ever going to be, right Joaquin? Even if we don't know what day it is …"

"So, the gang's supposed to arrive at 1 o'clock this afternoon?" she asked no one in particular.

"According to the plan," I said.

"To the warehouse–all forty-three of the crates at one time?"

"Yes," Grandpa answered.

"We're assuming that the truck has a lift gate, right? And I saw the floor lift, so we can maneuver the crates around once they're off the truck."

"Yes, and Lars got three cordless drills so we can undo the crates as quickly as possible–I'm thinking they're going to want to get out ASAP," Grandpa said.

"I think you're right. And then what?" Mad asked.

"Well, after all this by-the-numbers stuff, it gets a little freeform. Lars is going to drive the bus up to Mt. St. Helena with all the gnomes–but not until after dark so we don't arrive until Gob and company are awake. We'll follow the bus in Lars's rental car–if you're up for it–and make sure the reunion goes as planned."

"How long has it been since they've seen each other?" Mad asked.

"Well, Gob and his merry band of explorers stowed away on Capt. Niebaum's ship in 1879, so it's been, what? A hundred and thirty-four years?" Grandpa said. "That's in Uplander years. It's only about 13 years the way the gnomes figure it."

"How long does it take to get from here up to Mt. St. Helena?" Mad asked.

"Two hours, more or less. And I can see where you're headed, Mad," Grandpa said. "You want to know what we're going to do between the time we get them out of the crates and the time we take off in the bus for Mt. St. Helena, right?"

"You'd be surprised at how much of my old job was making sure all the details for bringing a group of professionals together went off successfully. I had people I could rely on to assist me, of course, but they needed pointing in the right direction. If there's one thing I learned, it's all in the details. So what *are* you going to do between one o'clock and eight or so? You can't just hang out in that warehouse, can you?"

"I'll be honest–I haven't thought about it," Grandpa said.

"The windows on the bus are tinted, aren't they?" I asked.

"Yes. Rock stars don't want lookie-loos watching their every move–unless they're on stage, of course. Why?" Grandpa asked.

"If people can't tell the bus is full of gnomes, why don't we show them around their new home–show 'em San Francisco, the Golden Gate Bridge, Muir Woods, Lands End. I bet Lars would be up for it. If you think about it, it would be kinda weird not to show them around a little. They're not in Finland any more," I said.

"What do you think, Mad?" Grandpa asked.

"As long as Lars is up for it, I think it's a good idea. And we can blow their minds and stop for pizza somewhere along the way and eat it on the bus–who doesn't love pizza?" Mad asked.

"Anything else?" Grandpa asked.

"Yeah—a hard one," Mad said.

"What?" Grandpa asked, trying not to sound alarmed.

"What do you think the chances are that the Voslakians are going to show up?

"Here?"

"Yes."

Grandpa was silent for a bit and then said "As much as I hate to admit it, I think it's a possibility. The fact that at least one of them speaks English—which we found out from Minna at the DHL office—doesn't bode well."

"Do you have a plan in case they do?"

"No. I don't know what to expect. I *do* know they'll be pissed because we tried to fool them and even if it didn't work completely, it worked enough to screw up their plans. It's a safe bet they're going to want revenge, but what they're actually planning to do, I have no idea. To tell you the truth, I bet *they* don't even know—how could they? They don't know the situation here. But they're not going to walk away from the gnomes' gold without a big fight."

"I think you'e right, Nick, but we even if we don't know what they going to do, we have to have some defenses in place, don't we?"

"If you're thinking of looking to anyone in law enforcement, remember we have a slight problem: we're bringing 43 people into the country without passports—no documentation whatsoever—not to mention they're gnomes. That kind of throws a wrench or two into the works," Grandpa said.

"Well, we're going to have to keep flying under the radar then. When did you say Signe's coming back for the gold?" Mad asked.

"Not until Tuesday—four days from now. And I'm not feeling great about that, either. I mean, I understand her reasoning, but it seems like a big risk to me—all that gold, with no one guarding it, in some DHL warehouse somewhere for four days. The fact is the Voslakians could show up, rob the gold, and be long gone without us even knowing it. It's like leaving the doors to the warehouse unlocked. I didn't like that and I don't like this, but it's Signe's call."

"Well, we'll have a chance to talk to her together this afternoon. Maybe she'll listen to an ex-banker," Mad said. "What time are we meeting Lars?"

"At noon, in the lobby," I said.

"All right. I'm going to go freshen up. See you at noon."

In case you don't know what a sauna is
– and before I go any further you should
know that it's pronounced *sow-na* (like a
female pig), not *saw-na*–it's like a steam
bath, but with dry heat instead of steam, although you can throw a ladleful of water on
the hot rocks to produce a cloud of steam,
if you want, which makes it feel really hot.
Folks jump in a lake, if there's one closeby,
after getting super-heated in the sauna, like
the one shown below. That's a typical sauna
stove *(right top)* and what Signe decided she'd
claim was in all forty-three of the gnomes'
travel crates, four to a crate, though why
anyone would need that many sauna stoves
was beyond me. I guess a bunch of sauna
stoves coming from Finland made some
sense and, true, it seemed to work, so who
am I to question the logic? Grandpa, Lars,
and I used cordless screwdrivers to make
short work of taking the crates apart and
got the gnomes out as quickly as we could.

Chapter XXX

172 Sauna Stoves

June 28, 2013, *continued*

Grand Hyatt hotel, San Francisco International Airport
Signe's warehouse at the industrial park, Millbrae, California

Joaquin writing:
Everybody was right on time in the lobby or, as Grandpa said, we were all "Johnny at the rat hole"–another saying of his which made absolutely no sense to me. He had so many of them, I was getting used to just not understanding any of them. Lars had a big canvas duffel bag over his shoulder that was impossible to miss.

"What's in the duffel?" Grandpa asked.

"Tools," Lars said. "Ones we need to open the crates."

"Don't forget I'm claustrophobic," a small voice said from out of nowhere.

"Yeah, and Matti," Lars said quietly, using his head to motion over his shoulder.

"You've got Matti in there?" Grandpa asked, matching Lars's whisper.

"I had to have some way of getting him in and out of the hotel," Lars said plaintively. "Let's get outside so I can get him out before he hyperventilates or something."

We hustled out of the hotel lobby to the parking lot and found the rental car. Lars put the duffel on the back seat and quickly extracted Matti, who looked more than a little distressed. "Are you okay?" Lars asked.

"I will be after I start breathing again," Matti said.

"Sorry about that," Lars said. "We shouldn't need to do that again."

"Fine by me," Matti said. "Are we going to meet up with everyone else?"

"Your friends are being delivered in a bit. We'll get them out of their crates–and then it's up to Mt. St. Helena, your new home."

"It will be good to see Whitbeck and Wycoff again. They were my best friends before they left. It's been a long time," Matti said.

"Well, let's get this show on the road," Mad said. "Maybe you should put your window down, Matti, and get some fresh air. Looks like you could use it."

"How do I do it?" Matti asked.

"Push that little silver button down."

"I've seen a lot of cars–especially since we moved to the factory, but I've never ridden in one before. There's a machine in front that makes it move, right?"

"That's right," Mad said, "but most Uplanders, like me, have no idea how the machine works–we treat it more like magic than mechanics."

"We gnomes know there are many kinds of magic," Matti said. "I'm guessing there are many kinds of mechanics, too. I think there's a lot to learn."

"I think you're right," Mad said, "for all of us.'

•   •   •

The trip from the hotel to the warehouse didn't take more than fifteen minutes, through some typical California urban areas, including a few miles northbound on Highway 101 that appeared to scare the daylights out of Matti. Once we arrived at the industrial park, we were surprised to see a large DHL truck and trailer already parked in front of the warehouse.

"They're early," Grandpa said, "I wasn't expecting that."

Turns out the driver was in the middle of eating a sandwich in the cab of the truck. After talking with him he said he decided to use this delivery as the place to have his lunch and not to worry–he'd start the delivery on time. Grandpa drove the rental car into the warehouse and ushered Matti into the bus for the time being.

At one o'clock on the dot, the driver opened the back of the trailer, lowered the lift gate and started pushing the crates around. One by one, he lowered them onto the floor jack and Lars moved them to the back of the warehouse. I wanted to start opening them up, but we decided it would be better to wait until the driver had taken off. It was hard to wait, though, as I knew how anxious the gnomes had to be to get out of their crates. At least all the "This Side Up" arrows were, in fact, pointing up.

The driver gathered up the paperwork and brought it over to Grandpa.

"Nick Sinclair?" he asked.

"That's me."

"You're the one signing for–what?" he said, looking at the bill of lading–"*172 sau-*

na heaters? Not that it's any of my business, but what in the world are you going to do with those?"

"Build 172 saunas?" Grandpa said, making it sound more like a question than an answer."

The driver had a quizzical look on his face and then decided to drop it. "Well, good luck with that," he said.

Before he had even started the truck up, I pulled the overhead doors down and Lars grabbed the cordless screwdrivers from the rental car. He handed one each to me and Grandpa and we started unscrewing the side panels Lars had designed as "doors" to the crates. It wasn't long before we had a good-sized group of gnomes all looking dazed and more than a little confused. Mad quickly became comforter-in-chief, introducing herself, handing bottles of water out, and showing them where the bathroom was. As soon as we started taking the sides off the crates, Matti stuck his head out of the bus and asked if he could get off. We said "Sure," and he kind of hopped from one foot to the other, anxious to be reunited with his friends. With each crate that we opened up, there was more hugging and kissing and slapping of backs all around. Signe's crate was one of the last ones we opened, so there was a lot of activity going on by the time she was set free. I introduced her to Mad right away and there seemed to be a natural rapport between the two of them. It didn't take long for Signe to pull herself together and gain control of the situation. Minutes after getting out of the crate, she was clapping her hands and telling everyone to listen up.

"We made the first leg of our journey successfully, with considerable help from our friends here," she said, her hand extended towards us. There was considerable clapping and whooping and hollering. "Please remember to give them your thanks. And now we are all going to get on that very fine bus over there and our friend, Lars, is going to drive us up to Mt. St. Helena where we will be reunited with Gob and the rest of his 'explorers.' I invite you all to board the bus and take a look at it. Before we take off, make sure you use the bathroom but, just so you know, I have been assured that there's also a bathroom on the bus."

This fact caused quite a stir. There was something about being able to go to the bathroom on a moving vehicle that excited their imaginations. Matti tapped on Mad's arm and she leaned over. I could hear him say to her, "I told you there were many kinds of magic."

To get to Tony's Pizza, we had to drive up Broadway through the North Beach neighborhood in San Francisco—a trip which included an un-planned-for view of Carol Doda's blinking anatomy *(bottom right)* which probably thoroughly confused all of the gnomes who were sitting on that side of the bus. I mean, how do you explain something like that? Matti was the only one who piped up, wanting an explanation. I bowed out and let Grandpa handle it. Seemed like the best thing to do. Luckily, the natural world was less perplexing: by the time we arrived at Ocean Beach *(above)* the gnomes got to experience fog like they'd never seen before. It was so thick it masked everything in sight, allowing everyone to get off the bus and onto the foggy beach without fear of causing a sensation. They had a ball—the total opposite of being cooped up in their travel crates for all those hours.

Chapter XXXI

The Magic of Moving Bathrooms

June 28, 2013, *continued*

One the bus, sightseeing: Muir Woods, Lands End, and the Golden Gate Bridge

Grandpa Nick writing:

While Signe was telling everyone to use the bathroom before we left, I realized I hadn't asked Lars if he was okay with taking the scenic route home to the valley. I quickly went over to where he and Joaquin were talking and said "I apologize, but I forgot to ask you something."

"What's that?"

"Would you mind driving the bus to a few of the local sights before we head up to the valley? We need to use up some time so we arrive after dark up on Mt. St. Helena. Signe had Gob informed we'd be arriving around 9:30 tonight."

"I don't know my way around, so I'd need a navigator, but sure, I'll do it," Lars said.

"I'll help navigate," Joaquin said.

"Are you sure?" I asked.

"No problem," he said, holding up his phone. "GPS knows the way."

"Okay. Mad and I will follow in the rental car. After we drop everyone off at Mt. St. Helena tonight, we'll all go back to my place in Rutherford–there's room for the bus–and us–but first, the tour. Joaquin knows what we talked about this morning–Muir Woods, Lands End, the Golden Gate Bridge–they're all fairly close together. And we thought we'd order a bunch of pizzas in North Beach and eat them on the bus. I know these names don't mean much to you, but Joaquin knows. Are you ready for this?"

"Seven weeks at the International Driver's School in Helsinki, and I'm ready for anything," Lars said bravely.

"Did they have a class on driving forty-three gnomes around?" I asked.

"I may have been absent that day," Lars said, "but I'll do the best I can," being far more cheerful than I would have in the same situation.

Although the idea of the sightseeing tour started as a means of using up some time, it quickly took on a life of its own. The gnomes were incapable of a disingenuous response, and it was deeply satisfying to see their reactions to the redwood trees in Muir Woods–hundreds of years old and hundreds of feet tall. The sheer majesty of the Golden Gate Bridge caused a wave of silence to fall over them, especially as we got to the middle of the span and they instinctively understood that there was nothing underneath them except the tension of suspension and a fine bit of Uplanders' own brand of magic. After a nano-second of hesitation, ten large pizzas from Tony's Pizza Napolitano were inhaled in what was, for all intents and purposes, a feeding frenzy. I'm still not sure if that was a good idea or not. Time will tell. The best, though, was arriving at Lands End just as the fog started rolling in, gently enveloping everything in its path, adding a layer of mystery to every turn. The long parking lot made for easy parking for the bus and the fog meant that any onlookers would mistake the gnomes for kids, so everyone was free to lose themselves on Ocean Beach, between the land and the crashing waves, running, twisting, jumping and rolling for the sheer joy of it. That we got everyone back on bus without incident is testimony to something I had absolutely no control over. All I can say is that once we were headed north on 101, I felt like the impromptu tour had been a good thing.

I said as much to Mad, who responded, "It's not every day you get to introduce forty-three gnomes to the joys of frolicking in the fog at the beach *and* pizza."

"Not to mention blinking nipples," I said.

"What?"

"Apparently Matti was sitting on the side of the bus that had a good view of the big neon sign in front of the Condor Club in North Beach–you know, the one of Carol Doda, the exotic dancer, with the red blinking nipples?"

"Kind of hard to miss–it's been there since forever," Mad said. "What did he say?"

"Not much. He just wanted to know if for Uplander women, that was a real thing."

"What'd you say?"

"I wasn't quite sure what to say, so I just said 'no' and left it at that. I couldn't tell if he looked disappointed or relieved."

"A little of both, I'd imagine," Mad said. "I hope it doesn't give him nightmares."

Right: Once you get to the town of Calistoga, at the north end of the Napa Valley, it's about 8 miles up Mt. St. Helena to the Robert L. Stevenson Memorial State Park trailhead, which is where we let the gnomes out to hike to their new home. As you can see, however, the turnout for parking *(middle right)* is on the opposite side of the road–and there's really no safe place to turn a bus around on the narrow road over Mt. St. Helena until you get to Middletown, which is another ten miles up the road. So off we went, over the mountain, to turn around in Middletown and back to the park's entrance to park the bus. The trail to the summit of the mountain is also the trail to the entrance of the gnomes' cave, with a slight detour or two. As you can see *(bottom)* most of the trail is well-trodden. The pile of stones in the photo is the marker commemorating the location of the cabin Robert Louis Stevenson and his new wife lived in during the summer of 1880.

Chapter XXXII

Covering Old Ground

June 28, 2013, *continued*

Mt. St. Helena, Calistoga
Grandpa Nick's house, Rutherford

Grandpa Nick writing:

Before leaving the beach at Lands End, I called Doyle and told him that Mad and Lars would be staying at the house. I hadn't asked Joaquin, but I assumed that he would want to see his mom and dad and spend the night in his own bed. I told Doyle not to wait up for us, knowing full well he would anyway. The trip from San Francisco up to Mt. St. Helena, which stood at the north end of the Napa Valley, took about two hours. As it often does with good friends, Mad and I picked up a conversation that seemingly ended a few hours ago, not the 45 years it actually was. Strange, that, but even our silences were comfortable, something that definitely *doesn't* happen that often.

I explained to Mad that, before taking off from the warehouse, Lars, Joaquin and I had talked about the logistics of delivering the gnomes to Mt. St. Helena. Before we even left for Finland, G said that, on the appointed night, it would be best to drop everyone at the turnout to Robert Louis Stevenson State Park, which was on the west side of the narrow road up the mountain. We would be traveling on the opposite side and the curves and narrowness of the road made turning the bus around in the middle of the road impossible. That meant that we'd have to drive all the way to Middletown–another 10 miles further up the road–to turn around and, ultimately, approach the turnout easily from the opposite direction.

We could have just parked the rental car at the turnout and waited for the bus to make its way back, but Mad and I decided to follow them. I hadn't traveled the route to the small town of Middletown in a very long time–in fact I avoided it, as it was the route my family took in 1958 when the accident took place that killed my brother and my parents. We had been coming back from a Sunday dinner with my mother's parents, who lived in Middletown. A deer jumped in front of the car not that far from the turnout to Robert Louis Stevenson Park. The first summer we met, in 1967, G told me he had used his power of levitation to get me out of the car and onto a bed of leaves on the side of the road. He also told me that he was the one who'd been chasing the deer we hit—a childhood game for him that ended in utter tragedy for me.

They, whoever *they* are, say that "time heals all wounds." I think that time maybe covers wounds with a callus or a scar, but the wound is still there. Over the years, I'd allowed the wound to cover over, but I had to be careful about banging into it—there was still a lot of hurt there—a lot of pain. Mad was silent for a while, finally saying, "That's a lot to carry, Nick. It's a fragile journey we're on, isn't it—all of us?

"Precarious," I said. "Seems to me the only antidote is to be fully present for the good stuff when it comes around."

"Amen brother," Mad said.

"I'm happy our paths crossed again, Mad. It's a good thing," I told her.

"Ditto that, Nick," Mad said.

We were right behind the bus as it finally pulled into the turnout and parked. Lars cut the engine and opened the hydraulic door with a swoosh. Joaquin was the first down the steps.

"These guys and gals are more than ready to egress this coach," he said, stretching his arms above his head. "Oh, look who's here."

Mad and I turned around and saw G standing in the shadows, waving with one hand and holding an old-fashioned lantern, lit by candle, in the other.

"You made it," he said with a big smile.

"Yessir," I said, "and Joaquin has just informed me that your cohorts are more than ready to get off the bus. Are you ready for this?"

"More than ready."

Joaquin stuck his head back in the bus and whistled very loudly and yelled "All ashore who's going ashore." He stepped out of the way as a wave of gnomes descended the steps in a disorderly dance—pushing, shoving, complaining, laughing,—none of it the least bit surprising. Signe was the last to get off, allowing a little space between the thundering herd and herself. She stood with us, watching the scene, shaking her head. "It's been quite the trip," she said. "Where's Lars?"

"Right behind you," he said, trundling down the steps of the bus.

"Thank you for everything you did to make this happen, Lars and just as importantly for all that you made *not* happen. Things could have turned out much differently if you hadn't intervened. And many, many thanks to you two, and you too, Mad," she said, looking at all of us individually. We're not quite done yet, but this right here is a milestone in our history and we couldn't have done it without you all. I'm not going to belabor my gratitude, because we all need to go to our respective homes now. It's been a long journey and we'll talk the day after tomorrow. We all need to take a day to pull ourselves together. I'll contact Remi and he'll get in touch with you with the last of our plan. Meanwhile, a most pleasant evening to you all. I'm needed, I think, to help my son get these gnomes herded to their new home."

With that, she bowed her head in our direction and stepped into the chattering shadows.

"What I wouldn't do for a tenth of her graciousness," Mad said.

"Oh, I don't know," I said, "I think you hold your own in that department."

"Shall we do it?" Joaquin asked.

"Do what?" I asked.

"Head back to the barn. I think it's time."

"I don't think you're going to find any disagreement," Mad said. "Let's go."

Within a half hour, we were in the home stretch. I instructed Lars to park the bus in front of the barn, where it would be easy to turn around in the morning. As I thought, as soon as he heard us arrive, Doyle was on the steps to the back door, welcoming us. There were hugs all around and then Joaquin ran off to his house to catch his folks before they went to bed. Lars had definitely done yeoman's duty and was ready to go "toes up," as he said. I got him set up in the guest room upstairs, where Doyle had already laid things out for him. By the time I got back downstairs, Mad and Doyle were already deep in conversation, the stained-glass lamp low over the kitchen table, the room softly lit and inviting. I pulled out a chair and said "I'm not interrupting, am I?"

"There's an empty wineglass with your name on it right in front of you. Mad and I were waiting for you," Doyle said.

"Doyle and I were talking about the last time we saw each other—at that barn burner of a party Hattie threw after we got back from Kauai," Mad said.

"The one where Katia lost her blouse on her flight to the stars on the hummingbird express?" I asked.

"I forgot about that," Mad said. "I put her to bed that night. I wonder if she was ever the same?"

"Hard to say with that one," Doyle said. "She moved back to Germany a few years later. We still send her a box of California citrus every year for the holidays and get a *danke* back, but never any news."

"Hey, isn't that the Quicksilver Sphere of Perfection?" Mad asked, pointing at the small, shiny globe hanging from the pull chain of the lamp over the table. "The one Gob awarded when he proclaimed us—what was it—'chevaliers?'"

"Indeed," I said. "Do you still have yours?"

"It's in my jewelry box," Mad said. "I should start wearing it. Maybe I'll get a chain for it."

We all sat silently for a moment, each lost in our own thoughts. There may have been only three of us sitting at the table, but we shared volumes of history, leading all the way to the present moment.

"I'd love to be a fly on the wall up on Mt. St. Helena right now," Mad said.

"How do you think it's going?" I asked.

"I was just trying to imagine that. Given what I read in your journal, I'm thinking the group is in for a major culture clash, don't you?" Mad said.

"Like what?"

"For one, the way you described how Signe and the rest of the tribe did up their rooms at the factory. Chandeliers, treillage, log cabin look-alikes, Victorian parlors—do you think they're going to want to go back to living underground? Not to mention Joaquin's suspicion that the digital world has landed in their midst, even though no one's admitting it? And, sorry guys, but don't forget that Gob and his gang have been on their own for what—130-odd human years? That's plenty of time for them to have fully embraced their manly ways—their hairy, smelly, belching, farting ways. I wonder how well that's going to go over with the women?"

"Well, now that you mention it…" Doyle trailed off.

"I have a lot of faith in Signe, but I think you're right, Mad, she may not have factored the hairy-smelly thing into her long-range plans," I said.

"Stay tuned, right?" Mad said, "Speaking of Signe, she said for us to take tomorrow off, right?"

"Right."

"Is it okay if I use the rental car for the day? I want to go explore Sebastopol—see what it feels like."

"What's in Sebastopol?" Doyle asked.

"My step-son and his wife. They're going to have a baby next month and I'm thinking about buying a house somewhere close by, so I can enjoy being a grandparent and maybe even be of some help."

"In all honesty, Mad, it's hard for me to reconcile 'grandma' with the general hip state of you, topped off with that radical-chic 'do,'" Doyle said.

"'Rad-Gran,' that's me," Mad said, swinging her hair. "Who I think should head off to—what was it Hattie used to say? To Bedforshire?"

"To Bed For Sure, that's right," I said. "Me too."

"Before we toddle off, I assume you have Chuy's number, don't you?"

"Sure, why?"

"I was thinking I'd give him a call tomorrow and see if he wants to go for a ride."

Remi showed up unexpectedly at grandpa's and said, casually, that we had a beautiful valley *(below)*. No fooling! That was a fact that was kind of hard to miss. *Bottom:* After bribing us with a huge breakfast, grandpa got us to wash Grandma Hattie's limousine. After Lars and I were done, it looked pretty good, if I do say so myself. Remi, of course, wanted to buy it, but grandpa said no.

Chapter XXXIII

The Limousine is Back

June 29, 2013

Grandpa Nick's house, Rutherford

Grandpa Nick writing:

My internal clock was still off and, after lying awake for almost an hour, I decided that 6 o'clock was an acceptable time to get up and go downstairs. I was in the middle of making coffee when Lars showed up in the kitchen, barefooted and bedheaded.

"I'd forgotten what it was like to sleep in the dark–without pulling the blackout shades," Lars said. "Let alone with an open window and the sound of crickets. I could get used to it."

"It *is* nice, there's no denying," I said. "What's on your list today?" I asked, putting a mug of coffee in front of him.

"Not much. Do you have something in mind?"

"I forgot to tell you last night–Signe wants you to sell the bus. She said they wouldn't be needing it any longer and she wants you to keep whatever you get for it."

"Really?" Lars said, eyes widening.

"I don't think Signe kids when it comes to the business side of things," I said.

"Man, that would be great. How do you sell something like that?" Lars asked.

"I found it for Signe on Craigslist. That's probably the best place to try and sell it again."

"Can I ask what you paid for it?"

"$64,000."

"Holy Moly! Really?"

"For real. I think you should list it for the same price–I mean, we didn't even put

100 miles on it, did we?"

"Probably not. Who actually owns it?"

"It's in my name," I said. "And I've got the pink slip–the certificate that allows you to legally transfer ownership–so you're good to go. I suppose you have Craigslist in Finland, don't you?"

"Oh yeah. I think it's everywhere," Lars said. "I'm going to take some pictures now, if that's okay."

"It's your bus, Lars; you can do what you want," I said.

"This is so cool. Hard to believe this started with digging a hole for a new outhouse…"

"The world works in mysterious ways," I said, as Lars headed out the screen door.

I sat down at the kitchen table with a fresh cup of coffee and hot milk, something I'd forgotten how much I liked until this last trip to Scandinavia. I proceeded to peruse *The New York Times*–something I hadn't done in a while. I was lost in it for thirty minutes or so when Lars and Joaquin came in through the back door and Mad came down the stairs at the same time, everyone talking at once. Mad wanted the keys to the rental car and didn't want coffee. She said she was late picking up Chuy.

Oh, that's right, I thought to myself. I'd kind of put that out of my mind. It seemed like Mad was being cagey, which I found unusual. Or it could be she just wanted to see Chuy on her own without me complicating things. Joaquin had tipped me off that she asked him what was up with the two of us not talking. I decided to leave it at that for the time being. There was nothing I could do about it at the moment anyway.

Mad took off in a cloud of heifer dust, as Hattie used to say, and Joaquin and Lars said yes to breakfast, about the same time as Doyle showed up in the kitchen and said yes, too. There was a tube of ready-to-bake biscuits in the refrigerator, so I got them going in the oven, made a skilletful of country gravy with sausage and poached a bunch of eggs. Split, buttered biscuits topped with country gravy and poached eggs makes for a mighty fine breakfast. It was JP, chef, friend and co-adventurer from the Kauai trip, who introduced me–along with Mad and Chuy–to the dish, only he would have made cornmeal waffles instead of cheating with what he called "store-bought" biscuits. Regardless, it was an industrial-strength breakfast, enough to satisfy anyone's hunger until dinner. Thinking of Hattie and JP put me in a nostalgic frame of mind and I decided to take the boys out to the small barn and get them to wash Hattie's old car which, as completely impractical as it was, I had kept after she died. We pulled the cover off the very long, black car–a 1967 Cadillac limousine–and Lars whistled.

"Now *that's* a car," he said.

"And a half," Joaquin added.

I handed Joaquin the keys and told him to back it out, something he'd done before. "I figured that maybe I could trade you guys that breakfast for a car wash. Whaddaya' say?"

"We're on it," Lars said. "As long as I get to drive it–at least down to the end of the lane."

"As much of a barge as it is, it'll feel small compared to the bus," I said. "I figured we'd take it when we go back down to San Francisco tomorrow. It hasn't been driven in a while."

"You've got your chauffeur, ready when you are," Lars said.

"I'll take you up on it," I said as my phone rang. I didn't recognize the number and there was no name. Usually I ignore such calls but something made me answer it.

"Hello, Nick here."

"Hello Nick, it's Remi. How are you?"

"I'm fine, Remi. Where are you?"

"I'm actually here in the valley–beautiful place. I was wondering if we could talk."

"I didn't know you were here. I assume you want to meet in person?"

"Yes, I think that would be best."

"Do you want to meet here, at my place?"

"That would be good, yes."

"When do you want to meet?"

"Can you meet now? I'm in your driveway."

Grandpa and Remi had some time to kill before they were supposed to have some big, hush-hush meeting with Signe after dark, up on Mt. St. Helena. So it was his turn to play tour guide and show Remi around. After seeing Mt. St. Helena *(below middle)*, Remi said he could see why Gob chose it as their new place to live. Grandpa also gave Remi a tour of our winery, including the wine aging caves *(bottom)* which, of course, Gob and his men carved out of solid rock back in 1879. He also showed him the sapphire and rhodium brooch Gob gave Capt. Niebaum in recognition of the BFF status between the two "families."

Chapter XXXIV

Special Agent Man

June 29, 2013, *continued*

Grandpa Nick's house, Rutherford
Sightseeing in the Napa Valley

Grandpa Nick writing:
No sooner had I put my phone back in my pocket than Remi came around the curve in the driveway, driving an anonymous, small, white car–so anonymous, I couldn't even tell if it was a Chevrolet or a Toyota. We stood in the bright sunlight and shook hands. Remi noticed Joaquin and Lars over my shoulder, waved, and went over to say hello.

"Nice ride," he said, admiring the limousine.

"It was my great-great-grandmother's, a 1967 Cadillac. Only 29,000 miles on it," Joaquin said.

"If you ever want to sell it ..." he said to me, trailing off.

"No, this one's staying put. I'll let Joaquin figure out what he wants to do with it when I'm gone," I said. At the risk of seeming rude, I couldn't help myself from commenting on his rental car. "Speaking of cars, after that boat of yours, I somehow didn't expect to see you in whatever that is that you just drove up in."

"I'm keeping a low profile," he said. "I hadn't planned on being here. Is there somewhere we could talk in private?" he asked.

"Sure. Let's sit on the porch," I said, walking towards the house.

"This is lovely," Remi said, looking around.

Fairly certain he hadn't come all the way from Sweden to enjoy the view, I was straightforward: "What's up?" I asked, as we both settled into the old wicker chairs facing the view of the surrounding vineyards.

"Some background first–all of which must stay between you and me–is that okay?"

"Yes, of course," I said.

"As you know, I'm a hawaladar. My great-grandfather started our family in the business and because of our long association with it, I've not only inherited a history but a reputation. Suffice it to say I'm privy to a lot of what goes on, particularly large, international transactions. Some twenty years ago I made friends with an American living in Stockholm. At first I thought our meeting was accidental, but I found out later he was sent to Sweden to establish a relationship with me. His name is Paul Wright. Paul, as I gradually uncovered, works for the U. S. Treasury as a Treasury Agent. It was news to me, but apparently there are American Treasury Agents operating everywhere around the world. His proposition to me was simple–basically I was to let him know of any activity I came across that didn't, as you would say, pass the 'smell test,' and he would let me know if anyone involved was a bad actor. Because hawala is based solely on trust, it is vitally important that all of our transactions are conducted at the highest level of honesty and integrity. I agreed to work with him because, as I said, I have an overriding interest in preserving our family's reputation. We are nothing without it. I have to admit, though, that Paul's and my relationship has always been a little one-sided, with me providing him with most of the information–until the other day."

"What happened?" I asked.

"Paul called me and said there was talk–in the darkest corners of the financial world–that an unfathomably large amount of gold was about to be moved. He wasn't sure from where to where, but wanted to know if I'd heard any rumblings about it."

"What'd you say?" I asked.

"I never lie to Paul, but I don't always come right out and tell him everything I know, so that's how I played it, hoping he'd tell me more. It's always a dance with him. You should know that over the years, over a glass of wine or two, I've tried to introduce him to the possibility of the reality of gnomes continuing to exist in our realm but, particularly as an American, he didn't want to hear it–*at all.* He was so resistant he accused me of deliberately trying to pull a joke on him, which he took offense at. So I gave up. But then, out of the blue, he asked, 'This doesn't have anything to do with the you-know-who, does it?' I asked him to clarify his question and he repeated 'You know–the you-know-whos.' He couldn't even bring himself to say the word, so I said it for him–'You mean the *gnomes*?' It obviously pained him, but he whispered 'yes,' to which I could only answer 'yes' in return. 'Well, tell them to be very careful, because word is that there's some very bad people following them closely and they'll travel anywhere in the world and use any means possible to do it.' I asked him if 'anywhere in the world' included the U.S., particularly California, and he said 'definitely.'"

"Oh man," I said. "Not good. I assume he was referring to the Voslakians, right?"

"Yes. And I know Signe didn't account for the possibility of the Voslakians following the gold here, to San Francisco. But then we didn't count on them downloading all the information from the DHL computer system onto a thumb drive, either."

"Do you know what's going to go down?" I asked.

"Only that they're intent on intercepting the shipment–wherever it is. I need to alert Signe and you're the only one who knows where she is, exactly. I mean, she told me Mt. St. Helena, but that was it. And I have no idea of how to use the local system of crows."

"Do you know when the Voslakians will show up?" I asked.

"No, but I don't think it'll be long. I think they're more sophisticated than we give them credit for," Remi said.

"Well, we can get Joaquin to send one of his pigeons with a message letting her know we're on our way, but our timing is off."

"What do you mean?"

"The pigeons don't fly in the dark and the gnomes are asleep until around 9 this evening. It's been my experience that once they're asleep, it's almost impossible to get them to wake up, so our best bet is to split the difference and send a pigeon off around 7:30 or 8–that way it will still be light enough for the pigeon to make its way to Mt. St. Helena and late enough for G to hear he's got a message," I said.

"How's that?" Remi asked.

"The pigeons are G's responsibility–he's what they call the Pigeon Master. The coop where they live is right next to where G sleeps. There's a bell that rings when a pigeon enters the coop, which is supposed to wake him up. I hope it still does. Let's wait until 7:30 or so and then get Joaquin to send the message."

"What now? Remi asked.

"It seems a little like whistling while Rome burns, but would you like to see some of what the valley has to offer? I can show you around the winery, too. Might as well see it while you're here," I said.

"I'm up for it," Remi said.

We spent the rest of the day touring the winery and wandering through the vineyards. It was a beautiful summer day, typical of the valley, hot but not too hot. It was good to see the valley through the eyes of a first-time visitor, but I couldn't escape the feeling of dread every time I thought of the Voslakians and what we might be facing tomorrow. With some effort, I decided the best approach was to focus on today, today and tomorrow, tomorrow. There was nothing I could do about tomorrow right now, anyway. So I took Remi to see the town of St. Helena and then decided to show him Calistoga, as well, so he could get a better view of Mt. St. Helena, where we'd be going later that night. It was a majestic mountain, prominently anchoring the northern end of the valley, every bit the silent sentinel standing watch over the lands below.

"I can see why the tribe likes it," Remi said. "It's beautiful."

On the way back I decided we should grill up something and eat dinner outside. My first thought was fresh salmon, but realized that's what Joaquin and I had cooked just *ten days ago in Helsinki? More like ten years*, I thought. Considering that there was still going to be business to attend to after dinner, I decided to keep it simple: grilled tuna steaks served on top of white beans with a basil vinaigrette over the top. A platterful of sliced tomatoes fresh from the garden and baguettes from the local bakery and I'd call it good.

While I was pulling dinner together, Remi, Joaquin, and Doyle got busy with the 'Pigeon Post.' Joaquin got what he needed from inside the house, returning with the capsule to hold the note, the Zig-Zag rolling papers and a very sharp pencil, and Doyle, who he introduced to Remi. Remi wrote the message on the thin paper and Joaquin and Doyle worked together to attach it to the pigeon's leg. Joaquin then handed the pigeon to Remi and said that since it was his message, he should be the one to send it on its way.

"Like this?" Remi asked, raising the pigeon above his head.

"Yep. Just give him a bit of a boost into the air," Joaquin said.

Remi lifted the pigeon above his head rapidly and let it go. It fluttered and headed northeast, towards Mt. St. Helena.

"Wow. Amazing," Remi said, with a big grin on his face.

It was hard not to be impressed with these working birds. Remi clearly was.

Just as I was about to yell "come and get it," Mad and Chuy showed up unexpectedly. Luckily it wasn't a problem because, as a matter of habit, I made some extra. Even though I hadn't seen Chuy in a long time, he was standoffish. Mad and Remi were the opposite, recalling they had met a few years back in Mombasa at a World Bank meeting about the future of Digital Financial Services—a subject in which they both had a professional interest. Talk about a small world. We sat at the long table under the grape arbor. Dinner was loud and fun, and it must have been good because everyone licked their plates clean.

After dinner, Mad drove Chuy home. As they were leaving, Chuy and I shook hands and did the polite thing, promising to get together, sooner rather than later. Mad looked on like she had a stake in the outcome, which actually didn't surprise me. No doubt she was up to something, but right now I had other things on my mind, like staying as many steps ahead of the Voslakians as possible. Chuy and I could settle what we had to settle after the gnomes and their gold were where they were supposed to be—deep inside Mt. St. Helena.

Everyone pitched in and helped clear the table and Doyle pressed Lars and Joaquin into service doing the dishes. Doyle said he had a television show he wanted to watch, so I took Remi into the library and showed him the pouch of gold nuggets the gnomes had left Gustave Niebaum as payment for the barrel of Charbono they stole from the winery back in 1896. I also showed him the sapphire brooch Gob had given Capt. Niebaum as a symbol of lifelong friendship.

"Well, that's certainly been the case," Remi said, inspecting the brooch up close.

"And then some," I said, handing him the letter Niebaum had written in 1901, explaining how he met the gnomes when they stowed away on his ship. "Here, read this. It will help you understand how intertwined we are—as you are, too. I'll be right back. I'm going to check on Joaquin and Lars. I'm thinking it should just be the two of us tonight, but we could probably use their help tomorrow. What do you think?"

"I think you're right. Depending on what Signe says tonight, we could wind up needing all the help we can muster."

"That's what I figured. Just one thing, Remi. You trust that your special agent friend is giving you the right information?"

"100 percent. I wish it were different, but he's the real deal."

"I figured you'd say that."

Grandpa told me the next morning that he and Remi's hike up to see Signe wasn't that bad because they had the light from a full moon to help them get there. Darren and I have made that trek in the dark more than a few times and I can tell you that, once your eyes adjust, any light really helps. As you can see by the photo *(right bottom)*, there's not a whole lot of room for mistakes on the trail. Even in the daytime, you've got to keep your eyes on where you're putting your feet. Grandpa didn't tell me everything that went down at the meeting with Signe, but did say that it had to do with an agent of the United States Department of the Treasury–a friend of Remi's–wanting to nab Bad Boris and any of the other Voslakians they could lay their hands on. I'd say the plot had thickened. A lot. Oh yeah, and that Treasury Department seal *(above right)* is from a one-dollar bill. Did you know it was there? I didn't.

Chapter XXXV

Night Hike

June 29, 2013, *continued*

Mt. St. Helena, Calistoga

Grandpa Nick writing:

It was about 9:45 when we parked at the entrance to Robert Louis Stevenson Memorial State Park, which was, as I've mentioned, nothing more than a not-very-wide spot next to the road, connecting to a barely noticeable path through the forest. Even though it wasn't that late, once the headlights were off, it was plenty dark. I had been on the path to the gnomes' cave enough times that it was familiar to me, but I doubt anyone would recommend a nighttime hike on a very narrow trail across the rugged side of a 4,000-foot-tall-mountain, but who in their right mind would recommend any of what I found myself doing since I started this quest or whatever you want to call it?

After about 15 minutes of walking, we came out of the forest onto the exposed western slope of the mountain and were greeted by a very full moon just rising above the western hills across the valley. It was a powerful sight and stopped me in my tracks; Remi practically ran into me and then, looking up from the path, caught sight of the moon as well and stood there silently. I did some quick arithmetic in my head and realized it was 50 years, almost exactly, since I'd walked this trail for the first time. It was Clyde, the old miner who had lived on the mountain, who pointed me in the right direction to the gnome's cave and then sent me on my way, wanting to have nothing to do with his neighbors. Clyde was a great guy. He had been gone for a long time, but he loomed large in my memory. That was also the night that scumbag Nigel Stayne decided to secretly follow me to the gnomes so he could complete his nefarious ends. At one point, I was climbing a rock face to spy on the gnomes who were about to stage a Midsummer Night celebration when I lost my footing and slid down the face, losing the amulet in the process. When I regained my senses, there was Nigel, gloating, wanting to "team up." I couldn't believe he he was there. I told him I didn't want to have anything to do with him and to get lost. It was quite an evening.

"Are you okay?" Remi asked, sensing my preoccupation.

"Yeah. I just took a little detour," I said. "50 years ago I followed this path and met the gnomes for the first time. There was a full moon that night, too. This is all a little much …" I said, trailing off. "Let's not keep Signe waiting," I said, turning to continue the narrow trail.

Just like that night so long ago, the full moon provided plenty of light to follow the path. After about ten more minutes of walking, we reached the stacked-stone corrals where Quicksilver, the miniature pony, had been held so long ago. Right next to it was the back entrance to the gnomes' cave, which is where we were headed when I smelled tobacco smoke and saw Signe sitting on the low wall of the corral, smoking her pipe.

"What are you doing here, Signe?" I asked.

"I could ask you the same thing," Signe replied.

"Didn't you get the message we sent by pigeon?" Remi asked.

"Yes, G brought it to me a bit ago, but I thought it was from Nick, not the both of you. I didn't know you were in California, Remi," Signe said.

"I'm here to see you, Signe. Nick was the only one who knew how to find you," Remi said.

"Well, it must be important. Is it?" Signe asked, puffing away on her pipe.

"It is. Do you want to talk here?" Remi asked.

"It's as good as anywhere," Signe said, "unless you have some objection."

"No, no, this is fine," Remi said, somewhat flustered. "Where to start?"

"How about the beginning?" Signe said sarcastically.

"Are you in a bad mood, Signe?" Remi asked.

"Sorry. I suppose I am. It has nothing to do with the two of you… it's… it's Gob."

"What's up with him?" I asked.

She was silent for a moment and then said "I think I may have left him too long on his own."

I admit to chuckling, because I'd seen this coming for a while.

"What are you chortling about, Nick?" Signe asked, like she had taken offense.

"It's just that I thought something like this might happen. Don't forget, Joaquin and I are the only ones who've seen both of you in your respective worlds and, you have to admit, they're worlds apart," I said.

Signe was quiet for a minute and then said, "You're on the money, Nick, but right now I'm not seeing anything amusing about it," Signe said.

"I have a lot of faith in you, Signe. You'll figure something out," I said.

"There's always murder," she said under her breath.

"Speaking of murder," Remi said, "I need to warn you, Signe."

"Surely not about murder," she said.

"No, at least I hope not, but the Voslakians are hot on your trail. They know the destination of the gold isCalifornia—and probably about it being delivered to the warehouse in San Francisco tomorrow."

"How do *you* know that?" she asked.

"I have a friend in Sweden," Remi said, "a highly placed American friend who, let's say, keeps tabs on the international comings-and-goings of large sums of money. The Voslakians have been on his radar for some time, but this latest chatter seemed different to him. He asked me if I was aware of anyone who was transferring very large amounts of gold from Scandinavia to the States. Because of the nature of our professional relationship, I had to at least acknowledge that I was aware of such a transaction."

"So what?" Signe asked, "You're a snitch?"

"If you want to put it that way, yes," Remi said. "But he's not interested in your gold—he's interested in shutting down the Voslakian network. It seems they've got a hand in everything that's bad—from drugs and arms sales to cybercrimes. And, so far, they've proven to be very slippery. This is a big opportunity for him—he's not in law enforcement, per se, but he can arrange to have the proper authorities there to apprehend them, but it's going to have to be a coordinated effort. For that he's going to need your cooperation. He asked me to ask you. So, do you want to work with the good guys to get rid of the bad guys?

"If it actually 'gets rid' of the Voslakians, as you say, of course. But this is late notice, isn't it? I mean, what's expected of us? And not to cause problems, but how sure are you that he's not interested in our gold? It's been my experience that *everyone* is interested in our gold. That's why we've taken every effort to turn our fortune into a myth—kind of like the gold at the end of the rainbow. And I'd like to keep it that way. A fairy tale. How sure are you he can be trusted?"

"Very sure. I have his word it's just the Voslakians he wants. Besides," Remi said with a smile, "he's got enough gold himself–he's with the Department of Treasury, Signe."

Signe puffed on her pipe and went silent again and then uttered a cryptic "Hm-mmm," and said "And I suppose you have to let him know right away, right?"

"Yes. It's early tomorrow morning in Sweden, so I have to let him know tonight whether or not it's a 'go'. He thinks the Voslakians may show up in San Francisco tomorrow. As soon as they board a flight, he'll be made aware and inform me immediately."

"All right. Let's do it. Getting rid of the Voslakians would be a very good thing. Go ahead and call your friend, Remi."

"What time is the shipment supposed to arrive at the warehouse?" I asked.

"At one o'clock," Signe said.

"How about we pick you up here at 10 o'clock tomorrow morning. That'll give us enough time to do whatever it is we have to do–although, I've got to say, I feel like we're flying a little blind."

"I don't disagree," Signe said. "I think we should take G and Into with us. And Aalto. We may need her abilities. Is that okay?" Signe asked.

"Yes, certainly," I said. "Not Gob?" I couldn't help but ask.

Even in the semi-dark, I could tell Signe had rolled her eyes. "I think not," she said wearily.

"Okay, we've got to go and get some sleep, Signe. Tomorrow's a big day. We'll see you in a few hours. Tell G we'll meet you all at the usual place–he knows where. Are you going to be okay?"

"You're kind to ask, Nick. Yes, I haven't come this far to be defeated–especially not by Gob – *or* the Voslakians. Go on now. Both of you. We'll see you in the morning. And thanks for coming. I know it took some effort."

"Not at all," Remi said, and we both waved goodbye.

We walked back to the car in silence, the full moon lower, but still lighting our way. Once we got settled in the car, I couldn't help but to ask Remi if he thought it was odd that Signe didn't want Gob on hand for tomorrow's operation.

"No. Signe's nothing if not practical. She probably thought he'd just be in the way."

"Are he and Signe married?" I asked.

"After a fashion," Remi said. "In the strict, Uplander sense of the word, gnomes don't get married; they mate and they take care of one another for life, but it's a little looser than our concept of marriage."

"But G *is* their son, right?"

"Yes," Remi said, hesitating and then added "In case you're wondering, Gob wasn't always the caricature he's apparently become."

"I can see that. Seems to me he's still living the life he did when he and his men left Åland in 1879. Seeing how Signe lived and operated in Finland was an eye-opener," I said. "I wasn't expecting her to be so 'modern.'"

Neither of us said much as we drove down the mountain, both of us lost in our own thoughts. I kept going over our conversation with Signe and finally asked Remi, "Was it just me, or did Signe… what? Not… *overreact* to the news that the Voslakians may be on her trail?"

"Well, she certainly didn't 'freak out', if that's what you mean by not overreacting," Remi said. "But she seemed to have a lot on her mind, with Gob and all."

"That's true, but what's at stake–their entire fortune and the threat from the Voslakian–it's a big deal. I mean, I'm not afraid to admit that the whole thing scares the hell out of me. Does she know something I don't know? Or does she just have nerves of steel?"

"I have no idea," Remi said.

As it turned out, she knew a lot.

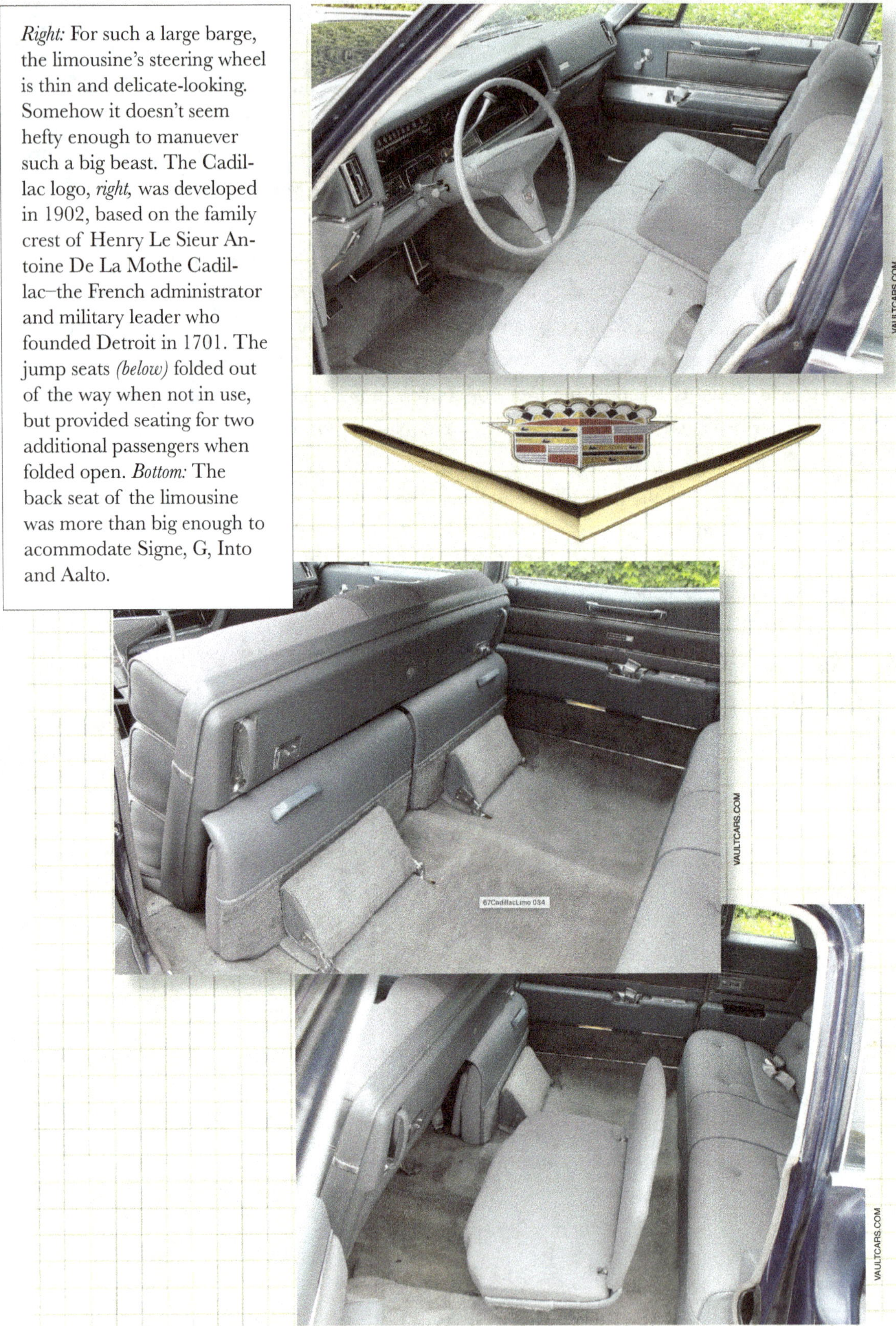

Right: For such a large barge, the limousine's steering wheel is thin and delicate-looking. Somehow it doesn't seem hefty enough to manuever such a big beast. The Cadillac logo, *right,* was developed in 1902, based on the family crest of Henry Le Sieur Antoine De La Mothe Cadillac–the French administrator and military leader who founded Detroit in 1701. The jump seats *(below)* folded out of the way when not in use, but provided seating for two additional passengers when folded open. *Bottom:* The back seat of the limousine was more than big enough to acommodate Signe, G, Into and Aalto.

Chapter XXXVI

Secrets and Shadows

June 30, 2013

Mt. St. Helena
Calistoga, California

Grandpa Nick writing:

As impractical as the old limousine seemed, it could fit everyone in our group and it *did* need to be driven–somewhere–at least once a month. So there were the seven of us: me, Lars (who was happy to drive us), Joaquin and Signe, G, Into, and Aalto. Remi had his rental car and would meet us at the warehouse; Mad said she'd ride with him. Doyle begged off, saying he had things to do at home. Frankly, I think he was looking forward to a little quiet time on his own after all the activity of the past few days.

To say a 1967 Cadillac limousine is not like today's cars is an understatement. In addition to it being very large, it just isn't as precise or responsive as the modern-day cars we've all become used to. The big black relic was so loosey-goosey it made me nervous whenever I drove it anywhere other than down the lane and back. It didn't seem to faze Lars, however. He was as happy to drive as I was to relinquish the duty, sitting in the front passenger seat instead, enjoying what Hattie used to call "the power of velour"–something I was only just beginning to understand some fifty years later.

We were right on time at the turnout on Mt. St. Helena. No sooner had we parked than Signe, G, Into, and Aalto appeared from the shadows of the forest and scrambled into the back seat of the limousine. Joaquin sat in one of the jump seats. The rear windows were tinted so passing drivers wouldn't be able to see our passengers, not that their heads were much above the bottom of the windows anyway.

Lars lowered the window between the front seat and the rear passenger compartment so we could all talk back and forth although, given the distance and the road noise, everyone had to speak up.

I asked Signe what arrangements had been made before she knew the Voslakians might interfere. She said the shipment from DHL was due to arrive at the warehouse in Burlingame at one o'clock. At 1:30, a dozen armored Brinks trucks would load up the gold and make their way up to Mt. St. Helena. Signe, Into, and G had all figured the road over the mountain was too narrow to accommodate a big tractor trailer and that multiple Brinks trucks could maneuver more easily. She said that they were planning on using the fire trail to the back entrance of their cave, the spot where Nigel had sunk the Caterpillar tractor back in 1968. Apparently the tractor was still there, a big rusting hulk.

"Why go in through the back?" I asked.

"So we can take advantage of gravity," Into said. "The fire trail is higher in elevation than the rear entrance to the cave, so all we did was dig a shallow trench from top to bottom and rolled–I mean we will roll–the gold down the hill, right to the entrance. We've asked the Brinks drivers to take the shot puts out of the boxes and send them on their way, down the hill. Of course, we're giving them very large cash tips for their effort. We're hoping that it will also cut down on the amount of gossip they engage in about so many boxes of shot puts being unloaded on Mt. St. Helena. We'd be the first to admit it's more than a little strange–hopefully it's so strange nobody will believe them if they do talk about it. We're guessing no one cares that much about a bunch of shot puts–at least that's what we're hoping."

"Solid gold shot puts," I added, "painted black."

"No easy feat, that," Lars said, remembering what it had taken to spray paint all the gold balls back in Helsinki, just a few days ago.

"No, none of this has been easy," Signe said, sounding tired.

"And not about to get any easier," I said, "although I'm glad to see you here, Aalto."

"Thank you, Nick, but in all honesty I'm not sure how much help I'm going to be," she said.

"She's being modest," G said. "She's awesome. Don't tell Dagywn I said this, but I think the student has surpassed her teacher."

"Not hardly," Aalto said, obviously uncomfortable with the comparison. "There's always more to learn, even after all this time."

"Do you talk to Dagywn?" Joaquin asked.

Aalto paused before answering and then said "As you might imagine, it's not easy for us to communicate with him being on an island in the middle of the Pacific, but we have our ways."

I know Joaquin was wondering the same thing I was—did those ways involve cell phones, by chance? Someday, after all this Voslakian business was behind us, we'd hopefully have the chance to talk about something else. Since getting back in touch with the gnomes, there'd been no mention of the their long-running debate about assimilation into the Uplander culture. I wondered how the tribe felt about it now? And what *were* they going to do about technology and the digital world—pretend to ignore it while secretly accessing it, like they were doing now?

Subjects for another day, I decided. Deliberately changing the subject, I asked Signe what she thought about Remi cooperating with an American treasury agent.

"Frankly, I'm surprised," Signe said. "Until last night, I thought I knew everything about Remi. He keeps his cards closer to his chest than I thought."

"I think he's at a level few of us can imagine," I said. "Full of secrets and shadows."

"As are we. But just between us, I'm thinking he knows more about our business than we do about his," Signe said.

The Federal Bureau of Investigation, the Secret Service, the San Mateo Sheriff's Department and the United States Treasury Department were all on hand at warehouse for the big Bad Boris takedown. In all the commotion, Signe observed that there was one too many law enforcement agencies on hand and she was right. Somehow she, with some help from Aalto, managed to stay out of the clutches of the Treasury Department, all while remaining in plain sight. It was definitely an event to remember.

Chapter XXXVII

The Stage is Set

June 30, 2013

Signe's warehouse in the industrial park in Millbrae, California

Grandpa Nick writing:

By the time we arrived at the warehouse, Remi and Mad were already there, standing outside, talking to someone I didn't recognize. Remi had parked his rental car in front of one of the rolling doors; Lars parked the limousine in front of the other one. I told him to just sit tight for a minute while I went and talked with Remi. The stranger turned out to be Paul Wright, Remi's treasury agent friend. Introductions were made and then Paul continued the discussion I had interrupted, namely the need to not draw any attention to the warehouse. He was concerned that one of the Voslakians might do a reconnaissance drive-by and get spooked. He recommended that we move cars inside the warehouse and keep the roll-up doors closed, which is what we did. He had parked his own car several units down in a guest parking area.

Once the warehouse doors were pulled down, Lars, Joaquin, Signe, G, Into, and Aalto all got out of the limousine and walked over to where we were standing. At the sight of the gnomes, the blood drained from Paul's face and I wondered if he was going to pass out. *Not my problem,* I decided, and proceeded to introduce everyone. If Paul was going to keel over, that's what he was going to do and there wasn't anything any of us could do about it. Mad made a beeline for Aalto, who she hadn't seen since we were all in Kauai, in 1968. The two of them went back into the warehouse where they could continue talking without disturbing anyone. Paul regained some of his composure and said, "This has all been very last minute. Why don't we share what we know so we can coordinate our plans? We don't have all that much time, so I'll go first. The goal of today's action is to apprehend as many of the Voslakian gang, led by Boris Bazarov, otherwise known as 'Bad Boris,' as possible. Just so you know, we have reason to believe that Boris himself is leading this operation. Mr. Bazarov and his associates are wanted on a number of crimes committed across international borders. Because of the scope and seriousness of their criminal activity, both the FBI and the United States Secret Service will be on hand, as will the local San Mateo County Sheriff's Department. I'm representing the United States Treasury Department but, just so everyone knows, I'm not here in any law enforcement capacity. Got that? And just to clarify, the shipment from DHL will arrive at approximately 1:30, correct?"

"That's what I arranged," Signe said.

"Just one truck?" Paul asked.

"A truck and trailer," Signe answered. "The Brinks company is sending twelve armored trucks, as well, all scheduled to arrive at the same time as DHL. The plan is to load the Brinks trucks directly from the DHL truck and trailer."

"Does Boris know about the Brinks trucks?" Paul asked.

"He can't," Signe said. "They have nothing to do with the DHL delivery. The arrangements with Brinks were made using the Bar… a friend's credit card—a friend Boris would have no way of connecting with me or this shipment. I'm certain of that."

Mad and Aalto had rejoined the group and Paul asked, "Would you briefly tell me what your roles are here today?"

Into spoke up first, saying "I'm here as Signe's assistant."

"I'm Signe's son," G said, "and I'm here to protect her—not that she needs much help from me."

"How about you?" Paul asked, turning to Aalto.

"She's insurance," Signe said, before Aalto could say a word.

"Well, okay then," Paul said, raising his eyebrows. "The local sheriff's department, the FBI, and the Secret Service will be here shortly… "

"My apologies for interrupting, Paul—may I call you Paul?" Signe asked.

"Of course," Paul replied.

"I understand your presence and that of the sheriff's department and the F.B.I., but what is the Secret Service doing here?" Signe asked.

"To be honest, I don't know exactly. When I was told they'd be here this morning, it was news to me. But it's unlikely you'll even see them because, as I said, we're trying to have the warehouse appear as normal as possible. Some of the agents will be on the surrounding rooftops, others will be inside neighboring warehouses.

Everyone will be in communication with each other via walkie-talkie. The Feds—the FBI and the Secret Service—would like to make this as clean an apprehension as possible. Instead of arresting the Voslakians for all their other crimes, they'd like to apprehend them in the act of stealing your shipment and charge them with the other crimes after they've been incarcerated. We're thinking that they'll incapacitate the DHL driver and attempt to steal the entire truck and trailer. It's anyone's guess where Boris is planning to take it, but if all goes according to plan, it won't be any further than the parking lot."

"I'll take that as a non-answer," Signe said under her breath.

"Do you have the Brinks paperwork, Signe?" Paul asked.

"No, but Into does," she said.

"With your permission, I'd like to call them and ask them to park their trucks in front and back of the DHL tractor trailer so it's boxed in."

"Of course," Signe said, motioning to Into to give Paul the papers, which he had in a small leather satchel.

"All right, I'm going to call Brinks. It's important that you all stay inside the warehouse and out of the way. And before I forget, the United States government thank you for your assistance in apprehending Mr. Bazarov and his associates. Your willingness to help is greatly appreciated."

With that, we all walked back inside the warehouse. Signe, G, Into, and Aalto decided to make themselves comfortable in the back seat of the limousine. The rest of us stood outside it, with the doors open, wondering what would happen next.

"Are you okay, Signe?" Mad asked. "You look worried."

"I *am* worried," she said.

"About what—besides the obvious?" Remi asked.

"I think this operation has one too many law enforcement agencies," she said.

I guess because Bad Boris was in California, he thought he had to go "full gangster" mode and get himself into an Escalade *(above)* with lots of dark, tinted windows and big wheels. Whatever floats your boat, Boris. He also brought his girlfriend along who was quite a bit taller than Bad Boris and, together, I swear they could have been mistaken for the cartoon characters of Boris and Natasha *(right middle)*. About as heavy and solid as Army tanks, Brinks armored trucks *(bottom)* are meant for transporting all manner of valuables, including the occasional few thousand shot puts.

Chapter XXXVIII

The Best Laid Plans...

June 30, 2013, *continued*

Signe's warehouse in the industrial park in Millbrae

Joaquin writing:
Grandpa said he had to do something so he turned the reporting duties over to me. We had to cool our jets for awhile, waiting for whoever was going to show up. I think I caught Signe nodding off more than once, but, in fairness, it *was* her nighttime. But, wham, as soon as it turned 1:30, everything went off like clockwork—except for the disasters, which were on their own timetable.

I had positioned myself at the small window in the front door of the warehouse, which was, conveniently, right at eyeball height—at least my eyeballs. I could see everything that was going on. First up was the DHL truck and trailer, which positioned itself parallel to the warehouse, parking in front of the roll-up doors. Luckily, the driver stopped short of the front door, so he didn't block my view. Immediately after the truck and trailer stopped, two guys—obviously Voslakian— appeared from around the corner of a nearby warehouse. They ran over to the DHL truck, one on each side of the cab, jumped up onto the running boards and stuck something through the open windows and at the driver and passenger. There weren't any shots, so I'm guessing they used some kind of a tranquilizer gun. They then proceeded to haul the DHL guys like a couple of rag dolls out the cab of the truck, onto the parking lot and dumped them into a heap. They then ran back to the truck and and jumped into the cab. Just as the Voslalkians were attempting to hijack the DHL truck and trailer, a parade of Brinks armored trucks showed up, one after another, in a continuous line. If anyone was watching, they'd have known in an instant that something major was going down. In the next heartbeat, a late model black Escalade with 24-inch chrome wheels and heavily-tinted rear windows showed up and parked across from the warehouse. I'm thinking it's gotta be Bad Boris, right? Sure enough, the rear window rolls down and Boris's ugly mug is staring out, taking in the action. It takes about a nanosecond for BB to pull a full-on shake 'n bake when he sees the Brinks trucks in the process of boxing in the truck and trailer filled with one of the world's largest fortunes in gold. He turned an unhealthy shade of red and was practically foaming at the mouth. He flew out of the backseat of the Escalade, making a beeline for the Brinks truck directly in front of the DHL truck-and-trailer. Bad Boris hadn't taken two steps before–BAM!–more cars than I could count showed up from every direction with flashing lights and sirens, all pointed directly in BB's direction. Officers of every stripe jumped out of their cars, guns drawn. I'm guessing here, but I'm pretty sure he soiled his drawers.

It was a lot of intense action in a very short period of time. So much so, I figured that had to be it. Arrest Bad Boris and his Voslakian cohorts and everyone goes home, but no–there was more to come. First, though, let me explain a few things. As ugly as the Voslakian men were, the country was known for its beautiful women. Go figure. A surprising number of internationally-known models were, in fact, from Voslakia. Two, and I'm guessing here, but I think BB wanted to show off in front of his girlfriend, letting her see in real time just how rich he was going to be after stealing a truck and trailer load of gnome gold. Or maybe she just came along for the ride. Who knows? But when everyone had their guns pulled on Boris, she jumped out of the Escalade, a pistol in her hands pointed at Boris, too. As much as it was something she'd probably been wanting to do for some time, she realized she'd made a mistake when several of the law enforcement folks laughed out loud. The closest agent on her left walked over to her, gun drawn, reached over her shoulder and removed the pistol from her grip. And that was that. Do I have to tell you she was beautiful–raven black hair, redder-than-red lipstick–and very tall, dressed in a short red dress and wearing teeteringly tall, black patent, high-heeled shoes? Of course I don't, but I want you to get the picture. The two of them must have made quite the pair in the crowds they ran with, especially considering she had to be more than a foot taller than Boris. Without the heels.

Understand that I was providing a running verbal account of what was going on for those in the group who were standing next to me, but who weren't tall enough to see out the window. Next in my color commentary was the two of them, Boris and... should we call her Natasha? Sure, why not? Anyway, the two of them wound up face down on the asphalt, getting hand-cuffed and read their rights, while another couple of officers managed to pull the Voslakian hijackers out of the cab of the DHL truck and trailer. In the next instant, emergency medical technicians were attending to the two DHL guys who, luckily, appeared to be coming back to consciousness. Meanwhile, to a one, the Brinks armored truck drivers looked on, mouths open, not quite believing what they were witnessing.

A male and a female agent escorted the Voslakian odd couple, Boris and Natasha, into the back of an unmarked sedan and took off, followed by a similar looking car containing the two Voslakian wannabe truck hijackers.

There were still a lot of vehicles haphazardly parked between the two rows of identical warehouses. Even so, my guess was the show was about to wind down.

Boy howdy, was I wrong.

The industrial park *(right)* near the San Francisco Airport, where Signe rented the warehouse, looked like any other of the thousands of industrial parks across the country–generic and anonymous–in complete and utter contrast to the multiple dramas that went down on that June day. *Below:* To give you an idea of the arrangement of all the players in the complex series of events that unfolded in a very short period of time in a very small space, I drew a map to give you a better idea of the situation. I was inside the warehouse, peering though the window in the front door, describing the action to everyone around me–who wasn't tall enough to see out the window. I didn't have room to fit all twelve of the Brinks trucks in the diagram and I have no idea where the single police car came from *(bottom left)* or why it was there.

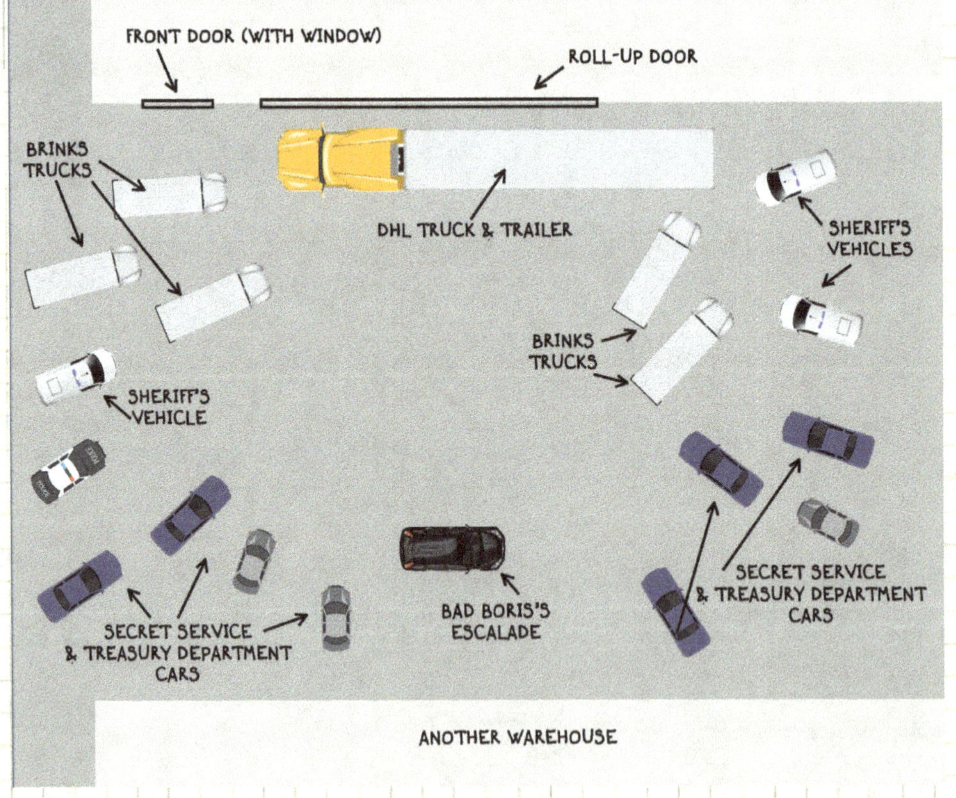

Chapter XXXIX

Uh-oh

June 30, 2013, *continued*

Signe's warehouse in the industrial park in Millbrae

Joaquin writing:

Finally, one of the Brinks drivers got out of his armored truck and went over to an agent who was leaning against his car, cell phone up to his ear. I heard him ask who had arranged for the Brinks pickup and the agent pointed over to where we all were, in the warehouse. I let him in and he asked who was in charge. I looked over my shoulder and both Remi and Signe started to walk forward. Signe looked up to Remi with a look that said "I've got this," and proceeded to add one more hard-to-believe experience to the Brinks driver's already unbelievable day.

"How do you do?" Signe said, holding up her hand.

"Pleased, I'm sure," the driver said, visibly nervous at meeting a gnome, presumably for the first time. "I… uh… was just wondering after all… this" he said, motioning in the general direction of the scene of the recent melee, "whatever just happened out there… ah… do you still want us to pick up and deliver your shipment?"

"Yes and no," Signe replied. "Instead of making the delivery to Mt. St. Helena, could you just deliver them here, to this warehouse?"

"If it's okay with you, it's okay with us," the Brinks man said.

"Yes, go ahead," Signe said, "thank you."

The Brinks guy went outside, held a quick meeting with his crew, and started unloading box after box labeled "Championship Shot Puts." No sooner had the first box been put in the warehouse, than some guy came striding over, holding a badge above his head, yelling "Whoa, whoa, whoa."

The Brinks guy looked up and, not wanting to provoke any trouble, held his hands in the air. "I'm just doing what my boss told me to do," he said, looking over at the guy who had just talked to Signe. That guy piped up, saying "And I'm just doing what the little lady told me to do."

"What little lady?" the guy with the badge said.

"The one inside the warehouse."

"Stop what you're doing and stand away from the truck," badge man said. He looked over his shoulder and summoned two of his buddies to come with him and headed for the warehouse. I saw Remi shoot Paul a look of alarm and Paul respond by raising his shoulders. By the time badge man and his two buddies had entered the warehouse, Aalto moved protectively in front of Signe.

"Who's the owner of the DHL shipment?" badge man asked.

"I'm the consignee," Grandpa said.

"And I'm the owner," Signe said, poking her head around Aalto.

Badge man asked them to come forward while signaling to his partners to put handcuffs on them both.

"What the…?" Remi said, stepping in between Signe and the agent. "Who are you, anyway?"

"Secret Service, sir. Stand aside or we'll cuff you, too."

"Secret Service?" Remi asked plaintively, looking at Paul.

Just when I thought things might go south, they went way south—*all the way* south. Aalto stepped forward resolutely. She planted her feet firmly, both arms held straight at her sides, fists clenched and looked up at the ceiling and then down again and, in an instant, Badge Man and his two partners were frozen in place, caught, unfortunately, with very strange, almost comical expressions on their faces. Signe, who was not frozen, simply looked peeved.

"Oh dear Aalto. Was that really necessary?" Signe said with some consternation.

"Well, if it saves our gold and keeps you out of jail, I'd say, yes, it was necessary," Aalto said.

"We'd better act fast. If the rest of whoever else is out there finds out there's a frozen trio in here, we're *all* going to jail," Signe said. "Do you have a plan?"

"Hold on a minute," Remi said, turning to Paul. "I thought you said there was no interest in their gold? That the FBI just wanted to nab Boris?"

"That's what I was told. Somebody must have blabbed to the Secret Service about the gold. I didn't even know they were going to be involved."

"Well, they sure are," Remi said with disdain. "Once they get un-paralyzed, I'd say they're definitely going to be involved. Big time."

"Let me ask the question again, do you have a plan, Aalto?" Signe said.

"Not really," she replied. "That's why I froze them—to give us a chance to come up with something."

"Whatever it is, you better come up with it quick, Aalto," Remi said. "The rest of them are making their way over here now."

Aalto ran over to the open door and looked out. Just like she did the first time, she planted her feet, held her arms straight at her sides with fists clenched and looked up at the sky, and then down again and—*poof*—everybody outside was gone. Like really gone. Disappeared. Even the Brinks guys.

Aalto surveyed the situation and summed it up with a simple "Uh-oh."

Government oversight organizations– like the Financial Crimes Enforcement Network (that's its logo, *at right*)–take monitoring activities like the movement of large sums of money and valuables in and out of the country, very seriously. Form 105 *(below)* is only a single sheet of paper and may, at first glance, seem like a fairly simple set of questions–simple, that is, until you don't fill it out and try to bring a bunch of money into the country–then things get seriously complicated in a hurry. I'm not sure of how aware Signe was of the legal requirements for moving money around the world, but she certainly managed a clever workaround with the old gold-balls-and-shot-puts switcheroo maneuver. Why am I not surprised?

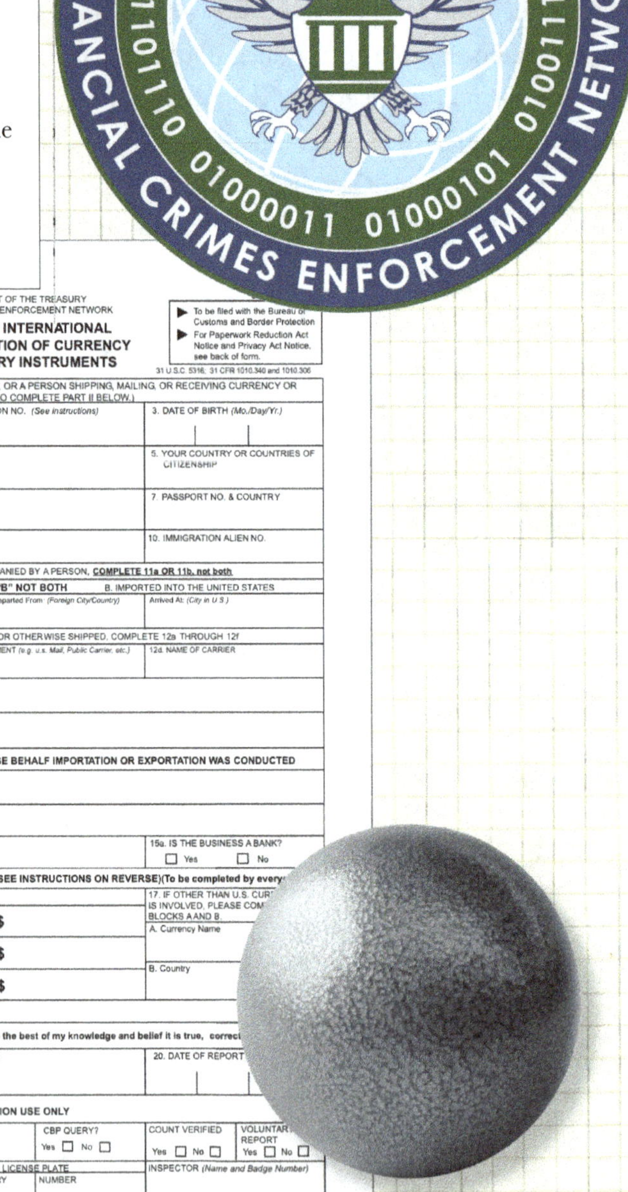

FinCEN Form **105**
July 2017
Department of the Treasury
FinCEN

▶ Please type or print.

DEPARTMENT OF THE TREASURY
FINANCIAL CRIMES ENFORCEMENT NETWORK

REPORT OF INTERNATIONAL TRANSPORTATION OF CURRENCY OR MONETARY INSTRUMENTS

▶ To be filed with the Bureau of Customs and Border Protection
▶ For Paperwork Reduction Act Notice and Privacy Act Notice, see back of form.

31 U.S.C. 5316; 31 CFR 1010.340 and 1010.306

PART I FOR A PERSON DEPARTING OR ENTERING THE UNITED STATES, OR A PERSON SHIPPING, MAILING, OR RECEIVING CURRENCY OR MONETARY INSTRUMENTS. (IF ACTING FOR ANYONE ELSE, ALSO COMPLETE PART II BELOW.)

1. NAME (Last or family, first, and middle)	2. IDENTIFICATION NO. (See instructions)	3. DATE OF BIRTH (Mo./Day/Yr.)

4. PERMANENT ADDRESS IN UNITED STATES OR ABROAD	5. YOUR COUNTRY OR COUNTRIES OF CITIZENSHIP

6. ADDRESS WHILE IN THE UNITED STATES	7. PASSPORT NO. & COUNTRY

8. U.S. VISA DATE (Mo./Day/Yr.)	9. PLACE UNITED STATES VISA WAS ISSUED	10. IMMIGRATION ALIEN NO.

11. IF CURRENCY OR MONETARY INSTRUMENT IS ACCOMPANIED BY A PERSON, **COMPLETE 11a OR 11b, not both**

A. EXPORTED FROM THE UNITED STATES   **COMPLETE "A" OR "B" NOT BOTH**   B. IMPORTED INTO THE UNITED STATES

Departed From: (U.S. Port/City in U.S.)	Arrived At: (Foreign City/Country)	Departed From: (Foreign City/Country)	Arrived At: (City in U.S.)

12. IF CURRENCY OR MONETARY INSTRUMENT WAS MAILED OR OTHERWISE SHIPPED, COMPLETE 12a THROUGH 12f

12a. DATE SHIPPED (Mo./Day/Yr.)	12b. DATE RECEIVED (Mo./Day/Yr.)	12c. METHOD OF SHIPMENT (e.g. U.S. Mail, Public Carrier, etc.)	12d. NAME OF CARRIER

12e. SHIPPED TO (Name and Address)

12f. RECEIVED FROM (Name and Address)

PART II INFORMATION ABOUT PERSON(S) OR BUSINESS ON WHOSE BEHALF IMPORTATION OR EXPORTATION WAS CONDUCTED

13. NAME (Last or family, first, and middle or Business Name)

14. PERMANENT ADDRESS IN UNITED STATES OR ABROAD

15. TYPE OF BUSINESS ACTIVITY, OCCUPATION, OR PROFESSION	15a. IS THE BUSINESS A BANK? ☐ Yes ☐ No

PART III CURRENCY AND MONETARY INSTRUMENT INFORMATION (SEE INSTRUCTIONS ON REVERSE) (To be completed by everyone)

16. TYPE AND AMOUNT OF CURRENCY/MONETARY INSTRUMENTS		17. IF OTHER THAN U.S. CURRENCY IS INVOLVED, PLEASE COMPLETE BLOCKS A AND B.
Currency and Coins	▶ $	A. Currency Name
Other Monetary Instruments (Specify types, issuing entity and date, and serial or other identifying number.)	▶ $	
(TOTAL)	▶ $	B. Country

PART IV SIGNATURE OF PERSON COMPLETING THIS REPORT

Under penalties of perjury, I declare that I have examined this report, and to the best of my knowledge and belief it is true, correct

18. NAME AND TITLE (Print)	19. SIGNATURE	20. DATE OF REPORT

CUSTOMS AND BORDER PROTECTION USE ONLY

THIS SHIPMENT IS ☐ INBOUND ☐ OUTBOUND	PORT CODE	CBP QUERY? Yes ☐ No ☐	COUNT VERIFIED Yes ☐ No ☐	VOLUNTARY REPORT Yes ☐ No ☐
DATE	AIRLINE/FLIGHT/VESSEL	LICENSE PLATE STATE/COUNTRY — NUMBER	INSPECTOR (Name and Badge Number)	

FinCEN FORM 105

Chapter XL

A Whole Lotta Shot Puts

June 30, 2013, *continued*

Signe's warehouse in the industrial park in Millbrae

Joaquin writing:

"Uh-oh?" Signe, Remi, and Paul all said at the same time.

The rest of us may not have said it out loud but we were all thinking the same thing: "Uh-oh? Really?"

Aalto ran over to Into and whispered in his ear. He quickly dug into his satchel and handed Aalto something which, for anyone with the barest knowledge of such things, knew had to be a cell phone. Aalto ran outside out of earshot and, presumably, made a call. My best guess was it was to Dagwyn, the former gnome wizard who was now retired in Kauai. If you haven't read *The Voyage of the Silverado*, book number two in the Silverado Trilogy, you need to know that Dagywn was the one, many years ago, who trained Aalto to take his place, teaching her everything (or perhaps, more to the point, *almost* everything) he knew. The look exchanged between Signe and Remi said to me that the whole cell phone thing was news to them but, given what else was going on right then, it was small potatoes. Aalto was back in the warehouse in just a few minutes, only to look over her shoulder and run back outside again. The next instant she was back inside again, asking G to hand her a couple of shot puts from one of the boxes the Brinks guys had already started unloading before all hell broke loose.

"Quick!" she said to G, who was struggling to open the box.

Finally successful and, obviously straining, he handed her two of the heavy balls. It all happened so fast, no one could remember how Aalto managed to do what came next. When she was outside on the phone, she had noticed two newly-arrived Voslakians skulking around the DHL truck, undoubtedly up to no good.

Much later, I found out that when Bad Boris was given his one jailhouse call, instead of calling his lawyer, he called one of his cohorts. Refusing to admit defeat in obtaining the gnomes' gold, Boris apparently had instructed this guy to grab one of his pals and get to the warehouse on the double to finish the job hijacking the DHL truck-and-trailer. For Boris, defeat was simply not an option. But back to the action: When Aalto ran outside, lugging the two shot puts, everyone in our crew ran outside too, not wanting to miss a thing. Considering Aalto had made everyone disappear, the two new-on-the-scene Voslakians easily moved two of the Brinks trucks out of their way and were now trying, without much success, to secure the rear door on the DHL truck-and-trailer so they could take off with the gold. Aalto put one of the shot puts on the ground and did a 360-degree arm spin with the other one, sending it flying to a direct hit to the back of one of the Voslakian's big head. Before he could figure out what had happened to his partner, Aalto launched the second shot put with the same amazing accuracy, felling the other Voslakian, just like the first. We all erupted in yells of approval and applause.

Signe was quick to give Aalto a hug and immediately asked if she knew how to get everyone back.

"Yes," she said, "but once they're back, do you know what you're going to do?" Aalto asked.

"I do," Signe said, "hand me one of those shot puts you so admirably pitched."

Aalto ran over and retrieved the closest ball and set it at Signe's feet. Signe put her foot on the ball to keep it from rolling away.

"Are you ready?" Aalto asked Signe.

"I am now," she replied.

"Okay, listen up everyone. I need your help. Everyone hold hands and try to hold an image of what this looked like out here before everyone disappeared. Can you do that? Quickly!" Aalto implored.

Everyone fell into line and held hands, closing their eyes and, presumably, imagining the scene with all the agents and law enforcement officers—not to mention the Brinks guys—back where they belonged. Aalto stood in front of us, not saying a word, but holding her arms out, palms up, and staring straight ahead. I swear I felt a vibration and then, like when you see a wobbly heat mirage in the desert, the scene in front of us took shape, at first kind of wobbly and then in clear focus, populated by everyone who wasn't there just a minute ago. Even weirder, they all just came to life right before our eyes, seemingly unaware any time had passed. They just continued doing before whatever it was they were doing before Aalto accidentally made them disappear. To say there was a collective sigh of relief would be a serious understatement.

However Aalto had managed to flip the switch back on again, it included Badge Man about to put handcuffs on Signe, only this time, there was a shot put under her foot.

"Before you put those on me, would you do me a favor?" Signe asked.

"What's that?" Badge Man said gruffly.

"First off, tell me what you're arresting me for?"

"You must complete a FINCEN 105 form at the time of entry for monetary instruments, including gold, worth over $10,000."

"What does FINCEN stand for?" Grandpa asked.

"Financial Crimes Enforcement Network. It's a bureau within the United States Department of the Treasury," Badge Man said assertively.

"And did you say 'gold?'" Signe asked.

"Yes ma'am," he said.

"What gold?" Signe asked innocently.

"I believe that would be some of it under your foot," Badge Man said.

"This?" Signe said, removing her foot, allowing it to do a slow roll in his direction.

"Yes," he said, picking it up.

"Do you carry a pocket knife, agent?" Signe asked.

"No," he replied.

"I do. Here," his partner said, handing him his pocket knife.

"Scratch the ball," Signe said. "Any gold there?"

Badge Man scratched, lightly at first, and then with more determination, without any sign of gold.

"Well?" Signe asked.

"Am I to understand all the balls are like this?" he asked.

"You're welcome to check each and every one, agent. They are as labeled: Shot puts." Signe said.

"I'm sorry. I'm a little confused here," Badge Man said. "What in the world would anyone want with a truck and trailer load of shot puts?"

"Good question," Signe said. "Why don't you ask them?" she said, motioning to the two unconscious Voslakians. "They seemed quite determined to have them."

Including the ones behind this caption box, that's 1,890 shot puts you're looking at—that's about all I could fit onto one page. Hard to believe, but what's pictured on this page represents only about one-quarter of the gnomes' cache of gold. All told, it formed 8,869 balls, each one weighing approximately 16 pounds for a total 141,904 pounds. That's a lot of gold! Or a lot of shot puts. Or both.

Chapter XLI

What Just Happened?

June 30, 2013, *continued*

Signe's warehouse in the industrial park in Millbrae

Joaquin writing:

"What happened to *them?*" Badge Man asked, genuinely baffled.

"Your guess is as good as mine," Signe answered. "Maybe they slipped and hit their heads."

"Right," Badge Man said sarcastically, his frustration visible. To make matters worse, he was certain he'd just been played. Wanting to get the operation over with, he ordered his agents to select random boxes of shot puts and do what he had just done–scratch the surface of the balls to see if there was gold underneath. There wasn't.

Meanwhile the San Mateo County Sheriff's Department called ambulances to pick up the two Voslakians who'd been beaned by Aalto's precision shot-putting. No one who witnessed that bit of athletic artistry is likely to forget it; I know I won't.

I continued to watch what was happening outside the warehouse. The crowd of various law enforcement folks began to thin, but Badge Man was still conferring with someone on his cell phone. He ended the call and spoke with two of his partners, then strode back to our group in the warehouse. Without looking directly at anyone, he said "You're free to go." Considering the alternatives, Signe was happy to leave it at that.

The only people left were the Brinks guys who were unloading the DHL truck and trailer, and the nine of us, in various states of confusion.

Mad was the first to speak. "Would somebody please tell me what just happened?" she said.

"Yeah," Remi and Paul said in unison.

"I know I'm late to the game," Mad said, "but am I right that there's been a major breakdown in communication here?"

"There had to be," Signe said.

"Why?" Grandpa asked.

"Because I needed to protect all of you. Protect you from knowing what the real plan was. Moving the gold from Åland to America was risky enough before the Voslakians were in the picture. Their presence changed everything."

"So what *did* just happen? Where's the gold? It's obviously not here," Remi said, pointing to the stacked boxes of shot puts.

"The gold is already on Mt. St. Helena. It was delivered before we arrived. The Baron and I came up with a last-minute change we knew would escape Boris's attention. It was the only way I could ensure success. I wasn't keeping anyone in the dark because I didn't trust them or their abilities. I did it to keep you all safe."

"So this was a 'used ruse,'" Grandpa said.

"What do you mean?" Into asked.

"Well, you already used it once, back in Eckerö, when you tried to make Boris and the gang believe the shotputs were actually gold. I can't believe you had them packaged up again and sent all the way over here. Who did it?"

"I had Minna arrange it. Right after you left the warehouse she had a crew come in and box the shot puts up and send them here. Those are some well-traveled balls," Signe said.

"I'm sure Boris thought you'd never try to pull that trick again. Who would? Wherever he is right now, he must be kicking himself," Grandpa said.

Everyone was silent, trying to process what had gone down. G finally broke the silence and asked "What are we going to do with all of them–the shot puts?"

"Good question," Signe said, "Good thing we've got this warehouse. They can stay here for the time being. We'll think of something. And G, will you be sure and remind me to ask everyone what they want done with their traveling crates? I bet some of them are going to want to keep them."

• • •

Signe settled into the back seat of the limousine, along with G, Into, and Aalto, and let out a big sigh. "That was quite the day" she said, with closed eyes. I took my position in the jump seat and Grandpa and Lars sat up front, Lars driving again. Remi and Mad were in Remi's rental car. Even though we hadn't physically done that much, the day had been draining, no doubt about it. Grandpa asked Lars and me what we thought of pizza for dinner, which we both agreed sounded great.

"Did someone say 'pizza'?" Into asked, overhearing our conversation. "I'm in."

"Me too," Aalto said.

"Me three," Signe chimed in.

"I'm for it," G said, keeping the silly pun going.

"Then it's settled. I'll call Doyle and ask him to order it and we'll pick it up on the way home."

Signe turned to Aalto and said quietly "About that cell phone …?"

"You're going to have to look on it as part of what I can do as a wizard, Signe. It would have been a completely different outcome today without it. It was actually Dagywn's idea, a long time ago."

"Is the phone yours?" Signe asked.

"No. Well, sort of. G and I share it. I know you call him on it."

"Only in emergencies," Signe said.

"Perhaps," Aalto said, "but you haven't been around to know how he uses it, have you? And you certainly appreciated it when you had to go around the crow network to tell him about the arrival of the gold. I know how you feel about them, but they can be an important tool."

"Yes, of course," Signe said with resignation. "I just don't want to see the day when all of our people are walking around with a phones stuck to their ears like the Uplanders."

"I'm not sure that will happen," Aalto said. "Most of the Uplanders are talking to their mothers. Our folks don't need a phone to do that considering that most of our mothers are within shouting distance."

"Even so, I'd appreciate your keeping the phone to yourself for the time being. It's one more thing we need to figure out about our future, isn't it? Oh, and before I forget to say so, even with your, ah, 'mishap,' I'm very glad you were along today, dear," Signe said, patting Aalto's knee. "Without your efforts, I would have been in the hoosegow right now. Jail is not for Signe," she said shaking her head. "And I must say, those were outstanding shots. Bravo. Those Voslakians never knew what hit 'em!"

Right top: Yep, that's Dr. Wilkinson, himself, up to his neck in hot mud, pictured on a postcard from his eponymous (how do you like that word? Look it up if you have to) hot spring resort in Calistoga. *Right middle:* That's the resort on the main drag of Calistoga, at the base of Mt. St. Helena. Grandpa liked the mud baths but, frankly, I think you'd have to be a little crazy to crawl into a tub of hot mud. Just sayin'. *Bottom:* That's the stone marker memorializing Robert Louis Stevenson on Mt. St. Helena. On the left side it says: "This tablet placed by the club women of Napa County marks the site of the cabin occupied in 1880 by Robert Louis Stevenson and bride while he wrote *Silverado Squatters.*" On the right are lines from a poem Stevenson wrote—*In Memoriam F. A. S.*— commemorating the death of an eighteen-year-old boy, Francis Albert Sitwell, who died of consumption in Davos in 1881 while Stevenson was staying there. Considering that Stevenson, himself, died at the young age of 44, the words could be about him: "Doomed to know not winter, only spring, a being trod the flowery April blithely for awhile, took his fill of music, joy of thought and seeing, came and stayed and went nor ever ceased to smile."

Chapter XLII

Mud, Tub and a Rub

June 30–July 1, 2013

Grandpa Nick's house, Rutherford
Dr. Wilkinson's Hot Springs, Calistoga

Joaquin writing:

During our impromptu pizza party back at Grandpa's house, Remi asked Signe the question he'd been wondering about ever since learning about the switchup in plans this morning, namely, how did they get the gold from the Brinks trucks to the cave? Remember that he and Mad were in the rental car this morning when Into told us in the limousine about how they were *going to* unload the gold–as opposed to how they had already done it.

Signe recounted how she remembered Gob telling her about the would-be thief, Nigel Stayne, trying to use an earth-moving tractor to dig a hole into the cave to access the treasure (see page 127 in *The Voyage of the Silverado*), and that he had approached the cave from a location above it. Having confirmed that the fire trail Nigel had used was still there, Signe instructed the gnomes to dig a shallow trench down the mountainside, from the fire trail to the rear cave opening. There wasn't much to it as the trench only needed to be a few inches deep. She gave the Brinks people instructions to take the "shot puts" from their boxes, place them in the trench, and let them roll on their own down the mountain. When asked if that was all they had to do, Signe replied yes, that once the shot puts reached their destination down the mountain, there would be someone there to take care of them. G reported that it went off without a hitch, but said that once the shot puts had made their way down the mountain, most of the black paint had worn off and the gold had started to show through but, by then, it didn't matter–the gnomes were the only ones who saw through the black paint to the gold below.

"We owe the Baron a big one," Signe said.

"Why?" I asked.

"If it hadn't been for his idea, back when, of forming our gold into balls, we'd never had been able to pull off moving it to Mt. St. Helena. No doubt, the worm will turn and we'll be able to return the favor one day. Right now, I'm glad the job is done and Bad Boris is behind bars and the gold is tucked away in the depths of the mountain. Let me get my feet under me and then we can have a celebration up on the mountain. Gob, as I'm sure you're aware, is always ready for a party." Signe was silent for a moment and then said with a chuckle, "I bet those Brinks guys go to their graves trying to figure out what the deal was with so many shot puts."

•　•　•

After the pizza-paloozza, Lars drove Signe, G, Aalto, and Into back up Mt. St. Helena and then came back to Grandpa's and spent the night, along with Mad and Remi. Figuring enough people were spending the night there, I walked up the lane and slept in my own bed for the second time in a week. It felt good.

By the time I got to Grandpa's the next morning, everyone was bustling around in the kitchen. The big news was that Lars already had a bite on his listing for the bus and was busy making arrangements to get together with the potential buyer. Remi and Mad were working out plans to return the rental car, get dropped off at the Napa Airport where Remi's plane was, and for Mad to get a rental car of her own. It was too confusing for me so I just stayed out of it and watched as Grandpa and Doyle flipped pancakes, fried bacon, scrambled eggs and warmed little pitchers of maple syrup and melted butter in a pot of simmering water. It was quite the production, but way worth it–so much so everyone had seconds. Darren made it over in time and managed to finish up everything that was still on the stove. I gave him the David Hasselhof *Knight Rider* t-shirt from Helsinki which he proclaimed as "boss–almost as cool as my *Vote for Pedro* t-shirt." He was speechless when I showed him the picture of Remi's speedboat. When he got his voice back, he wanted to know if I'd driven it, to which I answered "next time."

Everyone pitched in and helped clean up the kitchen. Remi and Mad took off–Remi for home in Sweden and Mad to pick up a rental car; she was going to stick around for a while. Even though Remi said his goodbyes, I somehow felt like we'd see him again, sooner rather than later. Darren and I took off on our bikes to parts unknown, but it was a beautiful day, neither of us had any chores we needed to do and there wasn't any school, so we were free to go where we wanted.

• • •

Nick, the old guy, back again. It's still the same day Joaquin was writing about. What a difference two hours makes: I am now up to my neck in a tub full of hot mud. No fooling. Doyle's in the same situation, in a tub next to mine. I was going to say something to him, but I knew he was on a different planet and it would be hard to reach him. So, like I said, I determined a little earlier that neither of us had anything planned for the day, so I got on the phone and called Dr. Wilkinson's Hot Springs Resort, an old-timey spa, on the main drag in Calistoga. I booked appointments for both of us—what locals referred to as a "mud, tub, and a rub," which translates into a mud bath (actually a combination of volcanic ash and peat moss), a bubbling hot mineral bath, and a massage. From past experience, I knew the package deal took about three hours and, when it was over, you felt like you'd been on the most relaxing two-week vacation you'd ever been on. Somehow, after all the action over the past few weeks, it seemed like exactly the right thing to do—and it was.

If there was ever a good time to put the clutch in and just let my mind wander, this was it. Heated by the volcanic steam below, the tub full of mud bubbled, gurgled, and hissed and made me think about the activity there was going on below ground in this little corner of the world—geysers and volcanic hot and warm springs all over the place. Like other hot springs around the planet, their presence made the town attractive to the weary traveler, of which I was definitely one.

Long before the first European settlers arrived, the local indigenous tribe, the Wappo, had trails going over Mt. St. Helena and considered the peak sacred. Now that same mountain was protecting an unfathomable treasure of gold, just like it had protected the natural deposits of silver and mercury from time immemorial. And now, along with precious ore, there was an entire population of gnome folk burrowed in the depths, calling the mountain "home."

As much activity as there had always been below the surface, there was a matching amount above ground. Sam Brannan arrived in the area around 1860 and, impressed with its beauty and the hot springs, promptly bought 2,000 acres and started building a resort town he called Calistoga. Less than twenty years later, Gustave Niebaum established his winery down the road in Rutherford in 1879 and the following year, looking for inexpensive (as in *free*) lodging and healthy air, Robert Louis Stevenson and his new wife, Fanny Osbourne of Oakland, honeymooned in an abandoned bunkhouse beside a defunct mine called Silverado, atop Mt. St. Helena. Gob and his men were already living on the mountain when Stevenson and Fanny arrived that summer of 1880 and, although they left him alone, they were well aware of the famous writer's presence on the mountain. With what I'd done with and for the gnomes over the last 45 years, I wondered if I'd have a place in this timeline of history. Or, because of the gnomes' desire to lead a secret existence, was I even part of the story? Did it matter? In the big scheme of things, I guess not. Worrying about what kind of legacy I was leaving was probably just another symptom of getting old. Truth be told though, I was still bridling at being told to wait forty-five years to publish "The Silverado Journals." And now, after being away from it for so long, being back in the middle of the gnomes' world–not to mention the writing of this third journal with Joaquin–has caused a lot of unresolved feelings to come to the surface. I hadn't come right out and asked G yet, but I suspected when I did, he would ask me to forget about publishing the journals at all. What with Lars's great-aunt and her sister wanting to make them into a side show and Bad Boris's failed attempt to steal their fortune, I couldn't blame them. It wasn't in my nature to go against their wishes and publish the journals whether they approved or not, so that only left one option: I was just going to have to forget about them and accept that it was time to move on. Bummer.

Long known for a variety of horticultural places of interest—from apple orchards to Luther Burbank's plant breeding efforts—the town of Sebastopol also features many beautiful, ancient oak trees *(above)*. Leave it to Mad to find an adobe house with a significant history, just waiting for her to take ownership *(bottom)*. That's Darren playing skittles *(right)*, putting some serious spin on the bat you throw to knock down the pins and earn points.

Chapter XLIII

Difficult Conversations

July 1–3, 2013, *continued*

Grandpa Nick's house, Rutherford
Sebastopol, Sonoma County

Still Nick here. After our "mud, tub, and a rub," Doyle and I were both feeling mighty relaxed and toxin-free. We were out on the sidewalk, in front of Dr. Wilkinson's Hot Springs, when I turned my phone back on. I had two text messages—one from Lars in San Francisco saying he was almost certain the bus was sold and one from Mad. Lars wrote that he was going across the bay to spend the night with a friend of his who was a student at the U.C. Berkeley College of Environmental Design. "If all goes well, tomorrow I will buy a car to tour the United States, including the Burning Man* festival." *Ah, to be young again,* I thought to myself. Mad's message was that she was on her way back and wanted to make sure it was okay for her to continue staying at the house. She also wanted me to go with her tomorrow to see a place she liked in Sebastopol. *Things are falling in place,* I thought to myself.

Neither Doyle nor I had the oomph needed to cook dinner, so we decided to pick up Chinese food on the way home. I called in the order from Calistoga so we

---

*Burning Man is a festival held every year in the Black Rock Desert in northwestern Nevada. The event derives its name from the symbolic burning of a very large wooden effigy, referred to as the Man, that occurs on the next to last night of the festival. The Burning Man festival is a gathering of bohemians and free spirits of all stripe. Radical self-expression and communal effort is expected of the participants, who design and build a wide array of art, activities, and events, including experimental and interactive sculptures, buildings, and performances. The festival started in 1986 with a handful of people; today, more than 70,000 attend the weeklong event.

wouldn't have to wait for it. I couldn't help but think about that time, forty-five years ago, when Doyle and I went to the Golden Harvest Restaurant and got a wheel barrowful of take-away for the night Gob, G, Whitbeck, and Wycoff all came to Grandma Hattie's house to negotiate the trip to Kauai (see *The Silverado Trail*, page 281). I remembered Hattie requesting an extra order of fried wontons–her favorite, so I added an order in her honor, although Doyle and I would be the only two who'd remember that bit of nostalgia.

Mad was already there when we arrived, as was Joaquin, who said if we were having Chinese food, he was staying. He texted home and afterwards told me "Just so you know mom said it was okay to spend the night at Darren's house."

Joaquin left for Darren's right after he'd cleared the table, which left the three of us–Mad, Doyle and me–at the kitchen table. It seemed like the perfect time to teach them the three-handed card game Lars had taught Joaquin and me at the tiny fisherman's cottage on that equally tiny island in the Åland archipelago, just a few weeks ago. Of course they wanted to know why it was called Jailhouse Gin, so I had to explain to them about his great uncle getting thrown in jail for driving to his favorite bar, drunk, on his riding lawnmower. Unfortunate for him, but not for the rest of us, because it was a good game, not to mention a good story.

We knocked off around eleven. Mad had won, handily, which I suspect wasn't unusual. I told her I'd go with her to Sebastopol; she asked Doyle if he'd like to go but he declined. Mad then asked "Is it okay if Chuy comes with us?"

Now there was a wrinkle I didn't see coming. I know Mad was trying to be considerate, but I didn't see a way to say "No, he can't come," so I said "of course." I wondered, though, whether or not this was part of something bigger Mad was working on. It was beginning to feel that way.

• • •

The next morning Chuy pulled in and met us in the driveway at 9 o'clock and we took off in Mad's rental car. Since I was most familiar with the route, I drove, first down the valley a few miles to Oakville and then over the western hills into Sonoma Valley, a twisty route if there ever was one.

No doubt about it, Sebastopol had plenty of charm and beauty, but it's about as small and rural as towns come. I couldn't help but wonder how Mad would fare after her high-flying professional career. Maybe she'd be happy to put her feet up, smell the roses, and dote on her grandchild? I reminded myself that it was her call and to keep my mouth shut, reminding myself of one of Hattie's favorite sayings: "The worst vice of all is advice."

The house she liked was certainly a find–parts of it were constructed of adobe brick, dating back to the mid-1800s. It was a beautiful oak-studded lot, not far from where the famous plant breeder, Luther Burbank, ran his experimental garden in the early 1900s. That she had found such an interesting property didn't surprise me at all; Mad and "interesting" seemed to go together. I also had the feeling that if anything had been wrong with the property, she certainly wouldn't have listened to either me or Chuy anyway, so she certainly didn't bring us along for anything like an "expert opinion." Like I said, I thought she was up to something else, and I was right. It started right when we got into the car for the trip home.

"So what's up between you two guys?" Mad said. "What's the no-talking thing about?"

Both Chuy and I were silent–a very awkward, loaded silence. Having thought about it a lot–too much, probably–I decided to start. I also figured by starting it, maybe I could end it, which was important to me.

I took a breath and started in: "Honestly, it feels silly to be talking about something that happened so long ago, when we were teenagers, but that's the way it is. I think it's best to keep this short, so that's what I intend to do. Chuy, you and I had been best friends from kindergarten right up until we went to Kauai to find Dagywn. We found Dagywn, but you and Mad also found each other and I felt like the proverbial third wheel. As painful as it was, I don't think it's all that unusual. I missed it being just the two of us, Chuy. I should have been better at dealing with it than I was, but I was jealous and that's never a good thing. I lashed out at you and that was wrong. It was hurt feelings talking. I realize that it's way too late, but I apologize–sincerely."

Chuy was silent. Mad finally said "Well?" looking at him.

"*You* didn't think twice about going off to boarding school, Nick. I was excited for you, I really was, but that's when *I* knew that we weren't going to be best friends forever."

Honestly, I didn't know my going to boarding school made much difference to Chuy one way or the other. He never let it show which, given that he was stoic by nature, shouldn't have been surprising. Self-absorption goes with being a teenager, but I should have recognized that my leaving had hurt his feelings.

"You know something, Chuy? I didn't know that. And I'm sorry for both of us that we weren't able to talk about it. If we had, I guess we could have made things better–or at least less hurtful. But now that it's out there, I think it's time to move on, don't you?"

Once again, Chuy was silent and then blurted out "Ah, just forget about it."

Guessing where he was taking the conversation, I said, "Yeah, let's leave it for now. We've got time." Right then and there, I didn't have it in me to talk about it. Mad stepped in and said "I think this session is over."

"How much do we owe you, doctor?" I asked, as light-hearted as I could muster.

"The first visit is on the house," she said. "It's the second one that's going to be expensive."

•   •   •

"Don't get mad," Joaquin said, sitting at the kitchen table. It was after four in the afternoon and he had just wandered down from his house, looking like he had slept most of the day, which was exactly what he *had* done. I was still in a kind of strange mood from the conversation with Chuy–"at sixes and sevens" as Hattie used to say–and wondering why Joaquin was prefacing what he was going to say the way he had. The way I felt, I couldn't guarantee him anything.

"What?" I asked.

"Darren and I spent the night up on Mt. St. Helena last night."

"Joaquin! Why didn't you tell me?"

"Because if I told you, we'd have to tell Darren's dad and he would never have let us go."

"What if something had happened, Joaquin?"

"I left a note upstairs in my room. If anything had happened, you would have found us. I had my cell phone with me."

"Argh."

"You did it all the time when you were younger than I am–and by yourself– without a phone."

"Yeah, but at least I told someone where I was going," I said, frustrated, knowing I wasn't going to win this argument.

"Well, I did, kind of, with the note," Joaquin said.

"All right, all right," I said, "but I'm going to have to have a talk with Darren and figure this out."

"It was a blast," Joaquin said.

"Yeah?"

"Yeah. G and Into taught us this game they call *Kyykkä*, only we've been calling it skittles. It's kind of like bowling, only there's no ball–just a short bat you throw at the pins."

"You throw the bat at the pins?"

"Yeah. It's wild."

"And I suppose you didn't get any sleep," I said.

"We didn't go up there to sleep, Grandpa."

"No, I guess not. How *are* things up there?" I asked.

"Okay. Only G said he thought things weren't all that great between Signe and Gob."

"Oh?"

"She told G that Gob was incorrigible, whatever that means," Joaquin said.

"Basically it means there's no changing him. I figured that was going to be a problem," I said, as much to myself as to Joaquin.

"And, oh yeah, Signe says she needs to talk to you."

"Does she want me to come up there?" I asked.

"No. She said she'd call you. I gave her your number."

I turned and looked directly at Joaquin to make sure I'd heard correctly. "She's going to *call* me?"

"Yeah."

Just then my phone rang. The caller's number was blocked.

Grandpa had to tell Signe about the lookout tower *(right)* on top of Mt. St. Helena, the sole purpose of which was to spot fires. Unlike Scandinavia, with its frequent summer rains, California's dry summers made the making of a bonfire out of the question. *Above:* The view of the Napa Valley from the lookout tower is a stunner, especially when a breeze blows the haze away.

Chapter XLIV

Wanted: One Very Large Bonfire

July 3, 2013, *continued*

Grandpa Nick's house, Rutherford

"Is that you, Nick?"

"It's me, Signe. Nice to hear from you–*and* a surprise."

"Well, I admit I'm not a huge fan of these phones, but there are times when they come in handy–like right now. I need your thoughts on something, but I didn't want to have you come all the way up here to talk–hence the call."

"It's fine by me, Signe, but isn't this the middle of your night? Shouldn't you be asleep?"

"I have no idea any more. Ever since leaving Finland, my body's been confused as to what it wants to do. I may just give in and sleep like you Uplanders do, when it's dark."

"Whatever you decide, Signe, I hope you get some sleep soon. You sound tired."

"Yes, I *am* tired, but that's not why I called. As you know very well, until recently I've had two major things to accomplish–get our folks safely moved from Finland to here, and to move our fortune at the same time. Now that Bad Boris and his henchmen–not to mention his girlfriend–have been locked up, I can safely say that I accomplished those tasks."

"Hear, hear," I said.

"Yes, indeed," Signe said. "Actually, there were three things I needed to do, but I overlooked the third. But now that the first two are done, the third has moved into first position. Are you following this? I'm afraid I'm not being very clear."

"No, I get it. So what's the third thing?" I asked.

"It requires some explanation. Do you have a minute?""

"I'm all ears," I said.

"Well, once every hundred years, our sort—you know fairies, elves, trolls, undines, and the like, put on a symposium."

"Hold on, Signe. *Undine?* What's that?" I asked.

"Basically a water nymph," Signe said, "slim little drippy things that complain all the time… oh, did I say that? Sorry. So every hundred years—your years, not ours—delegates are appointed from each elemental house and are invited to attend the symposium, the hosts of which are chosen on a rotating basis. The next symposium is, as you might have guessed, supposed to be hosted by us. I must admit that it's more than I care to take on right now, and to make matters worse, because I was so consumed with my other 'activities,' shall we say, I ignored it and now it's right around the corner."

"How close is 'the corner?'" I asked.

"The end of August."

"And what's your question?" I asked.

"Of course we've known it was our turn to host for a long time. From the beginning, we thought it would be a good idea to plan the move from Finland to California just prior to the symposium, thinking a celebration in our new home would be a good thing. Like I said, that was well before things became as complicated as they did. Even now, with my flagging enthusiasm, I know we'll manage to pull it off, except for one thing."

"What's that?" I asked.

"A bonfire. Make that a very large bonfire. It's the centerpiece of the entire symposium, staged on the last night. It's supposed to light the way to the next symposium, a hundred years in the future. It's not only important symbolically; all of us Elemental types seem to have a thing for bonfires, the bigger the better. It hadn't occurred to me until very recently that you, here in the New World, have a different attitude towards bonfires than folks in the Old World do."

"What do you mean?" I asked.

"Old World Uplanders are closer to the old ways, I think. They like bonfires, too, and take them in stride, no matter how big they are. Into told me yesterday that here bonfires can really scare people and if we do what we normally do, we're likely to call attention to ourselves."

"Sorry to say, Signe, but I think, no, I *know* Into is right. If you have a bonfire on Mt. St. Helena, you'll attract more than attention—more than likely, you'll get yourself in a whole lot of trouble. Have you noticed that tower on the very top of Mt.

St. Helena?"

"Yes."

"It's a fire lookout. There's a camera on top of the tower that constantly scans the surrounding area. There are people who monitor what the camera is recording and report smoke or flames the moment they see any. If you started a big bonfire—any size bonfire—you'd be busted in a New York minute," I said.

"What's a 'New York minute?'" Signe asked.

"Quickly, Signe, you'd be in trouble *tout de suite.*"

"Then what am I supposed to do?"

"I have absolutely no idea," I said.

"But that's why I called you," Signe said, sounding uncharacteristically pitiful.

"Wait a minute," I said, "Maybe I do have an idea," remembering something Lars had said to me. "Don't turn off your phone, Signe. I'll call you back in a few minutes."

Above: The Norwegian artist, Nikolai Astrup *(right)*, was obviously familiar with what Signe was talking about when she said "a very large bonfire." Astrup's painting, titled "Midsummer Night Bonfire," was painted in the early 1900s. People are dancing and celebrating around a huge bonfire, as are other partiers on other islands, which can be seen in the distance, their bonfires reflected in the water. Most of Scandinavia receives enough summer rain to lessen their danger, making such bonfires possible.

Chapter XLV

Giant Trolls and Obnoxious Fairies

July 3, 2013, *continued*

Grandpa Nick's house, Rutherford

Grandpa Nick writing:
"I've got a couple of questions for you," I said, having reached Lars on the phone.

"What's up?" he asked.

"Did you sell the bus?"

"Not yet, but the guy wants it. He's trying to put the money together, so we'll see," Lars said.

"And did you mention the other day you were going to Burning Man*?"

"That's the plan," he said.

"When is it?"

"The last few days of August through the first of September," he said.

"When's the big bonfire?"

"On the next to last night–September 1st, I think."

"Provided you haven't sold the bus by then, would you be willing to drive Signe and a few others down there?"

"Signe wants to go to Burning Man?" Lars said, surprised.

"Not exactly. Signe needs to piggyback on someone else's bonfire. I'll explain the situation later if you're willing to do it."

"Sure. Why not? Could be interesting," Lars said.

"I think that may be an understatement, Lars. Let me call Signe back. I'll let you know. When are you coming back?

"Tonight, if that's all right?"

"No problem," I said. "I'll talk to you then," and hung up and called Signe back.

"I may have found a solution, Signe," I said.

"Oh, I knew I could count on you," she said.

"Don't thank me yet," I said, "You may not like what I've come up with." I explained to her what Burning Man was and that Lars was willing to drive the bus there, that it would be a five-hour ride to get there, but it would definitely provide her and her symposium guests with a very large bonfire in a very festive atmosphere. And best of all, the timing was spot on.

"Let me mull it over," Signe said, "but on the face of it, I don't see how I can say no. We can hold the first part of the symposium here on Mt. St. Helena and then travel up to the desert in Nevada to mark the end of it. Are you sure Lars is wiling to do it?"

"Yes, but he'll be here tonight and I'll ask him again. Do you want me to have him come up and talk with you?"

"No, I trust you, Nick. And Lars. Just tell him I'll let him know for certain to-morrow morning."

"Will do. And, ah, Signe… you're going to have to tell him who the rest of your passengers are going to be. I mean, I don't think there'd be a problem, but it only seems fair to let him know, don't you think?"

"Of course, of course," Signe said, "However, I won't know myself for another couple of weeks who's actually coming, but as soon as I do, I'll advise him. The last thing I want to do is freak him out, as you Uplanders say."

"Not to put too fine of a point on it, Signe, but did you say there would be trolls attending?"

"Maybe. It's a possibility. All of us, what you call 'Elementals,' aren't that cohe-sive a group. And our communication is sporadic, at best. To tell you the truth, this symposium is one of the only organized things we do, if you can call it 'organized.' Why did you ask about the trolls?"

"Am I correct they can be either quite small or very large?"

"That's correct. I don't know if they're still around, but I understand there was also a tribe who lived on Galdhøpiggen, in Norway, who were the same size as you Uplanders, though practically no one ever saw them because they were so reclu-sive–that and they basically looked like any other Uplander."

"What type of troll usually shows up at the symposiums?" I asked.

"It used to be the giant type," Signe said. "But not any more. The only giant troll we know of for certain is Lucinda. I think I told you about her–she lives in Iceland and never leaves–but you can't tell. Even giant trolls need company now and then."

"Would Lucinda fit on the bus? I'm just asking," I said. "I want to make sure this bus solution will actually work for you."

"I understand. No, she wouldn't fit on the bus; she could lift the bus over her head though. That's how big she is."

"I get the picture," I said. "How would she get to the bonfire in Nevada then?"

"You don't ever need to worry about a giant troll–they get everywhere they want and get there quickly. They know every stretch of uninhabited territory on the face of the planet and can traverse it in no time. No, don't worry about a giant troll; if she wants to be somewhere, she'll be there."

"I don't know if I find that comforting or not," I said, "but I'll take your word for it."

"One last thing," Signe said, "Since we have to observe your rules now that we're living here, can there be drinking on the bus?"

"Drinking? Like what kind of drinking?" I asked.

"Like wine kind of drinking. Over the eons, these symposiums have come to be associated with a certain amount of consumption, if you will."

"Well, I'm not exactly sure," I said. "I know for certain that Lars can't drink and drive, but I'm guessing the passengers can–as long as they don't become a nuisance and imperil the safety of the bus."

"I'll make sure and have a stern talking to the fairies before we leave," Signe said. "They're a nuisance even when they're not drinking."

Above: I know these chapter opening pages are supposed to be put together by Joaquin, but when Signe talked about her symposium, with representatives of as many of the various Elementals as possible, my mind wandered back to the book that figured so prominently in the first of The Silverado Journals, *The Silverado Trail.* That book was titled *The Secret Teachings of All Ages*, written by Manley P. Hall in 1928. Signe's description of the symposium brought to mind, rightly or wrongly, the above image. It should be noted that the original book was filled with whacked-out illustrations, of which this one is rather tame. It shows a magician (oddly with a crown on his head), summoning all the Elementals, from undines to fairies (in the clouds).

Chapter XLVI

Making History

July 3–5, 2013, *continued*

Napa Valley

Grandpa Nick writing:

Summer proceeded apace, but not before I made an unusual commitment to Signe– for myself and Joaquin, and Mad and Chuy, as well–for a date in late August. More on that in a minute. Meanwhile, Lars explained to the potential buyer of the bus that he needed it to go to Burning Man, so it couldn't be sold until after he got back the first week of September. The buyer was fine with that as it gave him more time to come up with the purchase price. Signe let me know that everyone who had come from Finland wanted to use their traveling crates to incorporate into their new homes in the cave on Mt. St. Helena. The crates were still in the warehouse in Millbrae, along with about a gazillion shot puts which, apparently, weren't going anywhere for the time being.

Lars had been staying with his friend in Berkeley on the weekends and coming up to the valley during the week. When he was up, I told him about the traveling crates and he arranged to have them shipped up to the mountain and unloaded onto the fire trail that led to the rear entrance of the cave. How the gnomes maneuvered them into the cave, I have no idea, but they're plenty ingenious when it comes to moving stuff around.

Joaquin and Darren continued to go up and visit G and Into about once a week. Joaquin always told me when they were going and took his cell phone with him; I sat Darren down and told him he was on his own with explaining (or not) to his folks where he was. I asked Darren if he wanted me to take his folks up to meet the gnomes. He said he didn't think they could handle it, so we left the situation as it was. Not the best solution, but I wasn't sure what else to do.

Mad wound up buying the adobe house in Sebastopol. The deal was due to close the middle of September. Meanwhile she continued to stay at my place, which was fine, especially considering how much time she spent with Chuy at his place.

One time when Joaquin and Darren had gone up on the mountain, Joaquin came back with a message from Signe. She wanted me to know that she'd be calling me the next day at about 9:30 in the evening, which would be first thing in the morning for her.

Sure enough, the following evening, right at 9:30, she called. We made some small talk and then she said, "I've been thinking about this symposium. I haven't told you what the topic of discussion is, have I?"

"No," I said.

"You know we've been talking about the pros and cons of assimilation for some time now, and we thought it might be a good idea to see what the others think about it–although I can guess what their reaction will be."

"That would be a 'no,' right?" I asked.

"I think so. With the exception of the elves, the rest of them are stuck in their ways–very traditional. We gnomes have always marched to a different drummer, but there isn't uniform agreement within our tribe, either."

"But you're going to bring it up before the attendees?" I asked.

"Yes, but more than that, I thought it might put the issue in a different light if I invited you and Joaquin, Doyle, Lars, Remi, the Baron, Mad, and Chuy to the symposium as well. Let everyone see and be seen, as it were. Maybe the other Elementals will see that there're more similarities than differences between us and the Uplanders."

"Really, Signe? Are you sure that's a good idea?"

"To be honest, no, I *don't* know if it's a good idea. But where's the harm? If anyone doesn't like it, they can leave. The truth is, relations between our various races–elves, fairies, trolls, undines, and the like–have always been contentious. If it all blows up it's just one more example of how we've never gotten along all that well in the first place. Life goes on."

"Is there an upside?" I asked.

"What do you mean?"

"What if it *is* a good idea?" I asked. "What if they all agree to 'see and be seen,' as you put it? What then?"

"It would probably be a big step forward to ensuring all of our survival in the modern world. No one has wanted to address it for the past hundred years or so–in your time, Uplander time–but the world is changing in fundamental ways. We can't keep pretending that it's the same. Actually, we can, but ultimately, I think it would result in disaster. Sorry to paint such a gloom-and-doom picture, but it's what I believe."

"And you think that our being on hand for the symposium, mixing it up with the you and the rest of the 'Elementals,' would help show it's possible for us to live side-by-side, 'seeing' each other?"

"Precisely," Signe said.

"Hmmm… I can certainly ask the others, but I'm telling you now that getting Chuy to come is going to be a tough sell–he's still trying to process his last encounter with you guys back in the 1960s. And what do you think–does the Baron have it in him to make the trek to your cave? Parts of that trail are treacherous."

"We could carry him in from the fire trail in back, like we've done for the rest of the difficult stuff," Signe said.

"I suppose. Let me get in touch with everyone and I'll let you know."

"I realize I've been making this about me–about us–but tell everyone that it will be an interesting experience for them. Uplanders don't get invited to these kind of events, ever. We'll all be making history, one way or the other," Signe said.

"So what's the date for making history, Signe?"

"August 25th. We leave for the big bonfire in Nevada the next morning. If we can pull it off, it will certainly give us something to talk about during the ride there," she said.

"What time?" I asked.

"I'd like to make it easier for you, but tradition has it that the symposiums start at midnight. You can do it, can't you?"

"We can do it, Signe. Nothing that a nap or two won't fix. I'll let you know what everyone says."

"Don't forget, Nick, we're talking about a history-making event here."

"Got it, Signe."

Grandpa told Darren and me to get at the end of the line of hikers, just to make sure everyone stayed on the trail and kept heading in the right direction. With our headlamps, we looked like a bunch of miners headed off for the night shift, which we kind of were, except we weren't going to work; we were going to a party inside a mountain. Pretty wild. The picture below is of the turnout we always used to park whatever car we're driving. It isn't much of a turnout and easy to drive right past if you aren't paying attention. The trail to Robert Louis Stevenson Memorial Park comes in on the right side (which you can just make out in the photograph; there's a better picture of it on page 200), which is the same trail that leads to the gnomes' cave. In most places the trail is narrow enough that you have to hike in single file. Grandpa was in the lead of the parade of bobbing headlamps, one more strange experience in a summer full of all manner of weirdness.

Chapter XLVII

Seeing and Being Seen

August 25, 2013

The gnome's cave, Mt. St. Helena

Grandpa Nick here:

The summer was busy enough that the date for attending Signe's symposium snuck up on me. When it arrived, I realized I should have put more thought into it. When I finally told Signe who would be coming, I hadn't considered any of the details–simple things, like how dark it was going to be. I know that sounds stupid, but even though I had hiked the mountain at night many times before, this time it would be different. When I got around to looking it up, I found out that the moon would be waning on August 25th, which meant we couldn't count on it for providing much light to guide us along the path. That led me to the hardware store to purchase eight headlamps which, for some reason, I thought would be better than eight flashlights.

I wasn't sure if Remi was going to make it, but he wound up surprising me by showing up for dinner on the 25th–the day of Signe's event. I guess that's one of the advantages of having one's own jet, right? As I expected, the Baron had declined the invitation. And I wasn't sure whether Doyle would come or not, but in the end, he said he'd prefer to stay home and "keep the home fires lit," as he put it. I don't know how she did it, but Mad got Chuy to come, although I'm guessing it was under duress. Since Darren had become a regular on the mountain over the summer, Joaquin asked Signe if he could be invited to the symposium and she graciously said yes.

Considering the surreal nature of our outing, we decided what the heck, we'd continue with the theme and take the limousine. With the jump seats folded out in their functioning position, everyone fit, but it was a "full house," so to speak. Lars drove and I sat up front. I asked him if the car handled differently with the increased weight of all the passengers. "With a normal load, it's basically just a big barge. With the extra weight, it handles like a lead sled," he said. I took that as a cue to keep the conversation to a minimum and let him concentrate on driving.

He did an admirable job getting the lead sled up the mountain and to the turn-out where we always parked. Everyone clambered out into the darkness, stretched, yawned, and adjusted what they were wearing. I handed out the headlamps which everyone dutifully put on. Luckily no late night travelers over the mountain stopped while we were assembling next to the road; it would have been difficult to explain what we were doing. It was, after all, 11:30 at night.

As the one most familiar with the trail, I positioned myself at the head of the single line I had our group form and instructed Joaquin and Darren—the second most familiar with the trail—to bring up the rear, making sure nobody lagged behind or wandered off. If anyone had asked me, point blank, why I was making this yomp (as the Royal Marines say), I'm not sure what I'd say, other than "Why not? In for a penny, in for a pound." I'd come this far with the gnomes and even though nothing had turned out remotely as I thought it would, I was still committed to them. It also had something to do with getting older; lately I found myself more willing to do things that before I might have said no to. Rather than automatically shutting down, I was deliberately attempting to open myself up to the possibility of a surprise or two. After all, the big dirt nap loomed and I knew for sure *it* wasn't going to contain many surprises.

We got to the opening of the cave in about twenty minutes. I don't know exactly what I was expecting, but it wasn't *nothing*, which is what we were faced with—no greeter at the entrance welcoming us, no basket of flowers or sign pointing "this way." I wasn't certain, but I figured if they were having any kind of an event, they'd have it in what was basically the big main hall, off of which ran tunnels to the smaller caves and various rooms, so that's where we all headed. Once we turned the corner from what was basically the entrance cave, *nothing* suddenly turned into *Something*, as in *Something Else*. All seven of us stopped in our tracks and just stood there in a cluster with our mouths hanging open—not an attractive look, but I'm not sure there could have been any other response. The only one who actually spoke was Mad, and all she said was "Oh my." I had to hand it to them, the gnomes knew how to stage a spectacle. Somehow with just one look, I immediately understood its message: it certainly wasn't meant to impress us. No, it was some serious one-up-manship created to reinforce the gnomes' standing amongst the other Elementals as possessors of great wealth. After all it took to move their fortune halfway around the world, they were going to make sure it showed. And, boy, did it.

First of all, I've never seen so many candles in my life. They were attached to every nook and cranny of the main hall's towering rock walls, huge tables had equally huge candelabra along with heaps of beautiful fruit, loaves of bread in every shape, and one bouquet of flowers after another, not to mention every manner, shape and size of gold pitchers, goblets, plates and platters. Add to all this glitter the flitter of fairies in sparkling diaphanous gowns, undines scantily clad in crystal drips, elves draped in cloaks of actual flowers and leaves, and the gnomes in their multitude of layers of every type and pattern of fabric, everyone trying to outdo everyone else and doing a very good job of it.

With all the candles the hall was warm and it buzzed with an excitement any Uplander would recognize—just like its opposite—sudden silence, which is what followed our entrance into the main hall. If it was Signe's intention for all of us to "see and be seen," the Uplander contingent definitely accomplished it, right off the bat. The word "interloper" crossed my mind. Signe didn't waste any time, crossing the main hall, arms outstretched, saying "Welcome friends, welcome." There was an audible gasp across the hall. Signe had obviously not warned her guests that we'd be attending the so-called "symposium," which looked more like a serious party to me. There was nothing to do but smile and enthusiastically shake hands with Signe, signaling our friendship and familiarity. The knot our delegation had formed loosened and we managed to rearrange ourselves into a kind of receiving line for Signe to walk down, greeting us all as she went. Never lacking for surprise moves, Signe got to the end of the line where I was standing, turned around, put her two pinky fingers in her mouth and whistled for Gob—a very loud whistle. I learned later that she had grown tired of Gob's being so hard of hearing and had resorted to whistling for him like an Uplander would whistle for a taxi. It worked and Gob lumbered over, full of hail-fellow-well-met, dressed in a flowing tapestry robe trimmed in fur and what appeared to be rather dainty bedroom slippers. He was wearing his gold crown, but it looked as if it might be a bit too big and it was slightly askew.

After a few "ahems," Gob bellowed "In my official capacity as king of the gnomes, please allow me to welcome you all here to our humble new home." There was some polite laughter at the statement, considering the unbridled opulence of the setting. "I know you've traveled far and wide at our request and I would like to give most profound thanks to the team of Uplanders who so ably facilitated what was, at times, a challenging affair. I would call you out by name, but I'm sure to forget someone, so if you'd all just take a bow, I'd be most obliged. Sincere thanks for returning our dependents to us, their loved ones."

Because Signe was standing right next to me, I was able to hear her mutter "Oh my god, he's such a tool. *Dependents?*" Wanting to get it wrapped up, Signe stepped forward, clapping, which started everyone else clapping and sent Gob, with a tap to his crown, back to his throne.

Regardless of what he actually said, Gob's speech seemed to have the effect of returning the hall to some of its former buzzy bonhomie and, I'm guessing, made us a little more acceptable as guests.

I saw Joaquin turn to Mad, smiling, his eyes twinkling and overheard him say, "let's wade in; it doesn't look deep."

"You're a chip off the old block," Mad said, taking his arm. "Let's go."

The inside of the cave really had been transformed into a place of magic with countless candles on the stone walls and more flowers than I'd ever seen in one place before. They were not only beautiful, they added a fantastic fragrance, amplified by the warmth of all those candles. Add strains of woo-woo music bouncing and reverberating off the walls and it added up to quite the sensory experience, just shy of "too much."

Chapter XLVIII

Oh, What a Night!

August 26, 2013

Signe's Symposium, the gnome's cave, Mt. St. Helena

Grandpa Nick again. As soon as Gob left center stage, Signe came over and grabbed Remi's and my hands and said, "Walk with me," which we did. She walked us over to an alcove where there was a cluster of shimmering beauties I took to be undines.

"Excuse me ladies, if we could get through," Signe said, trying to create an opening between them. She finally succeeded and who was in the center of all the attention but the Baron, sitting on an elaborate chair, looking a bit flushed. One of the undines turned to me without hesitation and said "He's so *cute*. We all want to take him home with us."

"Calm down, girls, and give the Baron a little space," Signe said. "Do you need more wine, Eddy?" she asked.

"Why, I think I could use another barrel or two," he said, wiping his brow with a monogrammed handkerchief. Signe raised one hand over her head and made a circular motion with her index finger, indicating another round for the Baron. Presumably there was someone close by to witness the signal.

"Good to see you, Baron," Remi and I both said at the same time.

"Likewise, I'm sure," he said, "It's been quite the evening, I must say. Have you ever been carried in a litter before?" he asked.

"Not me," I said.

"Nor I," said Remi.

"Well, that's how things got started," the Baron said, accepting a glass of wine from a gnome I didn't know. "It was positively regal."

Signe had kept the Baron's acceptance of her invitation a secret, but she had followed through with her idea of bringing him into the cave's back entrance via the fire trail; carrying him on a litter is not something I would have thought of, but it made perfect sense.

"I couldn't refuse Signe's offer as I'd been meaning to come here to the Napa Valley for some time now. You know our family has an interest in a winery here? Not as old as yours, of course, but a good one, nonetheless," he said to me.

"Of course," I said. "Are you going to tell anyone at your winery about where you are right now?"

"You know, I think I *will* tell them, as matter-of-factly as possible. They can make of it what they want. They'll probably think I'm a crazy old man, but this is simply too rich to keep to myself. How about you? Are you going to chat this up?" the Baron asked.

"That's rather why we're here, isn't it? Signe told me the subject of the symposium was 'assimilation,' although I must say, it doesn't look like there's much of a discussion going on," I said.

"More like a lot of gossip and flirting," Remi said.

"Indeed. I think you and Signe may have saved me in the nick of time," the Baron said, chuckling. "I don't know the last time I was called 'cute'–perhaps when I was in diapers–the repeat of which I'd like to delay for as long as possible."

"Has anyone ever told you, you were scandalous, Baron?" Remi asked.

"Not so far today, but frequently, yes," he replied, clearly enjoying himself.

As the Baron was talking, I looked over his shoulder and saw G and Into standing together and waved to them. Behind them I noticed Chuy, by himself, leaning against a rock wall. He was taking in the scene, looking almost like he was enjoying it, which surprised me, although I have to say that you'd have to have an extremely hard heart not to enjoy all the delight that was front-and-center right at that moment. No sooner had I had that thought than I saw him jump straight up in the air, twisting to look behind him, with a stricken look on his face. In an instant, I knew there was only one explanation: Lucinda, the giant troll. What a place for Chuy to lean up against! After Signe had mentioned the existence of giant trolls, I did some research and found out that they're similar to chameleons in that they can transform their appearance to mimic whatever it is they're up against. It's how they, as big as they are, can completely disguise themselves. She was basically doing the same thing as Chuy was–being a wallflower and taking in the scene–only she was about a hundred times bigger than Chuy and caused a significant rock slide each time she made herself more comfortable. I pointed out to Remi what was going on just as Lucinda leaned over slightly and apologized to Chuy for disturbing him which appeared to freak him out even more. I wondered if he'd ever recover.

Above the buzz, I heard the tuning up of an orchestra and, sure enough, in a matter of minutes, melodic strains of music could be plainly heard. It made me think of that time in 1967, when I saw the gnomes celebrating Midsummer's Night, here on the mountain, in their amphitheater, dancing and playing their hypnotic music. No sooner had the memories crossed my mind than I saw the gnome musicians strolling onto the floor of the main hall, jumping, twisting, swaying, and spinning in time with the music. All the rest of the Elementals, with the exception of Lucinda, fell in behind the gnomes, dancing their own interpretation of the music. By this time, our Uplander group had found each other again and in an instant, Remi took Mad's hand, she took mine, I took the Baron's and the Baron took Darren's and Darren took Lars's and Lars took Chuy's and, shockingly, Chuy took Joaquin's and we joined the procession of dancers. I had underestimated Chuy; I thought his brush with Lucinda would have turned him off for the night, but he didn't hesitate to join in the dance. Then again, the amount of magic present at that moment in the hall was so overwhelming it may have simply been impossible for anyone to resist.

I have no idea how long we danced or how long the music played. I couldn't help but think of those old tales about being put under the spell of fairy music, lulled to sleep for a hundred years under a mountain. I was fairly certain that wasn't going to happen. Or maybe it already had. I was tempted to throw caution to the wind, but another reality crept into my consciousness. As hard as it was to believe, this group was due to get on the bus in a couple of hours for their appointment with a major bonfire in the Nevada desert. That brought me around in a hurry, thinking that Lars had to have some sleep before driving that bus on a five-hour journey.

I started rounding up our folks, whispering in their ears that it was time to go. In truth, it felt like the celebration was winding down anyway. Gob had nodded off in his throne, chin on his chest, mouth open, snoring, crown in his lap. There were only a few musicians left playing and various fairies, elves, and undines were flaked out in chairs, eyes closed. I saw Signe and started, at that moment, calling her, in my head, "Signe the Indefatigable," as she was the only one who looked wide awake and ready-to-go.

I explained to her that it was time for us to leave, especially because I wanted

Lars to get some sleep before embarking on the trip tomorrow. I thanked her pro-
fusely, as did the others. It was a moment of recognition and genuine appreciation.
No doubt about it, the evening had been, just as Signe predicted, "historic."

It's easy to see how a few fairies and gnomes, along with the other Elementals, might have been overlooked in the spectacle of the bonfire which ends Burning Man. The Elementals favored big bonfires–this one was big enough to be seen from outer space. No wonder they wanted to come back the following year.

Chapter XLIX

Symposium Postmortem

August 26–September 3, 2013, *continued*

Grandpa Nick's house, Rutherford

Grandpa Nick writing:

The next morning, while I was still half asleep, I heard the bus start up. I was impressed that Lars had managed to get himself going on so little sleep–one of the benefits of being 24 years old. Confident that things were going as planned, I rolled over and went back to sleep–one of the benefits of being 60-plus years old. It felt great. When I got up and more-or-less situated, I realized that my day-to-day responsibilities had been piling up, un-done. Before someone got ticked off due to my lack of attention, I decided to turn what happened next over to Joaquin.

• • •

Hello again, it's me, Joaquin. As expected, Lars rolled back into Grandpa's place late in the afternoon on September 3rd and parked the bus next to the barn. The bus was covered in a heavy layer of dust and dirt and Lars, himself, looked like he'd been pulled through a knothole. With only a weak wave, he made a beeline to the house and upstairs to his room. Grandpa told me and Darren later that no one saw him again until the next day at dinnertime–he had slept for twenty-four hours straight.

Once we knew they were back from Burning Man, Darren and I decided to go up and see G and Into before school started and things like homework and track practice started interfering with our free time. We waited until after dinner to go up, knowing that G and Into wouldn't be up and about until after dark. We had started stashing our bikes on the fire trail instead of next to the road on the turnout like we used to, thinking there was less of a chance they'd get stolen. From the fire trail, it wasn't that long of a walk to where we played skittles, on a court the gnomes called their amphitheater. It was a big space with a flat, packed-dirt floor, maybe twice as big as a tennis court and completely surrounded by massive rock walls probably fifty feet tall.

It was early evening by the time we got there, so we had to wait around for a while, but Into and G finally showed up just as it was getting dark. They each had one handle of the basket of skittles and were all smiles. They had traveled to Burning Man with Signe to provide whatever assistance she might need. They definitely looked better than Lars did, but then they were used to staying up all night, every night. We broke into our normal teams—me and G on one team and Darren and Into on the other. We set up the court with the skittles and lit the small lanterns we used to light the court. We played straight through until it was just starting to get light, around 5 o'clock the next morning. It was a marathon skittle session, that's for sure. Early on I asked how the trip had gone and Darren and I wound up getting an earful—too much to repeat in detail here, but here are the headlines...

• First off, I guess you could say the whole thing was a big success. Or maybe a "run-away success" is more accurate.

• Before departing for Burning Man, Signe asked G and Into to encourage everyone to try and be at their best.

• With the exception of Signe, and G and Into, no one behaved. At all.

• Without preplanning it, the festival schedule dovetailed exactly with the Elementals' natural routine. The desert was too hot for activity during the day, so all the action took place at night when Elementals were in their prime. G and Into agreed: It was a recipe for maximum disaster.

• Not only that, but the overall mindset of the participants of the desert festival matched that of the Elementals' natural inclinations, namely mischievousness and a fondness for partying hard. No pun intended, but the Elementals were definitely in their element.

• The farewell bonfire was the best any of the Elementals could remember and everyone—except for Lucinda who decided to return to Iceland instead of going to the desert—said they wanted to come back the following year, instead of waiting a hundred years for the next symposium.

After Darren and I got off the mountain and caught up on some sleep, I gave

Grandpa the headlines. All he said was "interesting." Lars was within earshot of my report to Grandpa and said "And let it be noted that they didn't behave on the bus, either."

"Will you and Doyle do me a favor?" Grandpa asked me.

"What's that?" I said.

"Will you send a message via Pigeon Post to Signe? I'll write it, if you and Doyle send it off."

"Sure," I said, wondering if the gnomes were going to get in trouble. Grandpa wasn't much of a scold, but it kind of sounded like that's what was going to happen. I think it's best to let Grandpa tell what happened next:

I wrote a short note to Signe and told Joaquin to find Doyle to help him attach it to the pigeon. I wanted Signe to get the note when she got up.

The pigeon was sent off and Signe called me at 9:30 on the nose, just like I had asked her to. I wasn't upset that everyone misbehaved–frankly, I expected it–it's just that I was curious and the gnomes had the annoying habit of letting things slide until you could barely remember what you were curious about in the first place. So, when I had her on the phone, I asked her point blank, how it had gone.

"Do we have to talk about it?" Signe said wearily. "I haven't recovered yet."

"I think we do, at least a little," I said. "Way back when, when I was a teenager hanging out with Gob, G, Dagywn and the rest of the men, there was lots of talk about whether to assimilate or not. *Lots* of talk. As far as I know, no decisions were ever made, one way or the other. And now, all this time later, you said the topic of your symposium was 'assimilation.' I was just wondering–did you talk about it?

"*Talk about it?*" Signe said with surprise, "We *did* it."

"You assimilated with the folks at the festival? Or they assimilated with you?" I asked.

"Both," Signe said. "I think we merged. Sometimes it's better not to talk about these things and just do them."

"So… so no one commented on your presence?"

"No–no more than anyone commented on anyone else who was there."

"So you're telling me you fit right in?"

"I'd say that's accurate."

"Fit right in with a group of… how should I say this? Progressives? Outsiders? Bohemians?"

"I'd call them 'free spirits,'" Signe said, warming to the conversation.

"Okay, 'free spirits' in a highly unusual, celebratory festival where there's a significant amount of merry-making going on, right?"

"Right. Don't tell me you have a problem with that?" Signe said.

"No, not at all, but you have to admit the circumstances under which you 'merged' were a little unusual."

"That doesn't make them any less real, does it? And you've got to start somewhere, right? Who cares if you start at an edge and work you way in. I don't believe in fate, but there was certainly something fortuitous about our need for a bonfire leading us to the desert and Burning Man. To tell you the truth, if she had decided to come, I don't think even Lucinda would have caused a commotion. Maybe next year..." Signe said.

"Next year? I thought the symposium was every hundred years?"

"Well, we're just going to have to call it something else, because everyone wants to do it again next year," Signe said.

"I think you may have to find another bus driver," I said.

"I was afraid we might have pushed Lars too far," Signe said. "The fairies always do that. I told them not to mess with his hair while he was driving."

"'*Mess with his hair?*'"

"They thought it would be fun to make a nest in his hair. I told them it was a bad idea, but bad ideas and the fairies seem to go together," Signe said.

"I think the less I know about it the better," I said–and meant it. "Has everyone gone home?"

"As near as I can tell," Signe said. "Thank goodness."

"What's next?" I asked.

"Let's let the dust settle a little," Signe said, "and then I think you, me, G, Aalto, and Into should have a symposium of our own. No bonfires. Please invite Mad and Joaquin, as well. Chuy, too, if he wants to come. I'll let you know when–let's say next week some time."

"What about Gob?" I asked.

"He'll go along with whatever we decide," Signe said.

"What's the topic of discussion?" I asked.

Signe was silent for a minute and then said "Next steps."

It's funny how things work out, especially considering that it all started in the bottom of a hole halfway around the world from Kauai. After Signe made some life-changing decisions, she contracted to have Lars build her a beautiful new house on the Menehunes' compound, where she had taken up full-time residence, together with her new partner, Keola. It was a goodbye to snow, ice, and perpetual winter darkness, but it was "hello again" to some familiar items, namely the shot puts she used to edge the garden beds of her new house—shot puts that, as Signe put it, "had more frequent flyer miles than any other shot puts in the world." At least they got put to good use and were in a spot where they were going to stay for the foreseeable future.

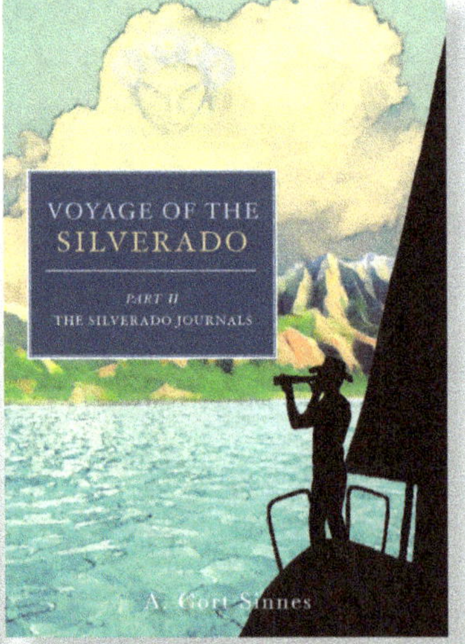

So, after 45 years, the story can be told in its entirety and shared with anyone else who might care to read it. How about that? It's been a long trip and an interesting one, that's for certain. I'd be the first to admit there were many times I wasn't sure if I'd ever see this come to pass, but now that it has, I admit I'm proud of sticking with it. And thanks for coming along, Joaquin. It's been a pleasure having you aboard. Smooth sailing, my friend. Grandpa

Chapter L

The Forty-Five Years are Up

September 12, 2013

Grandpa Nick's house, Rutherford

Grandpa Nick here:

For our own private "symposium," Signe and I decided to split the difference be-tween our sleep/awake schedules and get together at 8 p.m. the following Thursday–late in the day for us Uplanders and early in the day for the gnomes. We also agreed to meet at my house, considering hiking in the dark on Mt. St. Helena was starting to wear a little thin. Lars said he didn't mind taking the limousine to pick up Signe, G, Aalto, and Into and then taking them back again. I never thought the old barge would come in so handy so late in its life, but we were certainly giving it a workout.

I wasn't sure what "next steps" meant to Signe, but I sensed this meeting was more about talking and less about eating, so I just laid out a bunch of ap-petizers–or "puu-puus" as I had learned to call them that summer of 1968 on Kauai when G, Chuy, and Mad and I went looking for Dagywn. I'd been so involved in what had been happening over the last few weeks, I hadn't stood back and given our long, shared history much thought. From the beginning in 1967, it had been a story no one on the outside would have believed–no way, no how–and it was still that way. It had the effect of giving a major portion of my life a note of "unreality,"–an unsettling thought, especially this far up the escalator, so to speak. Signe interrupted my thoughts with her "yoo-hoos"–I may not have been able to see her, but she definitely made her arrival known.

It appeared that everyone had shown up at the same time–Signe, G, Aalto, Into,

Lars, and Chuy all filed in through the back screen door into the kitchen. Gob had decided to stay on the mountain, asking to be filled in when Signe returned. Joaquin, Doyle, and Mad were already inside. Since that's where the food and drinks were, we all just stayed in the kitchen–besides, nobody seemed to want to use any other room in the house any more anyway. Once everyone got situated, Signe characteristically started right in. "Look here," she said, "Here's what I've been thinking. You yourself, Nick, brought up how long we've been wrestling with the question of whether to assimilate with the Uplander culture or not. I'm thinking we've been talking about it for too long and, to my mind, our experience at Burning Man underscores that position."

"What do you mean?" Mad said.

"I think we're overthinking this. Take a look around right here: You, Nick, Joaquin, Chuy, Doyle, Lars–aren't you all Uplanders? And don't you see us and don't we see you?"

We all looked at each other, nodded, and made murmuring affirmative sounds.

"And that's not even including Remi and the Baron and Darren and all the people you were in plain sight with, G, that summer on Kauai. And speaking of Kauai, look what Dagywn and the Menehunes have accomplished. They may be more or less hiding in plain sight, but they are, in fact, in plain sight. And it seems to be working–especially for the children."

"Are you making a case for 'merging?'" I asked, somewhat facetiously.

"After a fashion, yes," Signe replied. "I think all along we thought assimilation was something we'd do in a big way–something we'd make as an announcement, although for the life of me, I don't know where we'd make it or who'd pay attention. But you get my point. Maybe our assimilation shouldn't be seen as a big deal. Maybe it's better accomplished gradually, like we're already doing? Ever since you've been involved with our tribe, Nick, we've been known to more Uplanders with each passing year. And, frankly, I see it continuing that way; why wouldn't it? And let's face it, the world is always going to be divided between people who see us and believe what they're seeing and those who will never accept us, even if we're right in front of their faces. That's just the way it is. You Uplanders have a saying that it's very hard to put the toothpaste back in the tube after it's been squeezed out. If we made some big announcement it would, indeed, be very hard to go back to the way things had been. But if we just let assimilation unfold naturally, like we've been doing, we'd at least have a better chance of putting the toothpaste back in the tube if it became necessary, for whatever reason.

"Before I hear what you tall people think, I'd like to hear from my folks—G, Aalto, Into—what do you think? Do you think this is the way forward?"

G spoke first, saying bluntly "That summer in Kauai was the best summer of my life. It's not that I wasn't scared sometimes, but way less than I thought. Most of the time it felt completely normal for me to be with all of you," G said, looking at us Uplanders.

"While we're all here and speaking plainly, I'd like to ask you a question, Chuy," G said.

"Sure," Chuy said.

"How is it that we spent that summer together and all that time on the sailboat getting to Kauai and then sailing back again and then, once you got home, you pretended like none of us existed? But you *knew* I existed—that *I* was for real. We were friends. Or at least I thought we were."

"Yeah, but you were different," Chuy said.

"How?" G said.

"I knew you. Nick introduced me to you way before we went to Kauai together. You were just one of us," G said.

"Well, yes and no, Chuy. In some ways I wasn't 'just one of you.' I'm a gnome and you and Nick are Uplanders. Assimilation or merging or whatever you want to call it is about acknowledging what's different as much as it is recognizing what's the same. Over that summer, I felt like we'd accomplished that, at least it felt that way to me and it felt great. But then something happened and it was like the gnomes just didn't exist for you any more."

Chuy was quiet for seemingly forever. Finally he said "I think I owe you an apology, G—you and the rest of your folks. A lot of strange things happened that summer after we got back from Kauai and I just sort of lumped everything together and erased it—it was easier that way. I didn't want to think about any of it, so I got rid of all of it. But whatever you bury, you bury alive and now here we are, forty-some-odd years later, and it's all coming around again—Mad's here, you're here, Nick's here and I'm here and we have a chance to clear things up. And just so I make myself clear, G, I'm sorry. I really am."

G looked a Chuy and nodded his head in acknowledgement.

"We *do* have a chance to clear things up," I said, "and I need to talk with Chuy. But just the two of us. You want to take a walk, Chuy?"

"Sure," he said, and we walked out the back door, away from the house and down the lane.

Once the door had slammed shut, Mad, sipping her wine, said "It's about time."

"How about everyone helping themselves to some food?" Doyle suggested. "They may be gone awhile."

• • •

"Let me start off by saying I wish I didn't have to have this conversation, Chuy. I didn't want to have it the other day in the car, and I don't want to have it now, but we have to get this resolved. I understand that I owe you an apology for the things I said to you, back when, that were intentionally hurtful. I'm sorry. I truly am, but they were the words of wounded youth. I'm sorry I said them. But you're angry with me for something beyond words, Chuy, and I cannot and will not apologize for myself any more than G could apologize for being a gnome, or you would for being Mexican. We're all just the way we were made, and that's that. Let me be me, Chuy. See me and accept me the same way I see you and accept you.

"It's not just Signe and G and the rest of the gnomes who are struggling with how they fit into the larger community–let alone figuring out if they *want* to. I've made decisions my entire life that have resulted in what could only be called a delicate balance–of how I know myself to be and how I'm perceived by others. Mad may be smart, straight, and white, but she's had to fight for every bit of ground she's won in a business world run by men. And your position in our community as a Mexican, Chuy,–granted a fourth-generation Mexican here in the valley, way longer than most gringos have lived here–is open for as much misunderstanding and prejudice as anything the gnomes, Mad, or I experience. I get that. We're all looking for respect and understanding, Chuy."

"Are you and Doyle…?"

"Yep. And have been for a long time. He's everything to me. Does that weird you out?"

"It used to. But…"

"But what?"

"My daughter, Veridiana, she's…"

"Really Chuy?"

"She's also pregnant with my first grandchild."

"Well then, Chuy, I'm telling you, being a grandparent is one of the best things the world has invented. Dude, you have no time to waste. You've got to get hip to the jive or you're going to miss out on some very serious fun with that grandbaby–not to mention your daughter.

"And one more thing before we go back–and don't get angry with me–but let me just say, if you don't ask Mad to marry you, you're crazy."

We turned around and started up the lane to the house. It was that beautiful in-between time–late evening, the asphalt road still radiating warmth, sounds of insects in the dry grass next to the road clicking and buzzing, the barn swallows still dipping and diving through the air, the earthy smells of tilled ground and some-where, deep behind it all, the fragrance of grapes and the harvest to come. I put my arm around Chuy's shoulder and felt him tense up and then relax. It was nice. We walked back to the house and didn't say a thing. We didn't have to.

• • •

By the time Chuy and I got back to the kitchen, the gathering was beginning to take on the feel of a party. I heard Signe say "Where's Remi and the Baron. We need them here to see this."

Having been lost in the moment, there was no way I was prepared for what happened next–Joaquin walking over to me as the room went quiet, saying "These are from all of us, with one more on the way." With that he handed me a smallish parcel, wrapped in plain brown paper and tied with cotton string. I was completely taken by surprise when I unwrapped it and discovered the first two volumes of what I had taken to calling The Silverado Journals.

"What are these?" I asked, dumbfounded.

"If you don't know, nobody does," G said, laughing.

"Hey, the forty-five years are up," G continued. "We took the liberty, with a little help from your grandson, of having your journals turned into books–books you're free to unleash on the world, Nick. And as soon as you and Joaquin finish the one we're all still living, we'll add it to these two and you'll have a trilogy, right?"

"I don't know what to say. I'd all but given up on ever seeing these in print. Is this part of your assimilation plan?" I asked.

"No," Signe said smiling. "Let's face it, no one's going to believe what you wrote anyway, Nick–I mean, come on–*gnomes*?"

And so, dear reader, if you're holding this in your hands, you know that Joaquin and I did, in fact, finish the third book. And Signe, Gob, G, Dagwyn, and the rest of the tribe lived up to their word and didn't stand in the way of the trilogy being published and made available to the public. As hard as it is for me to believe the three books are finally for real, it's up to you to decide about the gnomes.

Oh, and a postscript or two: From the time I was presented with the first two volumes of *The Silverado Journals* and Joaquin and I finished this final book, some things happened that will probably interest you.

Six Months Later: March 2014
Menehune compound, Kaumakani, Kauai, Hawaii

Grandpa Nick still here:
While Chuy was building up his courage to ask Mad to get married, she asked him and he accepted. They decided to live in Mad's new house in Sebastopol, but first there was a wedding to attend to–in Kauai–because Mad had decided it "just felt right." Chuy liked the idea too, seeing as how it was where they first met, back in the summer of 1968.

In the curious way of the gnomes, they all seemed to know about Mad and Chuy's upcoming nuptials at the same time without anyone actually telling them. G expressed an interest in going, especially to see how Leo (Dagywn's son) was doing and convinced Signe she should go, too, just to see what tropical life was like, considering she'd spent most of her life in the cold northern climes. Dagywn and the Menehune contingent in Kauai offered the use of the community hall on their compound for the wedding party. Signe asked Mad if it would be all right to invite Remi, not only because they were friends, but his private jet solved the problem of how to get to Kauai with the least amount of issues. Mad, always of the opinion "the more the merrier," said yes.

Mad and Chuy had gone ahead to Kauai the week before the wedding to take

---

* Some of the following may not make complete sense if you haven't read book number two in The Silverado Journals, *Voyage of the Silverado*, which is the story of our (me, G, Mad, and Chuy's) adventure during the summer of 1968.

care of details and to reacquaint themselves with the pleasures of that beautiful, "garden isle."* A few days later, Remi and his jet made an entirely out-of-the-way pit stop at the general aviation airport in Napa and picked up a motley crew of passengers: me, Joaquin, Doyle, Signe, G, and Lars, who had timed his cross-country travels to end in the Napa Valley in time to take off to Mad and Chuy's wedding. What a strange family we were—and, I should add, still are. But strange is a relative term, isn't it? So much of it depends on whose metric of strange you're using. It's been my experience that it's best not to buy into someone else's definition of "normal" unless it happens to coincide with what makes sense to you.

Once we'd landed, it didn't take long for it to become clear that forty-five years doesn't pass without all kinds of changes. If we'd thought about it, none of us would have expected things to be the same, but still… you know? In 1980, Hurricane Iwa, with its 100-mile-per-hour winds, licked the much-loved Garden Isle Beach Cottages off the face of the planet, washing it piece by splintered piece off into the ocean. On the brighter side, one of Mad's cousins had taken over Queenie's shave ice stand so it was still in the family, and Pokee was still alive but more of a recluse than ever. Although Mad's father had long since died, Mad had commissioned a plaque commemorating his time as director of the Kauai Historical Museum and held a small ceremony when it was installed honoring his service to the community. Life goes on.

Mad and Chuy's wedding was held on the beach in front of what used to be the Garden Isle Beach Cottages, just as the sun was setting. It was a familiar spot for us who had been there in 1968—a big horseshoe bay, the water made calm by a far-off breakwater. As old as he must have been, Pokee still lived on the tip of the point of land on the west side of the bay. He apparently got wind of the wedding and decided to put on one of his displays of fireworks in honor of Mad and Chuy's big day, but for some reason, they went off right as Mad and Chuy were reciting their vows to each other. Pokee's timing may have been off, but his sentiments weren't and we all watched and applauded and whooped and hollered and then got back to finishing the ceremony. Thanks, Pokee.

After the ceremony, instead of throwing rice—or bird seed as they do now—Joaquin and G released white doves from several cages, which was quite a sight. Someone had hired a bus for us all to get to the compound near Kaumakani, where the Menehune lived. The group was fairly raucous and once we got to the community hall, it didn't show any signs of abating. Over the years, the Menehune had transformed the compound into a what looked like a lush, slightly overgrown tropical botanic garden. It was seriously beautiful at every turn. The old community hall, which used to look, well, just like you'd expect a community hall to look, had been transformed into more of an inside-outside pavilion, with flowering vines of all kinds growing up and over the roof. The formerly very plain building now sported french doors on all four sides and a new, much wider porch around the entire building. There were lots of little lights everywhere, a Hawaiian band playing, and flowers and exotic scents everywhere and, I was told, there was a pig roasting over a live fire somewhere nearby.

Even though he was gnomish, not Menehune, Dagwyn had become the semi-official ambassador of the compound and, as such, greeted us as we stepped off the bus, presenting fragrant pikake leis to the women, while Hani, his 8-year-old niece, stood on a step stool next to him, presenting leis to the men. For those of us who knew Dagywn well, the formality of his greeting was a little surprising, but it didn't last long; within minutes he was doing a stylish solo two-step on the dance floor, showing us the *kalua pua'a* (pig in a pit), and getting everyone drinks. It wasn't part of the plan, but it also wasn't long before the entire Menehune community—young and old alike—arrived to take part in the festivities. There were line dances, and circular dances, and rock 'n roll and, I swear, what had to be the Hawaiian version of polka. It was an evening of too much of everything, including food, just as it should be. After a few hours, we were all just about worn out; by midnight the crowd had started to thin.

As we tottered off to our cabins, through the blooming, moonlit junglelike garden, I thought to myself that more than one loop had been closed that day—or maybe it was just one very big, intertwined loop—stretching back almost fifty years. The closure didn't make me sad; if anything, just the opposite. I figured we had all been lucky to have been part of the story for as long as we had and to have been able to see it through to one chapter's fitting end.

The end of a chapter, maybe, but not the end of the book…

• • •

My batting average for predicting future events is definitely no better than average, but I'll take credit for seeing this one coming from way back when we were in Helsinki. The differences between Signe and Gob were so obvious, I had to think there'd be some rocky times ahead. This is oversimplifying it, but it was as if Gob was stuck in the 1870s and Signe had decidedly moved into the 21st century. The gap between them, in the way they lived and how they thought, was huge.

Once we returned home from Kauai, I stopped going up to Mt. St. Helena–not for any particular reason but, as I said, I felt as if one chapter in my life had closed. Joaquin and Darren continued going up on the mountain, weather permitting, to play skittles with G and Into. Apparently Whitbeck and Wycoff had shouldered their way into the games and, in addition to considerable skill at skittles, they were both inveterate gossips, the substance of which eventually made its way to me, via Joaquin and Darren.

Before continuing, I should mention that, after Mad and Chuy's wedding, our departure from Kauai hadn't gone according to plan. The Scandinavian contingent, consisting of Signe, Remi, and Lars, had all fallen in love with the island and wanted to stay longer. Eventually we decided to split up, with Mad and Chuy, Joaquin, Doyle, and I taking a commercial flight home. It wasn't until Lars called a few weeks later asking if either Joaquin or I could sell his Subaru (which he had bought using the money from selling the rock 'n roll bus) that we learned he had decided to take up permanent residence in Kauai. Not only that, but Remi had decided to build a home there, on land he had purchased overlooking the Pacific. And then the real bombshell–apparently it wasn't just the island Signe fell in love with, but also Dagywn's wife's brother, Keola. Now *that* I hadn't predicted. Lars said she intended to build a house there, too, for her and Keola, on the Menehune compound, which is how Lars wound up with two major architecture commissions from two well-heeled clients. "Beats digging outhouses," he said.

One year later, March 2015
Grandpa Nick's house, Rutherford

Leave it to Signe to send a postcard via snail mail, inviting me to join her in a tour of her new house in Kauai via Zoom. In case that wasn't enough cognitive dissonance, the front of the postcard featured a classic, sand-and-surf beach scene, complete with palm trees, hammock, and surfboard with the caption "everything is here, wish you were beautiful." At least she was consistent in her unique take on the world.

The day arrived for our Zoom meeting. Joaquin and I were seated, not surprisingly, at the kitchen table in front of his laptop. Signe appeared to be in a garden wearing a flower print muumuu and a single pink plumeria blossom behind her ear. The tropical transformation suited her. I don't know about Joaquin, but it made me feel rather dull by comparison. We had a long conversation and a complete tour of the house. It was a beautiful, light-filled space, with a wide covered porch surrounding the house and open windows and doors everywhere. Taken altogether, it couldn't have been any more different from living in a cave, which I'm sure was exactly as she intended it. Joaquin and I got to meet Keola, who was in the middle of cleaning out their koi pond. We also got to talk to G, who was home on spring break from the University of Hawaii, where he was studying marine biology. He and Joaquin made tentative plans to get together over the winter holidays—in Kau-ai, of course.

As Signe digitally walked us through the gardens, I kept noticing something familiar along the edges of pathways and flower beds.

"Are those what I think they are?" I asked.

Signe laughed and panned her phone around the garden and then to a close-up of what could only be a black shot put—one of many. Many many.

"Yes, of course they are," Signe said. "I had to do *something* with them. The best traveled shot puts in the world. Like me, they've landed in a beautiful spot and they're staying put—no pun intended."

And so another loop, albeit a small one, was closed and we ended our call, but not without first vowing to take turns and check in with each other every other month. After signing off with Signe, I felt a twinge of guilt and decided that it was only right that I check in with Gob every couple of months, as well. Maybe that chapter wasn't quite as closed as I thought it was. The first time I saw him and his men, after more than a year's absence, I realized I had missed them. No doubt about it, they were almost comically old-fashioned, but I liked them for that. And the irony wasn't lost on me that in what they referred to as the "new world" (after escaping from Åland), Gob and his men would choose to cling so tightly to their old ways. Ironic maybe, but frankly, the older I got, the more I could see the attraction of keeping things as they always had been. Just as Signe found pleasure on new horizons, I understood the comfort of the broken-in and the familiar. Who was I to say what made sense and what didn't? To each their own, right?

Joaquin's just gotten back from playing skittles on the mountain, something I think he doesn't get to do as often as he'd like, now that he's back in school. Since he always hears the gossip when he's up there, I'll let him close this out with the latest news.

Alrighty then. Joaquin here. Like Grandpa said, Darren and I just got back from playing skittles with G, Into, Whitbeck, and Wycoff. It was fun, like it usually is; Darren and I actually won for a change. It had been a while since we were up there and a few things had happened while we were gone. Number one, Gob didn't actually retire as king, but he was named "King Emeritus" by the tribe which, I think, is basically the same thing as retiring, except with a new title. Whatever you make of it, it means that he's relieved of his official duties (whatever they were) and is free to spend his days the way he wants to. And he gets to keep his crown.

Although they didn't come right out and say it, both Darren and I got the impression that Aalto and Into had become an item. What *was* public knowledge was that the two of them had essentially taken Gob's place as head(s) of the tribe, each of them on equal footing in terms of power and decision-making ability. In other news, the role of "king as chief deceiver" for any inquiries the gnomes might field from the outside world was apparently being abandoned in favor of answering any questions from Uplanders as forthrightly as possible. The gnomes were notoriously slow to make any decision that involved change. These were big changes, made quickly. I don't know what to make of that, one way or the other, but Aalto and Into are both pretty cool customers, not to mention way smart. I think they'll make a go of it, on whatever path they take the tribe in the future. You'll hear from me when there's more to report, of which I'm sure there'll be plenty. Oh, I almost forgot. The last time Grandpa and I talked with Signe, she said she was instituting an exchange program between the tribe on Mt. St. Helena and the Menehune compound in Kauai: three young people from each tribe are going to spend a year living with the other's tribe. Leave it to Signe to come up with an idea like that. When Grandpa asked what she wanted to achieve with the program, she didn't answer directly. She just chuckled and said: "Let's just say I've seen the future and it's shorter, browner, and speaks a strange dialect of Esperanto with a Scandinavian accent."

I kind of get it, but I think you better stay tuned.

The End

It's not surprising that much of this story was inspired by the numerous treks my friends and I made to the summit of Mt. St. Helena back in the day, all of them magical, one way or another. What *was* surprising was the amount of detail that came flooding back from a trip I took to Finland in 1970 with my grandparents. Both of them had been born in Finland, emigrating to San Francisco in the early 1900s. Ostensibly the trip was to mark my graduation from high school, but it was more than that. They wanted me to be immersed in Finnish culture–of which they were understandably proud–the same way one jumped into the lake after a sauna–a deep, fast dive. We stayed for the summer and, some 50 years later, I think I can say it was a successful, memorable trip for all of us: Much of what is related in *Escape to Silverado* is a direct replay of events that took place on that trip.

Me, near the top of Mt. St. Helena, 1971

That my grandparents were in their mid-70s and I was 18 was a little strange, but we made it work. This was no minor achievement considering it included a 400-mile road trip to, of all places, Rovaniemi, the capital of Lapland, which happens to be above the Arctic Circle. Along the way, I really did hang out on my great uncle's miniature island in the Gulf of Bothnia, including spending the night in the one-room fisherman's cottage built amongst the granite boulders, with the midnight sun just barely dipping below the horizon before popping up again. And, after a long train trip from Sweden to Finland to see us, one of my cousins really did almost faint because she hadn't eaten any potatoes in 24 hours.

As far as the road trip to Lapland goes, one of my grandmother's well-heeled sisters loaned us a brand-new Saab. Grandpa, outfitted in his double-breasted suit and fedora hat, was the co-pilot. I was the designated driver with Nana comfortably ensconced in the back seat, clutching her handbag on her lap. I drove while my grandfather, the supposed navigator, dozed on and off. That said, it would have been hard to get lost, as there was only one highway we could take; as long as we didn't turn left or right, eventually we'd get to Rovaniemi. The fact that there was practically no traffic for the entire trip made me wonder, however, if I might be driving on another planet–a virtually *flat* planet with no mountains or hills, with the same trees mile after mile. There were times when it all felt a bit surreal, especially with Grandpa periodically bobbing his head into the fully awake position with a snort and a sputter and spontaneously breaking into song–that's how happy he was. His repertoire was limited to two songs–*K-K-K-Katy* and *Pie in the Sky* and he only knew the refrain of each:

> "K-K-K-Katy, beautiful Katy,
>
> You're the only g-g-g-girl that I adore;
>
> When the m-m-m-moon shines,
>
> Over the cow shed,
>
> I'll be waiting at the k-k-k-kitchen door."

Which folded right into:

> "You will eat by and by
>
> When you've learned how to cook and how to fry
>
> Chop some wood, 'twill do you good
>
> Then you'll eat in the sweet by and by."

His version contained the free-form lyric "and we'll have pie in the sky, by and by." No matter. With or without his vocal stylings, I think it's safe to say that, right at that moment, I was the only 18-year-old American driving his grandparents from Helsinki, Finland to Rovaniemi, Lapland, which only enhanced the out-of-this-world nature of the experience.

And for the record, "Napa," really does mean bellybutton in Finn. Unfortunately.

acorts@me.com

Me and my grandparents at the Kalastajatorppa Hotel, Helsinki 1970

Acknowledgements

Over the years it's taken to complete this trilogy, a veritable team of advance readers has evolved, each providing unique observations (and corrections!), all of which I greatly appreciate. Many thanks to Michèle Amendola, Patti Antonaccio, Nancy Barker, Karen Bergin, Anne Carey, Alan Freeland, Joël Hoachuk, Chris Howell, Hanna Norman, Kelly O'Hara, and Amy Troutner.

Special thanks to Gail Kenna for an extraordinary, fifty-year, student-teacher friendship that began at Napa High School and continues to this day. I'm still learning from you, Gail. A big shout-out to my friend Sean Behrens who never blinks when I throw him very strange questions and, impressively, always comes back with answers that make sense. And thanks to Gene Lyerla for his encyclopedic knowledge of the law enforcement profession and his continued willingness to part with it and Bill Haworth for providing the inside information I was looking for regarding international finance and its regulation, not to mention introducing me to the Gnomes of Zürich. Who knew? Special thanks, too, to Spencer Wheat who, over the years, posed for all three of the front covers, the last one done "over the horizon"–ah, the wonders of technology! Last, but hardly least, thanks Alan Freeland for your professional advice during the massively long time it's taken me to cross the finish line with this story. Prince of the City, forever.

About This Book

The body text of this book is set in Baskerville Regular. The typeface for some of the illustration captions is my own handwriting, transformed into a digital typeface using Calligraphr (Calligraphr.com). The color illustrations were done with colored pencil with ink accents. The pen-and-ink illustrations within the journal were created with a black Staedtler 0.5 pigment liner. *Escape to Silverado* was designed and composed on a Macintosh, using InDesign software.